Our Valentine Gift to You!

Harlequin celebrates the most romantic day
of the year with a delicious collection of
short stories...

Bestselling authors Meryl Sawyer,
Kate Hoffmann and Gina Wilkins
deliver three romantic, enticing tales
all wrapped up in a
mouth-watering chocolate theme.

And enjoy our very special gift for you...
a beautiful heart-shaped gold pin perfect for
Valentine's Day!

ABOUT THE AUTHORS

Meryl Sawyer

After graduating from U.C.L.A., Meryl taught gifted students in L.A. and wrote book reviews for the *Pacific Sun*. She also taught extension courses at Pepperdine University, and began writing children's plays and films. Because of her husband's job with a British firm, Meryl found herself traveling extensively with him. Inspired by the people she met and the interesting places she visited, she began writing novels that blend adventure, intrigue and human relationships. Meryl has seven books to her credit—one historical, the rest contemporary—which have been translated into over a dozen languages. Look for her new novel, *Unforgettable*, in bookstores now.

Kate Hoffmann

This talented author's first romance was published in 1993 and she's been going strong ever since. She's written ten books for Harlequin Temptation, three of which were the lead titles in the bestselling Bachelor Arms miniseries. She has also contributed two books to the exciting new continuity series Weddings by DeWilde. A native of Wisconsin, Kate lives in Milwaukee. Watch for her next Harlequin Temptation novel available in March 1997, *The Honeymoon Deal*.

Gina Wilkins

One of Harlequin's most prolific and well-known writers, Gina has written nearly forty books since she sold her first novel to Harlequin Temptation in 1987. She has also written for Silhouette Special Edition and contributed to two other short-story collections for Mother's Day and Valentine's Day. Gina and her husband and their three children make their home in Arkansas. Look for Gina's next Harlequin Temptation title, *The Getaway Bride*, in May 1997, the first book in the Brides on the Run miniseries.

VALENTINE *Delights*

Meryl Sawyer

Kate Hoffmann

Gina Wilkins

Harlequin Books

TORONTO • NEW YORK • LONDON
AMSTERDAM • PARIS • SYDNEY • HAMBURG
STOCKHOLM • ATHENS • TOKYO • MILAN
MADRID • WARSAW • BUDAPEST • AUCKLAND

VALENTINE DELIGHTS
Copyright © 1997 by Harlequin Books S.A.

ISBN 0-373-83324-5

The publisher acknowledges the copyright holders of the individual works as follows:

CHOCOLATE FANTASY
Copyright © 1997 by M. Sawyer Unickel

HIS SECRET VALENTINE
Copyright © 1997 by Peggy Hoffmann

GIFT OF THE HEART
Copyright © 1997 by Gina Wilkins

CONTENTS

CHOCOLATE FANTASY

Meryl Sawyer

Dear Reader,

What a thrill it has been to write a Valentine story. This holiday has such special meaning for me. My husband proposed with a ring in a box of chocolates just the way I've written it in the story. Only, in real life, I was afraid to ruin my dinner (he was taking me to a really fancy restaurant), and I wouldn't open the box. He tried coaxing me, but I resisted. Finally he opened the box, supposedly to have a chocolate himself, and I saw the red velvet jewelry box.

Since then, Valentine's Day has been our "special" day. On one occasion Jeffrey brought me a golden retriever puppy with a gold-foil bag of chocolates attached to his collar. Another time, he gave me a bottle of champagne that had been dipped in chocolate. We peeled off the chocolate, then drank the bubbly.

Last year, he brought me a jar of chocolate body paint. You can pour it over ice cream…or use your imagination. Trust me, this is the most fun you can have with chocolate. And it was the inspiration for my story, "Chocolate Fantasy."

Wishing all your chocolate fantasies come true,

Meryl Sawyer

PAPA VALENTINE'S PAPACCINO

Make Papa's wonderful coffee at home with this easy recipe:

Use one 8 oz coffee mug

Put a piece of your favorite chocolate in the bottom (bittersweet or milk chocolate)

Add ½ tsp of powdered vanilla and a dash of cinnamon

Heat 2 oz of milk (microwave is fine). DO NOT BOIL

Pour the milk over the chocolate and spices

Add 6 oz of your favorite coffee—Irish Cream is recommended—hot

Wait one minute, then stir

Top with whipped cream

Drizzle chocolate syrup over the top

Enjoy!

For Jeffrey.
Thanks for being my inspiration.

Chapter One

"OH, CRIMINY! There's chocolate on the sheets."

Gordon opened his eyes and peered up at Alexis Evans from the pillow beside her as if to say, "What do you expect? You're always eating chocolates in bed."

Allie couldn't help smiling at Gordon, who closed his eyes and curled into a tight ball, purring like a locomotive. Sighing, she set aside her laptop computer, aware that once again she was talking to her cat. Well, what else could she do? She lived alone and had her office in her apartment. Without Gordon, she would be talking to the walls.

"Some help you are," she told the cat as she surveyed the mess on her bed.

Dozens of pieces of what was supposed to be a child's fire engine lay scattered across the rumpled sheets. A technical writer who moonlighted as a restaurant critic, Allie translated assembly instructions written in foreign languages into user-friendly English, so that toys could be put together in a few easy steps.

"Ha! A few easy steps. That's a joke. Using the instructions they sent, it would take a rocket scientist to put together this fire engine."

Gordy opened one eye just a slit and glared at her again for interrupting his afternoon nap. Allie ignored him, searching under the various pieces of the fire engine for her chocolates. She found the small box under the glossy red hood. She yanked off the top. Empty.

"I guess this means I have to go to Valentine Delights and buy more."

Now she had Gordon's undivided attention. The marmalade-colored cat sat up and stretched, gazing at her as if he knew this was just an excuse to get away from her work.

"I'll think better after a *latte*," she said, knowing she would have one of Papa Valentine's sinful chocolate desserts or a hand-dipped chocolate to go with the *latte*. Undoubtedly her blood would be ninety-percent caffeine afterward. Oh, well, she had to pull another all-nighter, so that lucky parents across the land could put together the stupid fire engine next Christmas.

Dressed in sweats, Allie went out the door, not bothering to lock her apartment. Thankfully, crime in Cedar Ridge was rare. That was why she'd moved to the small town near Atlanta. She could dash around the corner for a *latte* without worrying about thieves.

Brick buildings and stately elm trees gave Cedar Ridge a quaint, historic character that appealed to Allie. She liked living in a beautiful place where people were friendly. When she'd moved here last year, Allie had thought she would miss the big city. Although Atlanta was close, she never went there unless she was reviewing a restaurant for her Sunday column in the *Cedar Ridge Tribune.*

Outside, the February sun cast long shadows across the cobblestone street. The air was cool, but if she hurried, she wouldn't be sorry that she hadn't taken the time to put on a jacket. She trotted down the sidewalk, dodging the stone urns filled with bright yellow and purple pansies as shoppers darted in and out of the shops lining the street.

Ahead she saw the bay windows of Valentine Delights. Papa Valentine's winning combination of wonderful desserts and chocolates available at a coffee bar made it a very popular gathering spot for those who lived and worked in the area. Allie smiled to herself, thinking of how often she came in for a treat and sat at one of the tables with a few pages to translate. Surrounded by the happy chatter, she felt less lonely.

She reached for the old-fashioned brass handle on the shop's door and caught her fractured reflection in the leaded glass. "You could haunt a house and charge by the room," she scolded herself aloud.

That morning she'd put her auburn hair into a ponytail on top of her head. Her hair was thick and ruler straight. Her habit of shaking her head as she worked had made the ponytail list to one side like a drunken sailor. Strands had come loose around her face. She rarely used makeup and today had been no exception. Even in the small squares of glass, she saw the shadows under her eyes.

Any fool would go home, she told herself. *No, just nip in and get out fast.*

"Hey, Allie! How's tricks?" Papa Valentine greeted her.

Tall and trim, Papa had a bald head fringed with white hair. And a welcoming smile that had won him as many customers as his delicious chocolates. Not for the first time, Allie thought about how lucky she was to be able to call Papa a friend.

"I'm having a devil of a time putting that fire engine together," she confessed.

"Keep working on it. You'll figure it out. You always do." Papa checked his watch. "Rudy's late."

Allie shook her head sympathetically, picturing the young man who had a gold ring piercing his nostril and an overbite that would have made a beaver proud. As an amateur stand-up comedian, Rudy didn't spare himself a few jabs during his comedy routines.

"I told him not to be late today—of all days."

Allie glanced around the shop, its warm woods and quaint antiques instantly cheering her. The pleasant aroma of freshly ground coffee filled the air. Then she saw the sign above the door. Happy Valentine's Day.

"Oh, great! Black Friday. I'd forgotten." She groaned, thinking about last Valentine's Day. She'd been happily living in Atlanta, planning a wedding. Of course, that was before Drew's betrayal. Her life was completely different now.

"Black Friday?" Papa echoed. "Allie, don't be such a cynic. There's nothing like love, believe me. Today's the day lovers celebrate their relationship."

"Fine. Let them celebrate. Give me a *latte* and—"

"Could you do me a favor?" Papa interrupted. "It's three and I have to deliver two dozen boxes of chocolates to different offices before they close. Could you wait on the customers until Rudy gets here?"

"Like this?" she cried, pointing to her chocolate-stained gray sweats and black grunge-style boots.

Papa beamed. "I like the message on your sweatshirt. 'Chocolate's Not Just for Breakfast Anymore.' It's perfect."

Trust Papa to put everything in the best light possible. No doubt if she told him about Drew, Papa Valentine would have comforting words. Part of her wanted to tell him about the way she had been jilted, but she couldn't bring herself to discuss it—even with someone as easy to talk to as Papa.

"I don't want to disappoint anyone," he said softly.

"I understand," she replied, imagining how thrilling it would be to receive a shiny silver box of chocolates with embossed burgundy script saying "Valentine Delights." You would know someone truly loved you.

Allie refused to feel sorry for herself just because this was Valentine's Day and no one had sent her so much as a card, let alone a box of hand-dipped chocolates. She counted her blessings and Papa Valentine ranked right at the top.

He was teaching her how to run a coffee bar. It was just a dream and a distant one at that, but one day she planned to say goodbye to the boring translating and open BrewHaHa. It wouldn't compete with Valentine Delights because it wouldn't have chocolates or desserts. What she had in mind was a small coffee bar in one of the office buildings along the road to Atlanta.

Not only was Papa Valentine teaching her the business, the small scab on the crown of his bald head proved how good a friend he was. Often he put on wigs and other disguises and accompanied her when she went out incognito as a restaurant critic. The last time, the self-adhesive tape on the wig had stuck to Papa's bald head, causing the scab. She couldn't refuse to help him now, just because she looked like something no cat would bother to drag in.

Allie marched around behind the counter. "If Rudy is more than five minutes late, I am going to personally pierce his other nostril with a...a knitting needle."

Papa chuckled as he dashed out the back door to where his van was loaded with the boxes of chocolate ready for delivery.

Forty minutes later, Allie had brewed seven cappuccinos, two decaf *lattes*, and served a dozen cups of the house blend—Papa's special combination of roasted Kona and sweet Javanese coffee beans. The vultures had cleaned out the pastry case, eating the last piece of Death by Chocolate Torte, which she'd planned to take home.

"Whew!" She cuffed the moisture off her forehead as the last customer left the shop, a box of chocolates for his sweetheart under his arm. "Where on earth *is* Rudy?"

Might as well refill the chocolate case, she decided. She grabbed the skeleton key off the hook behind the cash register and unlocked the storeroom. A blast of chilly air from the special cooling unit hit her when she opened the thick plank door. She filled a tray with an assortment of chocolates and noticed the Valentine's Day rush had almost wiped them out. Long before Papa closed at midnight, there wouldn't be a single piece left.

Oh, well. She helped herself to a Chocolate Midnight Fantasy. The bittersweet Belgian chocolate with the rich creamy raspberry center filled her mouth; it was sinfully delicious. She closed her eyes, allowing herself "a blond moment," imagining that she was a ravishing blonde. It was Valentine's Day and a handsome hunk—*her* midnight fantasy—had just given her a silver-foil box of Valentine Delights chocolates.

"Didn't you learn your lesson with Drew?" Allie scolded herself, still chewing. She backed out of the storeroom and locked it. She hung the key on the wall hook, balancing the tray on one hip. "You don't need a man. You need assembly instructions for a fire engine."

Ready to restock the chocolate case, she turned and saw him. Her stomach lurched, her pulse skittering alarmingly.

Oh, no. Not the studmuffin.

Allie had no idea what his name was, but she'd seen him around Papa's several times. Tall and powerfully built, he reminded her of the buff guys who wandered in and out of the Bad Dog Gym down the street. The gym's sign claimed: Our Trainers Are Real Animals. This guy fit the bill.

Chestnut-brown hair dusted the turned-up collar of the hunk's bomber jacket—the kind of hair that begged a woman to run her fingers through it. Twilight-blue eyes gazed at her through thick lashes several shades darker than his hair. Those intriguing eyes were fired by a hint of amusement, and she wondered if he'd heard her talking to herself.

"What can I get you?" she asked, justifiably proud of her cool tone.

His eyes took a leisurely tour of her body, starting with the lopsided ponytail and roaming downward so slowly that she felt a flush of heat creep up her neck. With it came a spurt of anger. Obviously, he was the kind of man who thought anything in panties was his type. *Not these panties.*

She ignored him, quickly refilling the nearly empty chocolate case.

"You've got chocolate on your lip." His voice was rich, heart-stoppingly masculine.

Guarding against looking at him, she swiped at her mouth with the back of her hand. *Great!* The remnants of the Chocolate Midnight Fantasy. Forget the piercing with a knitting needle. That would be too kind. She was absolutely, positively going to strangle Rudy when he finally appeared.

"Doesn't Papa Valentine worry about you eating all the inventory?"

She looked up and blistered him with the glare her father used to call the Stare from Hell. "I was merely checking to be sure the chocolates weren't stale."

He smiled a slow, easy smile that canted slightly to one side. A cocky, self-confident grin. A cute dimple appeared in his cheek. Didn't dimples come in pairs? She watched closely, expecting the other to appear. Nothing.

He was really adorable, and he'd laughed at her dumb joke. But he wasn't laughing now. He was staring at her. Actually, they were staring at each other over the chocolate case.

"You wanted some chocolates." Her voice faltered as a fresh wave of heat waltzed up her neck.

"Chocolates?" he replied as if hearing a foreign word.

She pretended to be looking at the chocolates, but through lowered lashes, she checked his hands. No wedding ring.

"I need a Valentine's present," he said. "What's the biggest box of chocolates you have?"

Of course. He needed a Valentine's present. Somewhere a gorgeous blonde was primping in anticipation of spending the evening with him. Allie hoped every chocolate the blonde ate went straight to her hips and thighs.

"The ten-pound foil heart is Valentine Delights' largest box."

"I'll take it." He gazed into the case while Allie pulled the box from under the counter. "Let's see, start with two white chocolate hearts. She likes those."

Allie plucked the chocolates from the tray and placed them in the enormous box. At this rate they'd be here all night. She looked up, ready to hear his next choice and found him gazing at her, not the chocolates. She clamped down on the inside of her cheek with her teeth to counter the silly leap of her pulse.

"Which kind were you eating?" he asked.

"The raspberry cream twice-coated with bittersweet chocolate. It's called Chocolate Midnight Fantasy."

His gaze slowly scanned her body again, finally meeting her eyes with a meltdown smile that would have tested a nun's vows. "Weird," he said, his voice pitched low. "My midnight fantasies have nothing to do with chocolate."

Allie could have shot back a great one-liner. Off-the-wall comments had made her "Restaurant Rita" column a hit. But why deliberately bait this man when she wanted to get rid of him? Now was the time to keep her mouth shut.

"I'll take two of those fantasy chocolates."

Two? Yes, they were going to be here all night, filling the blonde's box of chocolates. And Rudy was going to die a slow and painful death.

"What's that?" He pointed to a chocolate.

"A truffle. Dark chocolate rolled in cocoa, sugar and cinnamon. It's one of Papa's best. You're going to need six of those." Without waiting for a response, Allie pulled the truffles from the case and lined them up next to the others.

She looked up and found he was watching her again with that disconcerting gaze. Staring back at him with her drop-dead look did nothing more than encourage him. He grinned again, the adorable dimple reappearing. If she didn't know better, she would think he was trying to flirt with her. "When I came in, you were saying something about a fire engine."

Criminy! He *had* overheard her. "It's a long story. Trust me, you don't want to hear it." She reached into the case. "Does she like mandarin oranges in a dark chocolate shell?"

"She likes just about anything that's chocolate."

Allie couldn't help herself. She turned and grabbed a jar that had a silver-handled paintbrush tied to it with a frilly burgundy ribbon. "Why not try something a little different on Valentine's Day? How about this Chocolate Body Paint?''

That got him. Now the studmuffin was staring at her as if he suspected she'd been ingesting suspicious mushrooms. ''What do you do with it?''

She managed to keep a straight face as she pointed to the instructions on the back of the jar. ''It says you can pour it over ice cream.''

He winked at her. ''That's no fun.''

''Or—'' she paused to keep the smile out of her voice ''—you can use the brush to paint chocolate on your 'happy parts.' ''

''Happy parts?''

''That's what it says. What can I tell you? It's made in L.A. They probably meant erogenous zones, but couldn't spell it.''

''Happy parts, huh?'' He slowly ran the tip of his tongue over his lips.

Her stomach dropped to her heels and settled there. Suddenly, her knees were the consistency of Papa's Chocolate Mousse. She imagined this hunk licking chocolate off her body. Better yet, she would lick the chocolate off *his* happy parts. Every delicious inch of him.

''You're rather large,'' she said. ''It'll take more than one jar. Probably three. Trust me, this is the most fun you can have with chocolate.''

He grinned at her, the dimple deepening, his blue eyes fired with wicked delight. The laugh lines bracketing his mouth told her that he often smiled. He looked like a very naughty little boy—an endearing look some women found extremely sexy.

"Give me three jars of the milk chocolate."

"Ten pounds of chocolate and three jars of body paint. I guess she must be some valentine." The instant the words were out of her mouth, Allie regretted them. Her father always said her smart mouth would get her in trouble.

"She's the perfect woman," he responded automatically.

Of course, Allie thought, again experiencing a "blond moment." This stud had a glamorous blond girlfriend. What would it be like to have this man brushing chocolate over your body? He looked at her as if he'd read her mind, then his gaze dropped to her lips.

No doubt flirting was second nature to him. On one level she found his attention exciting, yet he irritated her. A man buying candy for his girl on Valentine's Day should be more loyal. No one knew better than Allie what it felt like to discover the man you loved had betrayed you.

"Hold everything! Put your hands in the air!"

Allie looked up at the sound of the urgent voice. A man stood aiming a deadly-looking gun—straight at her.

Chapter Two

KYLE PAXTON CURSED under his breath, spotting the young punk with a gun. A stickup. He would have bought the candy and been out of here before this jerk barged into Valentine Delights—if he hadn't been trying to flirt with Allie.

"Put your hands up!" yelled the robber.

Kyle raised his hands and watched Allie reach for the sky. He'd asked Papa Valentine her name after he'd seen her around the shop. He'd wanted to meet her, but she had an unapproachable air.

"Open the cash register," ordered the punk, waving the gun.

Kyle had been held up once when he'd been driving a roach coach, going from job site to job site, selling microwaved hamburgers to construction workers. He'd barely been eighteen then. Over a dozen years had passed, but he still remembered how frightened he'd been. Allie looked even more scared, her fingers trembling as she opened the cash register.

"Here." Allie gave the robber two fistfuls of bills.

He shoved the money into the pocket of his denim jacket, then pointed the weapon at Kyle's temple. "Gimme your money and your watch."

Kyle lowered his hands and pulled his money clip out of his pocket. Then he unfastened his watchband. He handed both to the kid, realizing he couldn't be a day over twenty. But dangerous as hell. His eyes had a wild, unfocused look that meant he was on something.

The young punk pointed the gun at Allie. "You're coming with me."

"Wait a minute," Kyle protested.

"I don't want nobody callin' the police," the kid told him, the weapon still trained on Allie. "She's my insurance."

Sweat peppered the back of Kyle's neck. He could not let this jerk take Allie hostage. No telling what might happen then. "Why not lock us in the storage room? Nobody else has seen you and it'll be hours before anyone gets us out. You'll be long gone."

The kid hesitated. Kyle didn't like the way the punk kept staring at Allie.

"Unlock the storeroom, Allie," Kyle instructed.

He gave her credit for coolly taking the key and unlocking the door. The kid stood watching, the gun aimed at her. Hands still in the air, Kyle walked behind the counter toward the storeroom.

"Lock us in and take the key."

Kyle didn't wait for an answer. He put his hand on Allie's waist and pushed her into the dark room, then slammed the door shut. A second later the key turned in the lock, and Kyle let out a breath of relief.

"You okay?" he asked, his hand still on the small of her back.

"Yes," she replied, but he didn't believe it.

He slipped his arm around her shoulders and felt her shaking. "I sure as hell was scared. Never can tell what a punk with a gun might do."

"You were frightened?" She pulled away from him and fumbled in the darkness for a moment. A small bulb filled the storage room with dim light. "You seemed pretty cool to me."

He watched her green eyes and saw the emotion behind her calm voice. She nervously hooked a wayward strand of sherry-brown hair behind one ear. She looked so damned cute standing there in baggy sweats, her hair a mess. And those shoes. Why would a woman with great legs like Allie wear boots intended for combat?

Even dressed as she was, Allie had unique appeal. Unusual hair that wasn't red and wasn't brown, either. Unusual eyes that were green with tiny stitches of gold. An unusual mouth with a full lower lip and upturned corners, like a Cupid's bow.

When he'd found her behind the counter today, he couldn't believe his luck. His heart had been thundering in his ears as he'd ordered the chocolates, deliberately taking his time. She'd warmed up to him gradually, and by the time she'd pitched the Chocolate Body Paint, he was on a roll.

"I said, you seemed pretty cool," she repeated.

"I wasn't," he responded with complete honesty. "I was afraid of what might happen if he took you with him."

Something flickered in her eyes, and he wondered if she knew how much they revealed. They were a gorgeous, subtle shade of green, but sadness lurked in their depths. Wariness. Someone had hurt her badly, he guessed.

"The storage room would never have occurred to me. If not for you, I'd be in a getaway car with that creep. How can I ever repay you?"

He had lots of ideas about how she could thank him—starting with a jar of that Chocolate Body Paint. He was a man who went after what he wanted—and got it. And he wanted Allie. "How about that jar of Chocolate Body Paint? My happy parts are all yours."

She ignored his joke, her expression completely serious. "You know my name. Out there you called me Allie."

"Papa Valentine told me."

"Oh." Her eyes widened, her lower lip trembling.

"You're shivering. No wonder. It's cold in here." He shrugged out of his jacket. "Let's get this on you. It might be a while before we get out of here."

She slipped her arms into the sleeves. His knuckles brushed the soft rise of her breasts as he helped her. The accidental touch made him freeze for a second. She felt so soft, so feminine. He realized with sudden clarity that, with this woman, one brush of his fingers wasn't going to be nearly enough.

Hot and hard, desire kicked in. Not that it hadn't been there earlier. He'd been staring at her across the case of stupid chocolates, wondering what it would be like to hold her, kiss her. Feel her beneath him.

His pulse picked up a beat, then zoomed into overdrive, heat pooling in dangerous places. He wanted this woman in an instinctive, primitive way. He didn't even know her, yet he wanted her on more than a sexual level, too. He wanted to make things right for her—and to protect her from jerks like the punk who'd just robbed the store.

ALLIE CLUTCHED the leather bomber jacket, wrapping her arms around herself. His body heat was still in the soft leather and it warmed her. Not that she'd been cold. She'd shivered because she'd been shaken to the core. Gun-wielding creeps were something she only saw on television.

She had almost been taken hostage. Allie shuddered again, imagining what might have happened next. She had been rescued by a guardian angel in the form of the man now looking at her so intently.

How could she have thought he was nothing more than a studmuffin too buff to have a brain? He had reacted quickly while she'd stood there, terrified. It wasn't just that he was a gorgeous hunk. He was witty and intelligent, too.

Every woman's dream. The perfect valentine.

He was still studying her, his expression strangely arrested, his pupils dilated so that his irises were almost entirely black. He reached toward her neck and straightened the collar of his jacket. He was so much larger that it hung on her like a choir robe. He lifted a strand of her hair, freeing it from under the collar, his fingers lingering a moment against her cheek.

"Thanks." Her voice sounded breathy. "You saved me."

He shrugged as if it wasn't any big deal. "I'm just glad Papa Valentine told me about having to put a lock on the storeroom door."

He was closer now, although she hadn't noticed him move. A scant inch separated their bodies and she caught his scent. It was a delicious masculine smell, like citrus laced with spice. She dropped her hands to her sides and ran her moist palms over the smooth leather jacket.

"I was here the day a lock became necessary," Allie said, smiling at the memory.

"Tell me about it," he said. A strange roughness had crept into his voice.

She realized he was trying to get her mind off the robbery and she went along with it. Her pulse was still pounding and she felt a little shaky, but she had the sudden urge to see him smile, to see the lone dimple again.

"Mrs. Dalwinkle came in with her six-year-old twins and a friend. I waited on them. Sometimes I help out Papa," she explained, not wanting to reveal her own dream of opening a coffee bar. "Mrs. Dalwinkle ordered a Papaccino. You know, that's Papa's version of a cappuccino."

"I know. I've had my share," he said.

She was extremely conscious of his virile appeal. He was standing so close that she was tempted to move another half step forward—into his arms. Instead, she rattled on, speaking too quickly. "The mothers were gossiping and dipping chocolate *biscotti* into their Papaccinos. That's when the boys slipped into the storeroom."

"Didn't you notice them?"

"No. I was trying to fill a dozen latte orders at once. Have you ever tried to get milk to froth?"

"It's murder." He rewarded her with that one-dimpled smile.

"Papa caught them, but not before the twins rearranged the lower shelves in here." She waved her hand at the stainless-steel racks, which held what remained of the day's chocolate delivery. "We couldn't tell the cream centers from the solids, the nut bases from the fruit bases. There was no way we could sell any of them."

"So what did you do?" he asked.

She threw up her hands and tried for a wide-eyed innocent look. "What *could* we do? We ate them."

He chuckled—a deep, smoky sound that seemed to vibrate in her own chest. It made her even more acutely aware of how close to her he stood. A brief shiver rippled through her, and he put a steadying hand on her shoulder.

"Are you okay?"

No. Her heart was hammering like a teenager's on a first date. All she could think to say was, "Cedar Ridge doesn't have crime. I can't believe this happened."

"There's not a place in America that's completely safe from crime." He gently squeezed her shoulder. "Something was bound to happen here sooner or later."

"I hope the police catch him. Papa Valentine had a lot of money. Today's one of his biggest days," she said, conscious of the vaguely sensual light in his eyes. Was she imagining it? What was he thinking? She kept talking, the words a bit rushed. "And your watch and money. I'm so sorry."

"Forget the watch. I can get another. And it wasn't much money. What's important is you're safe."

"How can I thank you? I don't know what I would have done if you hadn't rescued me."

He leaned closer and her heart stopped when she realized what he was about to do. She shivered as he cupped her cheek with his strong hand and lowered his head. A soft sigh escaped her lips as his mouth hovered over hers, his warm breath fanning the loose tendrils framing her face. Longing rose, swift and sure, from some place deep inside her.

"I'm glad I was here when it happened."

His lips brushed hers and a rough moan sounded from his throat. In a heartbeat his mouth possessed hers without any of the sweet foreplay usually preceding a first kiss. His kiss was bold, totally carnal, unbelievably erotic.

His demanding lips pressed hard against hers, his tongue stealing quickly into her mouth. Both his arms circled her, firmly anchoring her to his powerful body as his tongue mated with hers.

He subjected her to the most sexual, intimate kiss she'd ever experienced. It annihilated her defenses, her better judgment. She lost any inkling of resistance with an inward sigh and succumbed to temptation, leaning into the kiss.

The pressure of his aroused body made every nerve-ending tingle with awareness. An unfamiliar heat throbbed in her stomach, then languidly spread downward. Her arms were around him now, his size and solidity evident beneath her hands.

He pulled back, saying, "You taste like raspberries."

"That's Papa's Chocolate Midnight Fantasy for you." How she managed to say one word mystified her. A shocking wave of heat flared inside her, making her suddenly feel flushed.

"No," he countered, a sensual undertone in his voice. "*This* is a midnight fantasy."

He kissed her again, driving her up against the shelves of chocolate. His hands explored the loose strands of hair that had fallen from her lopsided ponytail. Soon all her hair was down, its weight tumbling around her shoulders.

And his hands were in her hair. She'd always thought of her hair as a nuisance—not an erotic plaything. But he showed her what she'd been missing. Running through her tumbled hair, his fingers furrowed their way to the base of her skull, then gently massaged her.

His hands were on her head, but she felt the tingling in her toes. He knew all the right moves, she thought. His was wondrously, magnificently masculine. She was out of her league here. Such an aggressive guy no doubt specialized in down-and-dirty sex.

He gathered her long hair in his fist like a silken scarf and drew her head backward to kiss the tender arch of her neck. A sigh escaped her throat.

He'd discovered a very happy part of her body—the sensitive spot just below her ear. He nibbled at it, running the moist tip of his tongue across the soft skin. She signed again, louder this time, the sensation tingling though her.

He answered with a low growl from deep in his chest. His hands were wandering over her back, and even through the sweatshirt, she could feel their heat, their strength. He explored even lower, while his lips were discovering the erotic area at the curve of her neck.

"Wait!" she cried.

In a matter of minutes, she was going to be flat on her back in Papa Valentine's storeroom—and she wouldn't be sampling chocolates—if she didn't stop this now. But her protest didn't faze him. He was too intent on kissing her neck.

She thrust her hands against the solid wall of his chest, finally pushing him far enough away to speak. "I'm grateful for what you did. But not *that* grateful."

"What's wrong?" he asked with all the enthusiasm of a man receiving the last rites.

"Here I am kissing you." She grabbed a chocolate from the shelf, trying to be cool. "I don't even know your name."

"I'm Kyle Paxton," he said, leaning forward to kiss her again.

She ducked under his arm. "Kyle?" She said the name slowly, disbelief etched in every syllable. "Kyle Paxton. Not *the* Kyle Paxton?"

Chapter Three

ALLIE SAGGED AGAINST the chocolate rack. *Kyle Paxton.* She'd been kissing a man she had no business even talking to. *Criminy!* How had she gotten herself into this mess?

As "Restaurant Rita" she went incognito to critique restaurants in Cedar Ridge and nearby Atlanta. From catering trucks to chic sushi bars, Kyle Paxton owned more places to eat than anyone else in town. Just yesterday, she'd handed her editor, Charlotte Keats, a scathing review of Kyle's expensive new restaurant, Reflections. Her "Restaurant Rita" column would appear in the *Cedar Ridge Tribune* on Sunday—two days from now.

"I guess Papa Valentine told you about me," Kyle said.

"Hmm," Allie hedged, popping the chocolate she'd been holding into her mouth. Papa had never mentioned Kyle even when they'd gone together—in disguise—to review Reflections.

"Papa told you about me helping him set up Valentine Delights, didn't he?"

Allie managed something that might pass for a smile and reached for another chocolate. Why hadn't Papa told her about Kyle?

Kyle grinned, then he chuckled, the rich sound filling every corner of the small room. "Okay, Allie. Now you know my name."

He leaned toward her, his lips parted. She thrust a chocolate in his face.

"Try this espresso truffle. It's delicious."

Kyle frowned, obviously not a happy camper. Amorous males spurned in favor of chocolates rarely were. He put the chocolate on the wrong shelf, staring at her as if ready to pounce. She turned her back on him and walked to the far end of the long, narrow room.

"What time is it?" she asked. "Shouldn't someone have tried to get us out by now?"

"I have no idea what time it is. The thief took my watch, remember?" From the sound of his voice, he was right behind her, but she refused to face him. "It was after four when I came in. It took a while to select those few chocolates."

"Then it must be between four-thirty and five," she said, turning to him. "Rudy should show up soon and let us out of here."

"Why? Do you have a hot date?"

"No. Do you?" Why had she asked that? Of course, he did. He hesitated, then said, "I have dinner reservations at eight. I imagine we'll be out of here by then."

She remembered the huge box of chocolates and his "perfect valentine." What would the blonde have said if she had seen Kyle kissing her? Anger mushroomed inside Allie as she remembered Drew betraying her in much the same way—with another woman.

She'd played right into Kyle's hands by letting him kiss her even though she knew he was involved with someone else. The scathing review set to run in the Sunday paper would serve him right; a man who would two-time his sweetheart deserved a bashing by Restaurant Rita.

"I want to go home," she said, more to herself than him.

"Was kissing me that bad?"

No. It was the most wonderful experience I can remember. She stared at the row of bittersweet chocolates, determined to ignore how attractive he was. That didn't work, so she walked over to the locked door. She rested her forehead against the wood, telling herself it wouldn't be long before she was out of here. She was disturbingly aware that Kyle had come up behind her. He was standing so close she could feel his body heat.

And she recalled with startling clarity what his powerful body felt like.

He put his hand on her shoulder, his touch light at first, then firmer. "Allie, look at me."

It was a voice accustomed to being obeyed. She slowly turned, not because she was the type to blindly follow orders, but because she wasn't a coward. She had to deal with this situation.

Kyle's face had a sheepish expression like that of a young boy who'd just been caught putting worms down a little girl's back. "I came on a bit too strong, didn't I?"

She defied any woman on earth to look into Kyle Paxton's blue eyes and not forgive him. "Yes," she said softly.

"I just wanted to take your mind off the punk who robbed the store."

She heard the amusement overriding his tone and couldn't help smiling. She forgave him for being a two-timing louse. After all, he'd saved her from being taken hostage by that creep. Kyle was some blond bimbo's problem, not hers. It had been nothing more than a kiss shared by two people still high after a crisis. That accounted for their intense reaction to each other.

Kyle dropped to the floor and patted the space beside him. "Might as well sit down. It looks like we're going to be in here awhile."

Allie hesitated, but felt foolish standing while he was sitting at her feet. The storage racks lined both sides of the narrow room. The only place to sit was in front of the door—right beside Kyle. She slowly sank to the floor and positioned herself as far away from him as she could get, which wasn't nearly far enough.

"Tell me about yourself," he said, sounding genuinely interested. "Sometimes I see you at one of the tables studying or something. Other times you've been behind the counter helping out."

"I'm a technical writer. I free-lance for a toy company, taking instructions written in Chinese and translating them into English. Then I 'dumb down' the directions into a few easy steps, so parents can assemble the toys they buy."

"Chinese?" he repeated, obviously impressed. "Wow! How did you learn the language?"

"My father served on various embassy staffs in the Orient. I lived there until I came to Los Angeles to go to college."

"What are you doing in a small town like this? You should be in Washington, translating for the government or something."

There was no way she was telling this man the humiliating story of her love life. She jumped up and grabbed another chocolate from the shelf. The white chocolate had a zigzag design of dark chocolate on it and a creamy mocha center. She silently offered him one, but he shook his head, then watched her eat it.

"Allie, it sounds like you're wasting your talent."

"I don't really want to spend my life translating. I just fell into it because I knew the language and so much is being made in China." She sat on the floor beside him again. "I'm saving money to..."

"To what?" he prompted.

"Well, maybe someday I'm going to start a small business of some kind," she hedged, not wanting to tell him specifics. After all, it was only a dream. "I like working with people."

He smiled his approval, the lone dimple winking at her.

"How did you get started?" she asked, intent on changing the subject. She didn't want to tell him more about her dream than she already had.

"I drove a roach coach around Atlanta going to job sites to sell hot dogs and soda pop. It took me a long time to save enough to move here and buy my own catering truck. I kept working hard and saving until I had enough to open my first hamburger stand."

"Why did you leave Atlanta?" she asked.

Two beats of silence. "I like a smaller town. My mother lives here." Another beat of silence and she sensed there was something he didn't really want to talk about, either. "So, Allie, how did you get from Los Angeles to Cedar Ridge? I'll bet that's an interesting story."

Interesting? No. Heartbreaking *would be the right word.*

He was gazing intently at her now, his blue eyes slightly narrowed as if he realized she was hiding something. She had never believed in lying, so she opted for a portion of the truth. "After college, I was offered a job translating for a small toy company in Atlanta. I took it. Now I free-lance for the same company, but I work out of my home. They pay me double to do the really difficult translations." She stopped there, hoping this would satisfy him.

"If you like being with people, why do you work at home where you're alone?"

"Well, I . . . I had some problems with another employee at the toy company. It's easier if I work at home."

"What happened?" he asked.

"One of the other employees took credit for my work."

"That's when you left?"

No. That's when I should have known I was involved with a creep, she thought. "Shortly after that, I moved here."

Again he smiled, and she had the feeling he smiled a lot. She hoped her explanation satisfied him. There was no way she could tell Kyle about Drew's betrayal.

"Allie, when you decide what you want to do, just go for it. Put your heart into it, work hard and go for it. That's my motto."

"Where does Reflections fit into your plans?" she asked, not concerned about making the reference since he already assumed Papa Valentine had told her about him. "Is it another step toward a big, splashy restaurant in Atlanta?"

"No, not at all," Kyle replied, his tone dead serious. "I started at the bottom of the business with a roach coach and worked my way up. Reflections is my dream. I want a five-star restaurant right here in Cedar Ridge. Why should people have to drive into Atlanta for a great restaurant?''

The sincerity in his expression and the excitement in his voice told her how important this was to him. This was the man who'd prevented her from being taken hostage. And Restaurant Rita was going to annihilate Reflections—his dream. A wave of guilt washed over her and she looked away, unable to meet his unflinching gaze.

The high-pitched screech of a siren announced the arrival of the police. Within seconds a percussion of muffled noises came from the other side of the door. Kyle and Allie banged on the heavy door, screaming that they were inside. Minutes later she heard a key turn in the lock. Police officers surrounded them when they emerged.

"Are you all right?" Papa Valentine asked as he pulled Allie aside and led her over to the espresso machine. "One of my customers noticed no one was in the shop, saw the open cash register, and called the police. I drove up just as they got here. Luckily I had another key to the storeroom with my store keys."

"I'm fine," she said, shrugging out of Kyle's coat. She ventured a look in his direction and saw he was talking to the police across the room. "I'm sorry the robber got all your money."

"Forget the money. At least he didn't hurt you or Kyle."

"Papa Valentine, why didn't you tell me you knew Kyle Paxton when we went to critique Reflections?"

Papa continued making a Depth Charge—two shots of espresso in a cup of coffee. "We were rating the restaurant, not the man. He isn't the chef. He's the owner."

"True," she said. "But he just saved me."

Papa handed her the steaming cup filled with the high-octane coffee. "Sounds like you could use this. Tell me what happened."

Allie took a sip of coffee and let the warm liquid soothe her. Then she gave Papa Valentine the details about the robbery.

"Kyle's one hell of a guy," Papa said when she'd finished. "He thinks on his feet. He outsmarted the crook."

"He was buying a box of chocolates. I'd just begun to fill it when . . ."

"I'll take care of it." Papa studied her, his expression concerned. "Allie, what went on in there? Your hair was up, now—"

"Don't ask. Just promise me you won't tell Kyle that I'm Restaurant Rita."

"You didn't tell him? Don't you think you owe it to him . . . considering?"

"I promised Charlotte Keats that I would keep my identity a secret," Allie said. "Since she's the editor-in-chief of the *Tribune*, she's my boss and I have to listen to her. You're the only person who knows I go out in disguise to critique restaurants. If people knew I was Restaurant Rita, I would get the red-carpet treatment and never know how the average person gets served at a restaurant.''

''Speaking of Charlotte Keats, she just walked in,'' Papa Valentine said. ''News sure travels fast in a small town.''

Charlotte Keats joined the large group clustered around Kyle just as a police officer walked up to Allie. ''Are you feeling better now, miss? I need to take your statement.''

Papa Valentine stood at her side while she explained to the police officer how a young man with a gun had robbed the store. Despite being very shaken by the incident, she found she could give a detailed description.

''Whoa, cops!'' Rudy burst into the shop, his black hair slathered with gel, the gold hoop in his nostril glistening. ''What's happening, man?''

''I'm out of here,'' Allie whispered to Papa.

She slipped out the backdoor into the alley. Dusk had fallen, and it was much cooler now than when she'd left home. The old-fashioned streetlamps were on, glowing in the gathering darkness, gilding the quaint storefronts and cobbled streets with amber light.

She hadn't had the energy to fight through the group around Kyle and say goodbye. What was the point, anyway?

An aching sadness swept through her. Black Friday. Valentine's Day. It had been almost a year since her engagement had ended in emotional disaster. She'd been lonely, sure, but she hadn't realized how lonely—until Kyle Paxton had taken her into his arms.

Forget that two-timing creep, Kyle Paxton. You have a cat to feed and a fire engine to assemble. She marched up the street toward the lonely apartment she called home.

"DID YOU LOSE MUCH MONEY?" Kyle asked Papa Valentine.

"It doesn't matter," Papa replied. "I'm just thankful you were here with Allie when it happened."

The police had left but the shop was jammed with people. Rudy was behind the counter serving coffee as fast as he could. Kyle looked around for Allie, but didn't see her.

"Where's Allie?" he asked Papa Valentine.

Papa studied him for a moment. "She went home."

Kyle grabbed his jacket from the counter, and asked for her address. Papa arched one dark brown eyebrow. It stood out, a stark contrast to the white fringe of hair around his bald head as he gave Kyle her address.

"Thanks again," Papa said as he handed Kyle the box of chocolates. "These are on me. Have fun tonight."

Kyle took the chocolates to his car and swung by Roses O'Grady. It took him almost half an hour to pick out three-dozen rare, exotic orchids and have them arranged in a crystal vase. When it was done, they reminded him of Allie. Unusual. One of a kind.

Her apartment was in a small, modest building on a side street not far from Valentine Delights. He rang her doorbell and waited. He rang a second time, positive she was home. All the lights were on and an orange cat with a tummy the size of the *Hindenburg* was staring at him from the window seat. Finally the door swung open.

Obviously, he'd gotten Allie out of the shower. She couldn't have looked sexier if she'd spent a week trying. She was dressed in a terry-cloth robe, her hair wrapped in a towel. Droplets of water clung to her cheeks and the shadowy vee of her neck exposed by the robe.

She stared at him for a second, then she saw the bouquet. "You didn't—"

"I had to," he said, inwardly breathing a sigh of relief at her pleased smile. "It's Valentine's Day and I've just met a very special lady."

"Kyle, how sweet." She took the vase and lowered her head to the dewy blossoms to take a deep whiff of one mauve orchid. "I didn't know orchids had any fragrance."

"The florist said only a few rare orchids give off a sweet smell." He didn't add that those orchids had prices hitting the stratosphere. It was worth every cent to see how touched she was.

"I'd invite you in, but it's getting late and I know you have dinner plans," she said. "Thanks for the flowers. They're lovely, so unusual. You didn't have to—"

"I know. I wanted to." He moved inside the door. "Nice place."

There was an awkward pause, and it bothered him. He didn't have trouble talking to women. But Allie was different. He'd gotten off on the wrong foot with her and didn't quite know how to change things.

She set the vase on a small table beside the door. His eyes lowered to the deep vee of the robe loosely belted around her slim body. An intriguing drop of water spilled out of the hollow of her throat and raced downward. Her hand immediately flew up to close the opening, and she swallowed hard.

Aw, man. Can't you do anything right? He was leering at her again like a man who had spent months at sea. "Would you like to go to dinner?" he asked. "I have reservations at Reflections at eight."

"Thanks," she said, looking puzzled. "I can't."

"Look, I said I was sorry that I came on so strong. I don't know what else—"

"Stop." She crossed her arms over her chest and glared at him. "I know you saved me, and I sincerely thank you. The blame for what happened in the storage room is as much mine as it is yours. But I know your type.''

''My type? Hey, hold it.''

''No, you just listen to me.'' She planted her hands on her hips. ''You're here now because I stopped you. Evidently you see me as some kind of challenge. Well, I think you're a class-A jerk. You already have a date with the blonde.''

''Blonde? What blonde?''

The orange cat had left his perch at the window and was now camped out on Kyle's feet, his bulk settled on the toes of his shoes.

''Don't do that, Gordon.'' Allie nudged the cat with her bare foot. ''Surely you remember the perfect valentine? You bought her ten pounds of exorbitantly expensive chocolates at Valentine Delights—and three jars of Chocolate Body Paint.''

The light dawned. So that's what had Allie upset. He waited for a long moment, inhaling the fragrant smell of shampoo and fresh soap. ''Oh, *that* blonde.''

A flush shot up Allie's neck, racing from where her slender hand held the robe closed, to the towel covering her auburn hair. ''Did you forget about her?''

''No. I love her. She'll be excited to have you join us for dinner. And you'll like my mother.'' Allie's head snapped up; the towel lurched to one side. She grabbed for it with both hands, and the robe gaped open. He had the decency—this time—not to sneak a peek. Okay, so he could see a tantalizing bit of cleavage without looking directly at her breasts.

"You bought those chocolates for your *mother?*"

"Yeah," he replied, unable to bank a swell of masculine pride. Allie was jealous. It meant she cared, and he couldn't help grinning. "But I never said anything about a blonde."

She regarded him suspiciously. "What about the Chocolate Body Paint?"

"I bought it for you. Any woman who can say 'happy parts' with a straight face is a woman I want to know better," he said with complete honesty. "Hey, I was coming on to you. I didn't want to admit that my only Valentine's plans were with my mother."

Allie's lips parted in speechless surprise. Kyle quickly moved in, taking advantage of the situation. He swept her into his arms and pressed his lips against hers, gently covering her mouth, testing its softness. She dropped her hands and the towel toppled off her head. It hit his arm and fell to the floor. Her hair, heavy and damp, swung across his arm like moist velvet.

He'd meant to make this a short, sweet kiss—the kind recommended by "sensitive" men in those women's magazines his mother read. But the instant her lips touched his and she arched against him, he lost it. A shock wave rocked his entire body.

They kissed, their tongues dancing together in darting little forays that sent a throb of pleasure surg-

ing upward through his groin. He twisted his body a
little. It wouldn't be his fault if the half-open robe
opened even more, would it?

Her arms slid up to twine around his shoulders in a
heated embrace. He shifted his stance again. This time
he got his wish; the robe parted, and the warm, moist
fullness of Allie's breasts melted through his light-
weight shirt.

Her breasts weren't huge, but they were high and
full. Perfect. He longed to cradle them in his hands;
better yet, kiss his way down the slender curve of her
neck, across her soft shoulders to those breasts.

Allie had gone completely still, evidently realizing
her robe was open. It took the fortitude of a saint to
pull away and smile as if he hadn't noticed. He stepped
back, breathing like a marathon runner. Stumbling
over the damn cat, he lurched into the doorjamb. "I'll
be back at quarter to eight."

Chapter Four

"DID YOU HEAR ME SAY yes?" Allie hooked the pin around the last electric curler. "I never said I would go out with him. Kyle just took it for granted. Gordon, are you listening?"

Of course not. The dratted cat was as bad as Kyle Paxton. Gordon was perched on the counter, staring at her with fascination. Well, no wonder. It had been months since she'd curled her hair.

Doubtless, Gordon had forgotten the pitiful sight. The hot rollers jutted out at odd angles, making her look like an alien from another galaxy. All she needed was a head like a lightbulb and a spaceship and she would be front-page news in supermarket checkout lines across America.

"A touch of makeup. That's all. I don't want Kyle to think I went to a lot of trouble for him."

She rummaged through a drawer containing a few cosmetics. Whisking on a little blush, she decided to apply a hint of eyeliner and green shadow to deepen the green of her eyes. Then she peered at her reflection.

"Close enough for government work."

She zipped into her small bedroom where the fire engine still lay in a pieces on the chocolate-stained sheets. Ignoring the mess, she threw open the door to her tiny closet, and groaned. Most of her evening clothes consisted of "blue-hair" dresses.

When she went out in disguise to do her "Restaurant Rita" column, she usually put on a gray wig and a dress suitable for the geriatric set. She couldn't possibly wear any of those tonight.

"How about this one?" she asked Gordon, who'd followed her. She pulled out a Day-Glo fuchsia T-shirt dress. "Like what it says? 'I'd Give Up Chocolate but I'm Not a Quitter'?"

Gordon twitched his tail in response, nixing the idea.

"You're right. Reflections is an elegant restaurant. Everyone will be dressed to the nines. I couldn't embarrass Kyle. After all, he brought me orchids on Valentine's Day."

A very special lady.

She leaned against the doorjamb, recalling his words. He'd brought her the most astonishingly beautiful orchids she had ever seen. And what had she done? She'd thrown a hissy fit only to learn the "blonde" was his mother.

"You let the past rear its ugly head and make you imagine the worst. Kyle and Drew are nothing alike." She rummaged through the closet for a minute, thinking. "I'm wrong, Gordon. Kyle and Drew are more alike than it first appears."

The marmalade cat now looked positively bored. Obviously, he'd rather find a yummy mouse than listen to her troubles.

"Both Kyle and Drew go after what they want with a vengeance. Blind ambition fueled by the desire to be successful. The only difference is Drew is sneaky. Kyle is up-front." She stared at the blond wig on the closet shelf. "I can't get involved with another ambitious man."

The pain of Drew's betrayal was still fresh, even though it had been almost a year since he'd broken their engagement. She took a minute to remind herself that moving here was the beginning of her new life. She'd learned her lesson with men.

What was she worried about? This was only a date, not a commitment of any kind. She had jumped to conclusions, imagining a nonexistent blonde.

She had become too emotional and lost sight of the real danger in this situation. She did not want Kyle Paxton to discover she was Restaurant Rita. She liked writing the column because it gave her a chance to be clever and funny. If Kyle found out who Restaurant Rita was, no doubt the whole town would discover her identity.

All she had to do was keep her secret safe for one night. And stay out of Kyle's arms. Her willpower seemed to evaporate the instant he touched her.

"Don't worry, he's bringing his mother. There's no surer way to render a man harmless than to have his mother in tow," she said, aware that Gordon had wandered out of the room. She was talking to herself, but it helped calm her frazzled nerves.

A flush of heat shot up her neck as she remembered kissing Kyle not so long ago. Her worthless old robe had parted at exactly the wrong time. Thankfully, he hadn't noticed. Thankfully, he'd left to change. Or heaven only knows what might have happened.

One of the electric rollers slipped from its mooring and bounced to the carpet. A loop of hair fell over one eye. She tucked the errant strand around another roller threatening to bite the dust. "What *am* I going to wear?"

She rifled through her wardrobe three times, coming back to the lavender dress again and again. It was a wispy silk gown she'd found marked down three times at Glad Rags. She'd splurged on it, spending some of her hard-earned savings on the dress and a blond wig.

When she'd gone to Reflections over two weeks ago with Papa Valentine, she'd worn the dress—and the blond wig. She doubted anyone there would recognize her with brown hair and another man, but she hated to court fate.

"Live dangerously, Alexis Evans. Live dangerously."

She dumped her electric rollers in the bathroom sink. Dropping her head forward so her hair fell to her knees, she ruthlessly brushed it. When she flung her head back, the heat-induced waves fluffed into a full mane of loose curls. They hung softly across the tops of her bare shoulders. She gave her hairdo two, three hours, tops, before the weight of her thick hair and its natural tendency to straightness wiped out her efforts.

With luck, she would be home by then. In bed alone.

"COME IN," CALLED ALLIE, and Kyle let himself into her apartment.

He stood in the empty living room and adjusted the tie he'd been saving for a special occasion. He couldn't remember feeling this excited in years. A wellspring of happiness rose in his chest. Maybe life had been getting too predictable, success too easy.

"I'll be right there," Allie called. "I'm getting a shawl."

Gordon spotted Kyle and trotted over. Instantly Kyle became the object of the fat feline's desire, and the cat circled his ankles, brushing orange fur on his dark trousers. Kyle tried to discourage him with a flick of his leg. That made porky "Gordo" even more amorous, rubbing for all he was worth against the dark fabric.

"I'm ready," Allie said softly.

"Allie?" he said, dumbfounded.

She wore a lavender dress with a low neckline that bared her shoulders and gathered across her chest, forming a knot of fabric just below her breasts. The skirt skimmed her hips and hung in soft, provocative folds around her legs. She'd curled her hair and it waved, lush and thick, to her shoulders where it settled, the ends of the curls brushing her bare skin.

Damn, she was sexy.

"Kyle, is this dress all right?"

No, it was not all right. Every guy around was going to be ogling her tonight. He realized he was staring, slack-jawed, like some Neanderthal. "You're drop-dead gorgeous. That's a dynamite dress."

She smiled, an arresting upturn of her lips that kicked up his pulse another notch. How was he going to make it through a night of dinner and dancing? He stood rooted to the spot, battling the urge to haul her into his arms and kiss her breathless.

Her lips were blush pink, soft and dewy. He imagined brushing his lips against their fullness, then marking every luscious inch of her bare body with his kisses. Why bother with dinner? Why not just trail hot, passionate kisses across her tender skin starting with the provocative curve of her shoulders?

He let his eyes wander downward as he anticipated making love to Allie. She must have read his mind—and had similar thoughts. Her nipples had contracted, clearly defined beneath the sheer fabric. Remembering how those nipples had felt against his chest earlier sent a fresh wave of heat to his groin. Allie swept an exotic-looking black fringed shawl around her shoulders and clutched it over her breasts. Killjoy.

"Did you leave your mother outside in the car?"

"Mom is really something," he said, stalling. He closed the door on the disgusting Gordo. "When she heard I had a date, she begged off."

Allie stopped dead in her tracks. The amber glow from her porch light haloed her hair, bringing out its red highlights. "You're kidding."

"Come on. We'll be late." He took her arm. "Mom thought she'd be a third wheel, so she insisted on staying home with the box of Valentine Delights. She's thrilled I have a date. I haven't been out in a long time."

Allie looked visibly shaken; she was the kind of woman who couldn't easily hide her feelings. "I have to be home early. I have a fire engine that's giving me trouble. I have to finish the project and have it in Atlanta by Monday."

He opened the car door for Allie, then settled himself behind the wheel, uncomfortably aware that she wasn't happy to be alone with him. *Why?* he wondered, more determined than ever to change her mind.

From the first time he'd seen her across the room at Valentine Delights, he'd been attracted to her. When he finally got to talk to her, what did she do? Pitched him the Chocolate Body Paint. Happy parts. Those words made him smile as he bullied his way into the traffic along Main Street.

He cast a sideways glance at her and saw her staring straight ahead. She seemed a little nervous to him, but it was hard to tell. She could be a smart-aleck one minute, then dead serious the next. She was a lot more complicated than he'd first suspected. A translator specializing in Chinese—of all things—and talented enough not just to put the directions into English, but to make those instructions easy for parents to understand.

Okay. Allie was smart and funny. And sexy as hell. But there was something more: a hidden current in her personality that signaled pain or loss. There was a missing link in the story of her life. His instincts said not to press it. Get to know her a little better, then she would tell him.

He pulled up to the valet parking station in front of Reflections. With pride, he surveyed the artsy chrome sign, then turned to Allie. She quickly smiled at him, but he could have sworn she'd been frowning.

Chapter Five

ALLIE FELT THE WARM pressure of Kyle's hand on the small of her back as they walked through the door into Reflections. She took a deep breath, determined to steady her nerves, but butterflies the size of eagles swooped through her stomach. She couldn't believe she was with Kyle. Alone.

Until she'd met Kyle Paxton, she had never believed in the kind of sexual attraction that was used by Madison Avenue advertising agencies to sell perfume or by Hollywood to peddle movies. It seemed too extreme, too overpowering, too primitive. Wrong. It existed and it was happening now.

Who could blame her for being attracted to Kyle? He was wearing an Italian-cut suit that made his shoulders seem even broader and an eggshell-blue shirt that emphasized his blue eyes. His chestnut-brown hair wasn't quite brushed into place, which gave him a slightly roguish air.

He moved with an athletic grace, projecting an aura of confidence that had a hint of ruthlessness. Yet his self-assurance was tempered by the humor lurking in his eyes—along with a glimpse of the mischievous little boy he must have been. There was a suggestion of stubbornness, though, in the square chin and firm jaw. But overriding it all was his winning smile, highlighted by the lone dimple.

"O-o-oh, Kyle. We've been expecting you," gushed the hostess.

"Sherry, how's it going?"

"We're overbooked, of course." Sherry glanced at Allie with a look suggesting cellulite was contagious.

"Kyle. Hey, I'm glad you're here," said a short man with a goatee.

"Henry, Sherry, meet Alexis Evans," Kyle said, then turned to Allie. "Henry manages Reflections."

"Good evening," responded Henry with a broad smile. He shook Allie's hand, studying her intently. "Have we met?"

"No. Allie's a technical writer. She's never been here, have you?"

Allie gulped. When she had been here with Papa Valentine, Henry had come by their table. She opened her mouth but was saved from a lie by Sherry.

"It's the dress." The blonde leaned toward Kyle, blessing him with a megawatt smile. "There was a blonde in here two weeks ago with the *exact* same dress. Henry couldn't keep his eyes off her."

Allie usually wore a gray wig when critiquing restaurants, but she'd always wondered what it would be like to be a blonde in a sexy dress. Well, she'd found out. Men had leered at her all night. It had made her acutely uncomfortable. She would stay a brunette, thank you very much, and save the "blond moments" for her fantasies.

Sherry couldn't pry her eyes away from Kyle. "The blonde was a trophy wife, fer sure. She was with an old dude in a gray toupee."

Allie bit her lip to stifle a giggle. Wait until Papa Valentine heard this. The humorous thought evaporated when she met Henry's hard stare. Why had she worn the same dress?

"I want to introduce Allie to the team in the kitchen," Kyle said.

Allie let out an audible sigh of relief as they walked away from Henry. *You're on borrowed time,* she told herself. Common sense said to be quiet about Restaurant Rita. Not only did she need the money the column generated, but she had no reason to expect this date to turn into something serious. Why reveal her secret unnecessarily?

"Dakota is our chef," Kyle told her with pride. "I stole him from an L.A. restaurant. He designed all the items on the menu."

"Really? What's his last name?"

"He just uses one name, Dakota."

Allie mustered a smile, deciding Dakota must be full of himself. Judging by the weird items on the menu that she'd noticed on her previous visit, he'd been in L.A. too long. Dakota should go back to southern California where no one could tell the fruits from the nuts. And no one cared.

"Dakota, meet a special lady. This is Alexis Evans."

Dakota lived up to her expectations. He was young with bushy, grizzled eyebrows and an attitude. But Allie barely heard him pontificating on the Valentine's Day menu. *A special lady*. This was the second time Kyle had called her special.

"Where's the pastry chef?" Allie asked. "I heard the desserts are to die for."

"Really?" Kyle said. "Where did you hear that?"

Allie managed a smile. When she'd critiqued the restaurant, she'd marveled at the wonderful desserts. "I think someone at Valentine Delights mentioned Reflections' desserts," she replied, hating to lie.

"Go on!" Dakota said. "What did they say about the food?"

Allie looked up at the copper pans hanging from the rack overhead, aware she'd painted herself into a corner. "They didn't mention the food—just the desserts."

A sullen expression replaced Dakota's smile.

"I'm sure that was because Valentine Delights only serves coffee and sweets." Kyle mollified his star. "No one was thinking of real food."

Dakota sniffed like a prima donna. "That explains it, of course."

Kyle led Allie over to the far corner of the kitchen where a young woman was diligently piping chocolate over an ice-cream mold.

"Marie, this is Allie. She's heard great things about your desserts."

"Really?" Marie said, obviously pleased. Then she glanced shyly at Kyle, and Allie realized Marie was quite taken with her employer. *Okay, ladies, form a line.*

"Tell me which dessert is your best, and I'll order it," Allie said.

"The chocolate pecan torte," Marie responded without hesitating.

"See you later," Kyle said, then he guided Allie toward the back of the kitchen.

"Where are we going?"

"I thought you'd want to see the storeroom."

"You're kidding, aren't you?" she asked as he led her around the corner.

Kyle winked at her, then grinned, his adorable dimple appearing. His smile alone did ridiculous things to her pulse rate.

"Of course, I'm kidding. We spent enough time in a storeroom today. I just wanted to get you alone."

"Wait!" she cried, realizing he was going to kiss her.

"I can't make it through dinner." He moved closer. "Just one little kiss."

Allie took two steps back, not trusting him. And definitely not trusting her traitorous body. No telling where "one little kiss" would lead. Getting involved with this man was out of the question.

Some men could be stalled, put off with a look or a word. Not Kyle Paxton. Once he'd made up his mind about something, he went after it with a single-minded determination that took her breath away.

"Why fight it, Allie?" He took another step forward. She edged away until her back hit the wall. "Something clicks between us. I feel it. You feel it." He braced his hands against the wall on either side of her head. "Don't you?"

Not trusting her voice, she shook her head. But she knew exactly what he was talking about. He exuded charm and a compelling sensuality that she was almost powerless to resist.

"Tell the truth, Allie." He trailed one finger up the curve of her throat, barely making contact although his eyes never left hers. "You want me to kiss you, don't you?"

She gazed at him, unable to look away. The searing blue of his eyes seemed to envelop her body, heating it. And making her yearn for his kiss. It took all her willpower not to confess how very much she wanted him.

He was so close now, his body brushing the tips of her breasts. His eyes swept over her face, silently challenging her. Then his gaze dropped to her chest, and she knew, without looking, what he saw. Her nipples were tingling, pushing hard against the lacy cups of her bra.

"You're worried about your makeup, aren't you?" Kyle asked in a husky undertone.

Makeup? If she hadn't been trembling, anticipating his kiss, she would have laughed. "Yes," she said, breathlessly, seizing the opportunity. "And my hair. It took forever."

"Okay," he said with a grin that would have made the devil proud. "We'll work around it."

Before she could protest, his lips were on the sensitive curve of her neck. At the damp, velvety touch of his mouth, a warm current of pure pleasure pulsed through her. She flattened her palms against the wall, knowing that if she touched him, their chances of making it to the dinner table would be nonexistent.

He didn't put his hands on her, either, but he adjusted his stance until his legs straddled hers. Even though he wasn't touching her, it was a blatantly aggressive, sexual gesture that she found exciting and a bit frightening. She sucked in her breath and held it for a second.

His mouth prowled lower, trailing moist kisses across her bare skin. *I have to stop this!* her brain screamed. But not one single word of protest came out of her mouth. She experienced an all-consuming urge to lose herself in the moment and forget what tomorrow might bring.

Moisture coated her palms, which were still clinging to the wall, and her toes curled. He continued to softly kiss her, his hands planted against the wall on either side of her head. Still, she got the message. Take no prisoners. That was what it would be like to make love to this man. He wouldn't settle for ordinary lovemaking. He would give it everything, and expect the same in return.

"There you are," Sherry interrupted them, her voice falsely cheery.

Allie blushed so hard, the roots of her hair felt singed. With this woman as a witness, the news would be around the restaurant in a heartbeat. Then if anyone discovered she was Restaurant Rita, it would be professional disaster.

"Your table is ready, Kyle."

Chapter Six

KYLE PICKED UP A GLASS of expensive French champagne. Over the special candles he'd ordered for Valentine's Day, his eyes met Allie's. "Here's to us. Here's to Valentine's Day."

She put down the menu and picked up the flute of champagne. The rims of their glasses kissed, and he smiled, feeling happier than he had in years. But he could tell Allie was still embarrassed. Okay, he'd come on too strong. Again. Well, hell, he was a man, wasn't he? A man who was more than just a little attracted to this woman.

"So what do you think of Reflections?" He waved his glass to indicate the room. Talking was good; women liked to talk.

"Interesting."

Interesting? Couldn't she say something more enthusiastic about a restaurant that had cost a fortune to build? "It's a minimalist design. High-tech. That's why it's all black-and-white. I flew in a decorator from Los Angeles to do the interior," he said. "Personally, I think it's a little stark, but that's the rage in L.A."

Allie rewarded him with a suggestion of a smile.

He kicked back the rest of his champagne, thinking how much he wanted her to like Reflections. Sure, he wanted to rip that dress off her sexy bod and make love to her until dawn, but he wanted more than that. He needed to share just what Reflections meant to him. Yet, as much as he could joke with people, it wasn't easy for him to expose his weaknesses.

He poured himself another glass of champagne. "Maybe we should order. What looks good?"

"Well," she said. "Everything is so... different."

He watched her lips moving. *A kissable mouth. Yes, most definitely a kissable mouth.* He scooted across the suede banquette, closing the small space between them.

"How about an appetizer?" he asked.

She leveled those magnificent green eyes on him. "I think I'll skip the appetizer to save room for Marie's chocolate-pecan torte."

"Good idea," he said. The last thing his aching body wanted was a long, drawn-out dinner. *Skip the appetizer. Skip the entrée. Skip dessert. Let's go home.*

She pointed to the menu. "What's *nouvelle* Cajun tofu?"

"*Nouvelle* is French for new—"

"I know. I speak French. This just seems like an unusual way to serve tofu."

"It is unique," he said, trying not to grimace. Tofu. The thought alone made him gag. "It's rolled in Cajun spices and served hot on a bed of cilantro. Believe me, you have to acquire a taste for it."

Allie gave him a look that said hell would freeze over first. "What about this lacquered duck with a spicy espresso sauce and grapefruit chutney? I like duck but I'm not sure about serving it with spicy espresso and grapefruit."

"Hey! I give up. Dakota designed the menu. I was responsible for the menus in my other restaurants, but I wanted Reflections to be special."

"Well . . . I'm going to have the snapper with the lemon grass and garlic-mashed potatoes."

"Good choice," he assured her. "I'm having the seared *ahi*—that's tuna—with a mustard-basil crust and sweet garlic *jus*."

"Garlic *jus*. Garlic-mashed potatoes. I guess we won't have to worry about vampires, will we?"

Kyle chuckled, but wondered if there wasn't a note of disapproval in her tone. This was a side of her that he hadn't yet seen. There was so much more to know, and he reminded himself to slow down and take his time. But it was really tough when all he could think about was holding her.

He ordered their dinners and a bottle of French wine. "Let's dance. I told Henry to move the tables back so we could have a dance area for Valentine's Day."

Allie hesitated, and he grinned, calling on the killer one-dimple smile that had coaxed more than his share of women into bed. "Hey, what can happen on the dance floor?"

"Promise to behave?"

"Sure," he said, but he had his fingers crossed.

The dance floor was crowded as he gently pulled Allie into his arms. She held herself stiffly erect, a good hand span from his chest. He pulled her closer, saying, "Don't fight me. Just relax. We're dancing, that's all."

She relaxed and effortlessly followed his lead, her smaller body fitting perfectly against his. They danced in silence, and he couldn't help wondering what she was thinking.

She put her head on his shoulder and almost bowled him over. He couldn't figure her out. One minute she was set to run out the door, the next she had her head on his shoulder.

"I was up all last night trying to write the instructions for the fire engine," she told him. "One glass of champagne and I feel like putty."

He was glad her head was on his shoulder and she couldn't see him grinning. Despite the champagne's effect, he sensed this woman was going to fight him every inch of the way. Even now, he remembered her clinging to the wall, refusing to touch him as he kissed her.

She'd sighed. She'd moaned. But she had kept her hands on the wall.

ALLIE RESTED HER HEAD against Kyle's shoulder, aware that they were moving in place—not really dancing. The floor was a sea of lovers, dancing and murmuring sweet nothings. She had no idea how to handle this man and come out the winner.

She was exhausted and the glass of champagne had hit her like a knockout punch, reminding her of how late she'd been up these past nights. She'd kept going on the caffeine boost from chocolates and double *lattes*.

Yes, she blessed Kyle Paxton for saving her from being taken hostage. But she knew a hopeless situation when she saw it. Kyle had one thing on his mind—sex with a capital *S*. When he wasn't thinking about sex, he seemed to be obsessed with his work.

Just like Drew. True, Kyle was a nicer person than Drew, but she knew blind ambition when she saw it. On a physical level she was attracted to this man, but she'd been through enough heartache in the past year to last a lifetime.

All she had to do was get through the evening. Then she would never see Kyle again. Eyes closed, she danced in the protective shelter of his arms. His hand strummed down the back of her neck.

"You okay?" he whispered and chills raced across her nearly bare shoulders.

"Fine," she murmured, aware the light was very dim, the dance floor even more packed than it had been.

His arms tightened a fraction, taking her breath away. She couldn't recall being this languid, yet totally aware of her body. As they danced, his thigh brushed hers, igniting a flare of warmth that spread with devastating swiftness through her whole being.

His hand shimmied down her back to the base of her spine and lingered there, sending yet another wave of heat through her entire body. She felt like rubber, yet he was all steely muscle, well-honed, ready for action. She peered up at him, wondering what he was thinking.

Looking at him was a big mistake. The sensuous light in his eyes mesmerized her. She had never found another man who was quite this captivating. Every nerve-ending in her entire body was responding to the sexual magnetism that made him so attractive.

His hand slid down to her buttocks, and she wiggled to free herself. But short of making a spectacle of herself, it was impossible. The dance floor was so crowded, no one could see his hands—even if they had cared to look—but she was shocked by his audacity.

His sex pressed against her, and every muscle in her body tightened. She inhaled what she hoped would be a stabilizing breath, but the air brought with it the tantalizing aroma of Kyle's after-shave.

"Don't you think of anything but sex?"

Kyle playfully pondered her question, the whole time pressing against her. "Once in a while I think of something besides sex."

"Go on, you can't mean it." Her tone was bitingly sarcastic, but her mutinous body was loving every inch of him—virile, hard, undeniably masculine.

"Yeah. Now and then, I think of food." He grinned. "They're serving our dinner right now."

Chapter Seven

"RESTAURANT RITA," Kyle said.

Allie's head snapped up, and she stared at him with utter astonishment.

"Pretend you're Restaurant Rita, the hotshot reviewer for the *Tribune*," Kyle said. "Rate Reflections for me."

Allie toyed with her snapper, pushing aside the lemon grass with her fork. She'd been quiet since they'd sat down again. Obviously she was upset with him. Granted, he had no one to blame but himself, yet he couldn't keep his hands off her.

"Well, the service is excellent," Allie said. "And this snapper is delicious."

"But you don't like the lemon grass or the garlic-mashed potatoes?"

"What about that stuff?" She pointed with her fork at his plate. "You ate one bite of it."

"It's fried horseradish. I don't eat much fried food." He smiled at her, happy just to get her talking. "Hey, what can I tell you? I'm just a poor boy who made good. So I'm not up to speed on stuff like lemon grass and fried horseradish. That's why I had Dakota create the menu."

"Who designed the menus at your other restaurants?"

"I did, but I wanted Reflections to be special." He picked up his glass of wine, thinking he could tell Allie a lot more about himself, but didn't know her well enough. Until he did, it was best to focus on his accomplishments—not on the past.

"Sunday's the day," Kyle said, anxious to keep the conversation going. "I'm expecting Restaurant Rita to review Reflections this Sunday. He usually reviews new restaurants four weeks after they open."

"He?" Her expressive eyes widened. "Isn't Restaurant Rita a woman?"

"The Rita bit is just to throw people off. Have you read one of his reviews?"

"More than one, trust me."

"Notice the tone?" Kyle asked. "He's really Restaurant Rambo."

"Why do you say that?"

"Take his review of Prime Cuts. It said the steaks were like old tires and to beware of a restaurant whose most popular entrée was a T-shirt," Kyle said. Something flickered in Allie's eyes, and if he hadn't known better, he would have sworn she was angry. "'Course Rambo had a point when he said the food sucked. The waitresses the owner calls his 'hooter girls' bring in a fortune selling hooter T-shirts. Wish I'd thought of it."

The waiter cleared their table and they ordered coffee and dessert.

"Rambo has razor-sharp wit," he told her. "It sounds like a man."

"You're saying women can't be funny?"

He winked at her, realizing she had a spark of temper. He liked that in a woman. He'd never been attracted to the weak, simpering types who agreed with everything he said. "I think it's a man, and I'm not alone."

"Really? Who else thinks Rita is a man?"

He seized the opportunity to lean closer, and lowered his voice. "There's a group of restaurant owners who meet once a month at a secret location to discuss the business."

"You meet at Prime Cuts, right?"

He smiled, thinking Allie was really sharp. "How'd you know?"

She looked up at him from beneath lowered lashes, and he had the distinct impression she was baiting him. "I'll bet most of the owners are men, and they just *adore* the steaks at Prime Cuts."

He chuckled. "Okay, so they like to gawk at the hooter girls. Anyway, we figure Rambo changes his appearance with wigs and fake mustaches. And he comes in with different women to throw us off."

"What makes you think Restaurant Rita isn't a woman with a stable of studmuffins?"

He chuckled and she laughed along with him. She had a terrific sense of humor. "We've all been on the lookout for Rambo, but no one's ever spotted him. Believe me, he's good at disguises."

"Isn't remaining anonymous a good idea? If owners knew a critic was in the restaurant, he would get the best service. The chef would knock himself out."

"True," he conceded. "This way, Rita sees what it's like to be an average person in a restaurant."

The waiter brought their coffee and a slice of chocolate pecan torte for Allie. She took one bite and closed her eyes, obviously savoring the dessert. He studied her wild mane of sherry-brown hair, imagining it spread out over his pillow.

"I'm not worried about Restaurant Rita reviewing Reflections. He's always liked what I've done. The Foggy Bottom Burger was rated the best burger in town."

"Isn't that the yummy burger with the peanut butter and plum sauce on it?"

"Yes, I used to eat them three at a time when I was a kid. I don't touch them anymore, though. Too fattening."

"You didn't order any dessert. Are you watching your weight?"

He shrugged. "Sort of. I work out every morning at the Bad Dog Gym. Keeps me in shape."

"My idea of exercise is phone tag."

He laughed. Not only was she pretty and smart, Allie had an off-beat sense of humor he found refreshing. With too many women, what you saw was exactly what you got. Allie was full of surprises—and that was exciting.

"You were saying this man who calls himself Restaurant Rita likes your restaurants."

"Yes. Earlier this year, I took two big gambles. I opened Wok on the Wild Side and Kosher Nostra Deli. He liked them both. He said the Thai food at the Wok was the best in town."

"You designed those menus, didn't you?"

"Yes," he admitted with pride. "Rambo had lots of other good stuff to say and gave them each five stars. But that was nothing compared to the raves about the Kosher Nostra Deli. He said only a genius would combine a New York-style deli with pasta."

"You're the genius with the innovative ideas."

"I've been lucky—so far." He tried to sound modest. If there was anything he hated, it was bragging, but he couldn't help being proud of himself. "Reflections is supposed to be an L.A.-style restaurant. I figured if Cedar Ridge went for Thai food, it was ready for Reflections."

"Thai food isn't much different from what's served in the Chinese restaurants already in town. I just wonder if Cedar Ridge is ready for lacquered duck with spicy espresso sauce and grapefruit chutney."

He chuckled. Man, oh, man, she was sharp. He was going to have to keep both eyes on her.

"Seriously, opening three places in one year is a risk. I'm strung out for cash. If Restaurant Rita trashes this place, it'll drive me out of business."

"You don't mean that, do you?"

She looked so genuinely upset for him that he could have kissed her, and he might have, except that she'd just forked in the last of the torte.

"A bad review didn't kill Prime Cuts," she said.

"No one goes there for the food. They get drunk, drool over the hooter girls, and buy T-shirts."

"Maybe you ought to get a few hooter girls in here." For a second, he thought she was serious. Then she licked the fork and said, "I would kill for Marie's torte. She's fabulous."

"Pray Restaurant Rita likes Reflections. Marie is a single mother who doesn't have much education. She was working as a cleaning lady and baking desserts for a fast-food stand when I discovered her. Her dream was to work for a classy restaurant. I think you made her day—her year—when you showed so much interest in her."

ALLIE STARED OUT THE window of Kyle's car as he drove her home, battling a queasy feeling that had nothing to do with what she'd eaten. Marie was getting a chance to fulfill her dream. If Reflections closed, what would happen to her?

How bad were Kyle's financial problems? She told herself that both of them were talented, and they would survive. But until now she hadn't really considered the negative impact a review could have.

She tried to write the column, using her wit. Now she wondered if some of those remarks weren't downright cruel. The review set to appear in the paper the day after tomorrow was cutting, even for Restaurant Rita. Of course, when she'd written it, she hadn't known Kyle or any of the others. Now they were real to her, and she could almost feel the pain they would experience when they read the review.

"You don't have to walk me to the door," she said as his car pulled to the curb.

He chuckled, but didn't sound the least bit amused. "My mother would kill me if I left a lady on the sidewalk."

Allie heaved a sigh and waited for him to get out of the car and walk around to her side. Exhaustion overwhelmed her, and the last thing she wanted was to fight him off. They walked up to her door shrouded in an awkward silence. She noticed that she'd forgotten to turn on the porch light.

"Good night," she said. "Thanks for a wonderful evening."

"Aren't you going to invite me in?"

"No, I'm really tired and—"

"You weren't tired when I was kissing you in the back hall."

"You're wrong. I was tired then," she said, her voice stiff with embarrassment. "It didn't mean anything."

"No? I'm going to have to do something about that."

He lowered his head, and she raised her hands to fend him off. Too late. Her hands were trapped against his chest as his mouth came down on hers and he hauled her into his arms. Instantly his heat engulfed her, for the night was cool and only a flimsy shawl covered her sheer dress.

She swayed against him, overwhelmed by the pressure of his arms. Against her hands his heart beat in heavy, rapid thumps, a counterpoint to her own pulse, thrumming in her ears. A little dizzy and weak with pleasure, she parted her lips. He angled his head to one side, spiraling his tongue around hers with knee-weakening audacity.

Allie couldn't resist him. She honestly couldn't, and she wasn't sure it mattered anymore. Then a distant bell tinkled in some dark corridor of her brain. For her, a physical commitment was a mental commitment. What would happen if she slept with this man?

She would fall hopelessly in love with him. Where would it lead? Nowhere. She'd been hurt once, and history wasn't repeating itself, thank you very much.

She jerked away, inhaling a calming breath. "Can't you take no for an answer?"

Kyle whacked his forehead with the palm of his hand. "That was no? Say yes. I *dare* you. This I gotta see."

"You keep forcing yourself on me," she said, knowing full well she'd done more than her share to encourage him.

"And you hated every second of it." He raked his fingers though the hair that had fallen across his forehead. Even in the dim light, she could see him staring at her as if she'd just arrived from Jupiter.

"I'm not making love with you and that's final." She knew she sounded a little too prim after wantonly kissing him, but it was the best she could do. She was totally out of her league with this man. "I'm not *that* attracted to you. I'm just grateful for what you did when that man robbed Papa Valentine."

She quickly took the key out of the evening bag swinging from her shoulder, turning away from him. She tried to jam it in the lock, but missed. A second try was successful and the door clicked open.

From behind, his arms encircled her, and one hand manacled both her wrists. He surrounded her, his bigger, much more powerful body clamping against her. It would be so easy to turn and surrender into those strong arms. To be taken by storm. That was what it would be like—a once-in-a-lifetime experience.

One hand still held her wrists captive in his strong grip. With the other hand he slowly lifted her hair off her shoulder, and cool air rushed over her heated skin, bringing goose bumps by the dozen. And a flare of anticipation.

His moist lips caressed the sensitive skin at the nape of her neck. She steeled herself, aware of how tempted she was to turn and taste his lips. He took his sweet time, kissing her neck and nibbling and nuzzling his way up to her ear.

"Don't try to sell me some damn bridge." His voice sounded gruff as his heated breath fluttered across her ear. "You can say you don't know me well enough to make love with me. Or you can say you don't do it on first dates. I'll buy a lot of bull, but don't you dare say you're not attracted to me."

He released her hands and had the door open before she knew what was happening. He gently pushed her inside.

"See you tomorrow," he said as he shut the door.

Allie sagged against the closed door. *Tomorrow?* Her knees buckled and she slowly slid to the floor. She sat there, her feet at an uncomfortable angle, until she heard his car door slam.

Gordon trotted up to greet her, purring for all he was worth, ever hopeful of getting another meal. She managed to pick herself up and stumble into the bathroom with Gordon dogging every step.

"He's not going to be easy to get rid of," she informed the cat.

Gordon had jumped up on the counter, but seemed more interested in scratching his ear than listening to her.

"'Restaurant Rambo.' That's a laugh," she said as she undressed. "Kyle thinks Rita is too sharp to be a woman. Well, if that isn't just—exactly—like a man." She peeled off her panty hose with a sigh of relief. "Kyle has his faults. But how can I be angry with a man who's worked so hard to make something of himself?"

She tossed her clothes in a heap over the rim of her bathtub. It had been an exhausting day, and she was too tired to tackle the stupid fire engine. Anyway, who could concentrate? His parting words kept echoing in her ears.

I'll see you tomorrow.

After pushing aside pieces of the unassembled fire engine, she climbed into bed. Gordon jumped up beside her and began kneading her tummy. She nudged him aside and turned out the lights.

The apartment was dark and quiet and lonely. *Tomorrow.* She stared at the ceiling, admitting to herself that she wanted to give this relationship a chance. It was a one-in-a-million shot, but her sixth sense told her to go for it.

"Don't be silly," she said aloud, the logical side of her brain countering. "You can't date him without telling him who you are. He'll tell all his buddies at Prime Cuts, and Restaurant Rita's cover will be blown.

And don't forget Drew. Ambitious men are ruthless men.''

Still, something inside her wouldn't give up. She'd been attracted to Kyle from the first moment she'd seen him across the room in Valentine Delights. She'd been eating a slice of Death by Chocolate Torte when she'd spotted him. She'd finished the heavenly piece of cake without even realizing it, because she couldn't take her eyes off him.

The telephone rang—a loud, shrill sound in the silent apartment. She flinched, then peered at the digital clock glowing in the darkness. Since it was after midnight, it was probably a wrong number.

"Hello," she said, then heard heavy breathing.

Great! An obscene phone call. Hardly the perfect way to end Valentine's Day. She went to slam down the receiver, but stopped when she heard the familiar masculine tones.

"Allie, are you in bed?"

The sound of Kyle's voice poured though her like warm fudge, hot and sweet. She couldn't help wishing he were here beside her instead of the dumb fire engine. And a cat who never really listened.

"Of course, I'm in bed." She tried her best to sound snippy. It was dangerous to encourage this man. "I'm dead tired."

"Really? You should have mentioned it sooner." The hint of humor made her smile. "What are you wearing?"

Hearing this made her wonder what he might be wearing. Just the thought of Kyle Paxton without clothes did naughty things to her body. "I'm wearing a night-shirt that says: So Little Time, So—"

"So many men."

She squirmed under the covers, totally aware of her body. And how much it wanted his. "Get your mind out of the gutter. So Little Time, So Much Chocolate."

"Hmmm," he responded. "Speaking of chocolate. I saved that Chocolate Body Paint for you and your happy parts."

Every part of her seemed to melt as she thought of him licking chocolate off her. She knew what wonders his tongue could do—without chocolate. "Be serious."

"I am serious," he said. "Dead serious. I'm under the sheet buck naked. What I have here is a very unhappy part."

She laughed—or tried to. She longed to touch him or slowly lick off some sweet chocolate. "I have a suggestion." Her words came out in a breathless rush. "Dip that unhappy part in the body paint."

He chuckled, but there was a raspy quality to the sound. "I really called to ask you to dinner. I always go to Mom's on Sunday night. She left a message on my machine. If I don't bring you, I'm dead meat."

His mother? He wanted her to meet his mother. He'd saved her, brought her orchids, taken her to an expensive dinner on Valentine's Day. Now he wanted her to meet his mother. How could she? The devastating review would appear in the Sunday paper.

Chapter Eight

CHARLOTTE KEATS HADN'T yet arrived at the *Tribune,* but Allie waited in her office, every nerve on full alert, until the editor-in-chief sailed through the door.

"Allie, what are you doing here? We don't want anyone to suspect you're Restaurant Rita."

"I wouldn't have come except I have a problem. I saw you at Valentine Delights just after the robbery. You're doing a story on it, right?"

"Sure, it's our banner headline." Charlotte nodded, and her dark hair fluttered across the shoulders of her brightly-colored silk blouse.

"Why wasn't the story in this morning's edition?"

"We didn't get it in time. It'll be the lead in the Sunday edition. The presses have already run the back sections. Sam wants to get the paper on the street this afternoon to take advantage of the story," Charlotte said while she logged on to her computer.

"On Saturday?" Allie groaned and closed her eyes, thinking about Sam Harper, the publisher. She might have talked Charlotte into rerunning the back section where her "Restaurant Rita" column was, but Sam was too good a businessman to waste paper. "Has my column already been printed?"

"Yes . . ." Charlotte stared at her with brown eyes that missed nothing. "Oh, Allie. I see the problem. Kyle helped you and your column blasts his new restaurant. Don't tell him who you are. He never has to know."

"It's not that simple. I went to dinner with him last night. I found out how hard he's worked and how much is riding on his restaurant. Charlotte, can't we do something? Restaurant Rita is negative and mean-spirited in that review."

"People love your reviews. This is one of your funnier opening lines." Charlotte clicked twice, then peered closely at the computer screen. " 'Reflections is so L.A. that you expect a drive-by shooting any second or, at the very least, someone to jump out from behind a fake palm and spray graffiti on the stark black-and-white decor.' Now, what other reviewer would think to start a review like this?"

"I don't want to ruin Kyle's business. Not after all he's done."

"Reflections can't be ruined by one review. People deserve your honest opinion. I have the bills you submitted. It'll cost the average person a week's wages to eat there. If it's not worth it, they need to know."

"I have to tell Kyle who I am."

Charlotte held up her hand. "Restaurant Rita's identity has always been confidential. Sam and I insist. If everyone knows you're a reviewer, you'll get the royal treatment. Can you trust Kyle Paxton to keep this secret?''

Allie hesitated, thinking about Kyle and his cronies who met at Prime Cuts to drool over the hooter girls and talk about the business. *Would he tell them? No,* she thought. Then she remembered Drew. She wasn't sure if she could trust her judgment when it came to men. Which meant, she couldn't necessarily trust Kyle.

''Maybe I'd better keep Restaurant Rita's identity a secret, but I'm still not comfortable about the tone of that review.''

''Allie, never be sorry you told the truth,'' Charlotte said, sympathy etching every line of her beautiful face. ''Just be sorry the restaurant didn't live up to your expectations.''

Allie left the *Tribune* and rushed over to Valentine Delights. The wind had picked up, bringing sullen clouds with leaden underbellies and the scent of rain. The turn in the weather matched her mood.

''Any word on the robber?'' she asked Papa Valentine when she found him behind the counter cleaning the espresso machine.

''No, but the police are working on it.''

''I hope you didn't lose too much money.''

Papa shrugged, smiling his usual smile, but today it didn't cheer her up. ''Valentine's Day is always the biggest day for chocolates. Next is Mother's Day. I'll have a chance to make it up then.''

"I'll be glad to help you."

"I'm going to take you up on your offer. It'll be good practice for you."

Papa really expected her to open a coffee bar. To her it was a dream like a mirage that beckoned in the distance, but you never quite reached. About as far as she'd gotten was saving a little money and helping Papa when he needed it. Anyway, she was too depressed about Kyle and the terrible review to think about her dreams now.

Papa Valentine studied her with a concerned expression. "Is something wrong? Are you still in shock over the robbery?"

"What am I going to do?" Allie asked. "Kyle bought me a beautiful Valentine's bouquet and took me to dinner. Now he wants me to meet his mother."

Papa nodded slowly. "You're serious about him."

"I don't know. We just met, but—"

"Let's sit down and talk about it," Papa said. He came around the counter and led her over to a table by the window. "Kyle saw you in here and asked about you several times. If you hadn't been Restaurant Rita, I would have introduced you, but I thought it would be a conflict of interest."

"He did?" She smiled and Papa smiled back. "I noticed him, too."

"Allie, love finds a way. This will work out. You'll see."

"I never said I was in love with him. It's too soon. We just met."

Papa's blue eyes sparkled as he said, "I remember meeting Harriet. We were the last two contestants in a high-school spelling bee. I let her win. But when we walked off that stage, I knew she was the one for me."

"You still miss her, don't you?" Allie asked.

"She's been gone almost ten years," Papa said. "But there's not a day that goes by that I don't miss her. Opening this shop was our dream. If only she could be here to see it and meet all the wonderful people I've met." He reached across the table and put his warm hand over hers. "Dreams are meant to be shared. Never forget that."

"Allie, there you are." Kyle breezed through the door, wearing the same bomber jacket he'd lent her yesterday—and a heart-stopping smile highlighted by the adorable dimple. He swung a chair around backward and sat at the table with them. "I went by your place to help with the fire engine, but you weren't there."

"OKAY, LET'S SEE WHAT you've got so far," Kyle said when they entered her apartment.

The tubby feline rushed up to greet Kyle. At least the cat was glad to see him. Allie had been polite, but hardly encouraging. A less determined man would have walked away from this situation. Gordo stood on his hind legs, front paws in the air—no mean feat, considering his size.

"Gordon wants you to pick him up."

If he hadn't been anxious to please Allie, he would never have picked up the porker. The cat snuggled against him, purring like he'd been into the catnip as Kyle followed Allie into the small bedroom.

"Eating chocolate in bed, huh?" He looked around the room, noticing the chocolate-stained sheets and dozens of pieces of what could only be the fire engine.

"I have lots of bad habits, believe me."

He deposited chunky Gordo on the empty chair by the bed. His navy shirt was coated with tangerine-colored fur. "Let's gather up all the pieces and take them into the living room," Kyle said, picking up an armful. He happened to glance up, catching sight of several wigs lined up across a shelf in the closet. "Do you belong to a theater group or something?"

Allie shouldered the door shut, frowning intently. "I—I used to be in a theater group when I lived in Atlanta."

There certainly was much, much more to her than he'd originally thought. He remembered the first time he'd seen her walk into Valentine's Delights. Sexy, he'd decided in an instant. But now he saw there was a power and a depth to her that fascinated him.

He dropped the pieces of the fire engine on the living-room carpet. "Let's see what your instructions say so far."

Allie dumped the pieces she'd been carrying onto the floor, then went over to her laptop computer and booted up. Over her shoulder he read the first line of the assembly instructions. DON'T PANIC! YOU CAN PUT THIS PUPPY TOGETHER IN NO TIME.

"Are you really going to start the instructions like that?"

"I always do. It's my trademark. Easy steps. A little humor."

Kyle plopped down on the floor beside the unassembled pieces, and watched Allie. Today her hair was down and nearly straight, with only a suggestion of curl remaining. And it was thick and full. Sexy as hell.

She wore faded jeans that gloved cute, round buns. Her T-shirt had been washed dozens of times, but he could still read the message: My Life is Like a Box of Chocolates—Full of Nuts.

"Shoot," he said, then listened to her translate the first instruction. Gordo ambled over and began batting around one of the engine's wheels.

They worked through lunch, taking just a short break for tuna sandwiches. It was late afternoon and pouring rain before they finally finished. By then

Gordo had lost interest and was snoozing, belly up, in the middle of the living room.

Kyle worked on the floor, while Allie sat at the table. Concentrating on the assembly process, he didn't think about sex. Okay, maybe once or twice. Who could blame him? She was only a few tempting feet away.

He longed to thread his fingers through that mane of long hair. Better yet, spread it across a pillow. Then . . . Get your mind back on the fire engine.

"Thirty-three easy steps," Kyle said, surveying the fully assembled fire engine. "Not bad."

"Thanks for your help. I couldn't have done it without you." She looped a strand of auburn hair over her ear.

Their voices awakened Gordo and the cat cocked his head. He hunched over on all fours, then hacking sounds erupted from deep in his gut.

"Poor Gordie." Allie dropped to the floor beside the cat. "He has a hair ball."

Gordo gagged and coughed up a wad of orange fur and slime smack onto the hood of the red engine. Then he waddled off toward the kitchen. A small chrome disk lay on the floor where the cat had been.

"Oh—" Kyle stopped himself before he said a few choice words that would have made a construction worker blush.

"Where did that come from?" Allie moaned.

Kyle lay back on the carpet. "That's an unhappy part, if I've ever seen one."

Allie giggled, then laughed harder and harder. She was on her back beside him, her breasts thrust upward, jiggling from laughing so much. He forgot all about dismembering fat Gordo.

He rolled onto his side. "I think I know where it goes. Back at step thirteen or fourteen. There was a spot on the axle that didn't seem quite right."

She turned her head to look at him. "I can't believe I missed it. The instructions must have..." With each word her voice had become lower and lower. She stopped, gazing at him as if she wanted to tell him something. Either that or she wanted him to kiss her.

He scooted closer and put his arm around her waist. Her only resistance was a slight tensing of her muscles. The T-shirt had hiked up, revealing a slim band of skin. He slipped his hand under the cotton fabric. Her skin was warm and baby soft, utterly feminine.

"Kyle, there's something I want to say."

Here it comes, he thought. She was going to lecture him, but he refused to let her. He trapped her words with his lips and she went still for a second, then her arms circled his neck and pulled him against the lush fullness of her breasts.

She nipped at his lower lip—a sweet, flirtatious gesture. He teased her bottom lip with his teeth in return, catching it in a gentle grip. Lightly caressing her lips, he dampened them, hoping to make her hungry for him. At the moist velvety brush of his tongue, her lips parted. An arrow of pure pleasure shot through him, pooling in his groin.

"Oh, Kyle," she moaned.

He kissed her ear, slowly tracing the ridges with his lips. His hand was still at her waist and he edged it upward a scant inch at a time, savoring the soft, womanly contours of her body. Reaching the rim of the silky bra she was wearing, he stopped.

"Your skin's as soft as a baby's."

Allie gazed up at him, lips parted, her pupils dilated, the irises nothing more than thin hoops of green. She wasn't resisting him the way she had last night, rebuilding the barrier that she'd seemed determined to keep between them. Every muscle in his body went taut with anticipation and he eased his hand upward.

Through the silky fabric, her skin felt warm, and his thumb gently massaged the hard nub pushing against the bra's lacy cup. Her hands were in his hair now, bringing his head down for another scorching kiss. He managed to slip his fingers into the bra. Her breasts were incredible: not centerfold material, but nicely round and full.

He broke the kiss long enough to push up the well-worn T-shirt and uncover a shell-pink bra. Beneath the sheer fabric, nipples like baby rosebuds lured him closer, begging to be kissed. He couldn't disappoint them.

"Beautiful," he said. "So beautiful."

He lowered his head and nibbled at one pert nipple. It took a second for his tongue to moisten the fabric. Then he sucked deeply, bringing the tight bud into the heat of his mouth. His tongue spiraled around it, his lips gently nibbling, his hand kneading the soft mound beneath.

Allie rewarded his efforts with a low, purring mmm of delight. Her fingers raked through his hair, furrowing against his scalp, and her body squirmed beneath him. She surged upward, offering herself to him.

He transferred his attention to the other nipple, dampening the fabric and stroking the taut peak as he sucked. Suddenly, a thumping noise rose above the sound of their breathing. Allie pushed at his shoulders.

"It's Gordon. He needs to go out." She jumped up and rushed to the door.

Kyle expelled a long breath, silently promising to get that freaking cat. It was raining outside, coming down harder now, by the sound of it. The rush of cold air from the open door took some of the heat off his skin and brought him to his senses. He hadn't slept a bit last night, with his mind on Allie and how to get through to her.

Sex was not the answer, although his body disagreed—big time. He had to give something of himself, to show her that he truly cared. It was a little early in a relationship to do this, but things seemed to be moving at supersonic speed.

He walked over to the table and sat down. "Come here, Allie. I have something to tell you." She took the seat opposite him, her eyes wary. He reached across the table and held her hand. "You know what's nice about a small town like Cedar Ridge? People know you."

"You're right," she said. "That's why I moved here from Atlanta."

"I've lived here for eleven years, but no one really knows me except my mother. I grew up in a small bend in the road west of here. When I was eight my father died."

"Really?" Allie's expressive eyes widened. "My mother died when I was ten. We were living in Singapore, and she caught some strange virus and died."

In her quiet voice, he detected a familiar heartache and knew Allie still missed her mother even though many years had passed.

"Even now, when I look up and see—"

"See what?" he prompted.

"Nothing. It's silly."

He squeezed her hand. "No, it's not. Please, tell me."

"The night my mother died, my father told me she was up there...up in heaven," she said softly. "I looked out the window and saw the star-spangled sky. One star twinkled, and I was sure that it was my mother signaling that she loved me. Over the years, I got in the habit of checking the night sky. When a star winked, I knew it was my mother, watching over me.''

Her words left him unexpectedly touched. ''Allie, I know what you mean. Sometimes I feel my father's spirit with me—especially when I've accomplished something special, like opening Reflections. I know he's there, cheering for me. It's difficult for me because... He hesitated, then told himself not to be a coward. *Just say it.* ''Because I was responsible for my father's death.''

''What do you mean? You were just a child.''

''I was a class-A brat,'' he insisted. ''We lived on a farm, and I would hide so I didn't have to do chores. One day, my father came after me. I could hear him calling, but I wouldn't come. He started to cross the road to get me and was struck by a speeding truck. He died instantly.''

She squeezed his hand, her eyes misting. *Aw, man, don't cry,* he thought, *or I'll cry myself.*

''I'm so sorry,'' she said. ''You can't blame yourself. You were only a child. Kids do things like that. Your father would be so proud of you now. Look at what you've become.''

He shrugged it off. ''Naw. I was a loser most of my life. I didn't have the grades to go to college. When my father died, I went into a tailspin. I ditched school and sat out in the fields most of the day. Worse, I overate until I became a tub of lard. The kids used to tease me all the time, calling me Fat Boy and a lot of other names that aren't repeatable. I never had a date. Girls headed the other way when I came along.''

Allie squinted at him as if seeing him for the first time. ''Really? You seem so...so together. I never would have thought—''

''Trust me, I wouldn't make this up. After high school, we moved to Atlanta and I got a job driving a roach coach. I ate more than ever. Then, one night I had a dream. In it my father told me to make something of myself, to make him proud. So I stopped eating, worked out at the Y and began to save money.''

Allie smiled with unmistakable warmth. ''Good for you.''

''I was determined not to be a loser any longer. I started going after what I wanted instead of being the fat kid everyone laughed at. So if I'm too aggressive sometimes, it's because I don't want to be that slob again. I want to be a winner.''

''You are a winner. Never doubt it.''

''You're the first person I've shared this with. Look, I know this is happening fast, but last night I couldn't sleep. I thought about my life, and what I want for the future. You're the woman I've been waiting for,'' he said with complete honesty. ''I want you to understand me, and I want to understand you. Please tell me what happened in your last relationship. He hurt you badly, didn't he?''

Chapter Nine

HE HURT YOU BADLY, didn't he? The words echoed through Allie's head. Kyle Paxton had recognized the pain she thought was well hidden. His sensitivity made her even more ashamed.

How could she destroy his dream by trashing Reflections? What she should tell him—right now—was not about her past. Instead she should confess that she was Restaurant Rita.

"Allie, it's all right. You can tell me."

She longed to throw herself into his comforting arms and rest her head against his broad shoulder. If he'd been nothing more than a studmuffin interested only in down-and-dirty sex, she could have turned her back on him.

But he wasn't.

True, Kyle had his faults. He was determined to the point of being stubborn. And ambitious. She needed to know him better before she trusted him with her secrets, but fate had thrown them together in a heartbeat. Their relationship seemed destined to happen quickly.

"Allie, are you okay?"

"I'm fine. I—I..." *Be careful,* commanded the logical side of her brain. *You must not get close to this man. If you do, you'll have to tell him everything.*

"Hey, you can trust me," Kyle assured her.

Trust me. Exactly what Drew had said. Granted, the situation was different then. Drew had convinced her that he knew exactly what was good for *them*—which meant him. Kyle was only trying to understand her.

But she could still remember the weightless, numbing sensation that had been with her for months after Drew's betrayal. Trusting a man again was risky business—especially a man she hardly knew; a man she shouldn't even be seeing. She honestly didn't know if she could do it.

"Allie, when that robber wanted to take you hostage, I would have done anything to stop him. You trusted me instinctively and walked right into the storeroom. Can't you trust me now?"

She gazed into his blue eyes, remembering how terrified she'd been. She'd stood like a pillar of stone while he'd reacted quickly and saved her from heaven only knew what fate. She could tell him, keeping it simple, not letting her emotions show.

"I was raised abroad," she began, her voice pitched low to hide her inner turmoil, "in countries where America is a four-letter word. I didn't have a normal childhood. I was lonely, especially after my mother died."

"We have a lot in common," he said quietly. "I don't ever remember not being lonely."

"I came home to America for college. That's when I met Drew, an engineering major, and we were together for years."

He frowned slightly, saying, "You must have loved him."

"I thought so. I had no other relationship to compare it with," she admitted. "Then my father died. I didn't have anyone. After graduation, Drew was offered a position with a small toy company in Atlanta. Most of the toys were made in the Orient, so they needed a translator."

"You moved to Atlanta with him."

"Yes. That's when I discovered that I didn't really like the rote work of being a translator. I began to play with the instructions, making them what they call 'user friendly.' You know. Easy, funny."

"Don't tell me," he said sarcastically. "Sales soared."

Allie couldn't help being proud. "Yes, sales went up, but I didn't get the credit. Drew claimed he needed 'a career move,' a way to get ahead of the other engineers."

"You let him take credit for your work?"

She had learned a valuable lesson the hard way. Now that she was discussing this, she found Kyle was much easier to talk to than she'd anticipated. His expression reflected his concern and understanding.

"Drew convinced me that his career—our future—was more important than taking credit for humorous instructions. Since we were engaged, and I didn't really like my job, I kept quiet while he took credit for my innovative work."

He clasped her hand in both of his, earnestly gazing into her eyes. "I don't care if you were engaged. The creep was taking advantage of you."

"I know," she said, bitterness underscoring her words despite her best efforts to keep it out of her voice. "One day Drew announced another 'career move.' He was marrying the owner's daughter."

Kyle's jaw tightened, emphasizing its angular line. "You're still working for this toy company. Why?"

"I need the money," she said defensively. This was worse than she could possibly have imagined. What she saw in his eyes was disappointment. "I do some translating for the university, too."

"That's good," he said, but she could see that he now thought less of her.

"I'm thinking about opening a *latte* bar in one of the office complexes—a mini version of Valentine Delights," she blurted out, attempting to redeem herself.

"Really?" He grinned. "That's a great niche in the market. Why didn't I think of it?"

"It's hardly an original idea," she conceded. "Many office buildings have snack bars, but this would be more like the coffee bars that they have on the West Coast. I'm going to call it BrewHaHa.''

He rewarded her with his one-dimple grin. ''Allie, what a great name. I'll help you—''

''No. I need to save more money.'' Talking about her dream made it seem more real, more attainable, but she didn't want him to expect immediate action. Opening a *latte* bar would mean a major change in her life, and a financial risk of immense proportions. She wasn't quite ready.

Kyle studied her for a moment, then slowly nodded. ''I understand.''

They sat quietly, Kyle's hands still covering hers, listening to the drumbeat of the rain on the roof. A sense of intimacy and understanding cloaked them and the rest of the world seemed very far away. But Allie knew that the Sunday paper must have hit the stands by now.

KYLE GAZED AT ALLIE, pleased with himself in a way that he could never have explained. He'd found the chink in Allie's emotional armor by sharing his own secrets. This woman was special. He'd known it from the first time he'd looked up from his double espresso at Valentine Delights and spotted her.

She trusted him, he thought, realizing how difficult it had been for her to tell him about her past. But she had. She trusted him now. That was what counted. After all, he'd trusted her with his secret.

A thunking noise rose above the rhythmic beat of the rain. Allie jumped up, saying, "It's Gordon. He'll need to be dried off."

"I'll start a fire." He let her tend to Gordo while he took a log from the basket on the hearth and built a fire.

"That's so sweet," she said, bringing the cat over to the fireplace. "You curl up here, Gordie, and dry off."

He waited until she'd put the cat down before reaching for her. "I didn't light the fire for the cat. What's more romantic than making love in front of a fire while it's raining outside?"

Her beautiful eyes widened and she willingly moved into his arms. She was incredibly small, almost fragile, and oh, so soft. He pressed his face into the curve of her neck, and held her, enjoying the welcoming warmth of her body and the feeling of emotional closeness that was so new to him.

Her breasts pillowed into his chest, the pert nipples hard against his shirt. His pulse kicked into high gear. He adjusted his body to fit against hers and lifted her chin. Their mouths brushed and her thick lashes fluttered shut.

He kissed her, his hands exploring the curve of her back until he came to her hips. "Perfect," he whispered against her sweet lips. "Just perfect."

He sank to the floor, and she came with him, kissing his neck and nibbling at his earlobe. His breathing sounded harsh above the soft crackle of the fire and the steady drumming of the rain. Allie was breathing hard, too, gazing at him with those matchless green eyes that reflected the glow of the fire. The flames brought out glints of red in her amber hair and did wonders for the peach tone of her skin.

He wanted Allie with such blind need that all he could feel was the scorching heat generated by their bodies, and the blood rumbling through his head like thunder. He had to have her.

DON'T THINK ABOUT tomorrow, Allie told herself as she gazed at Kyle, determined to memorize every detail about him. The firelight tempered the masculine planes of his face and muted the darkness of his hair, but it brought out the twilight blue of his eyes, firing them with inner light.

He slid over, making room for her on the rug in front of the fire. She slipped into the inviting curve of his arm and rested her head against his shoulder. She inhaled deeply, savoring the faint scent of his citrus after-shave.

"Let's see, where were we when Gordo interrupted us?"

He tugged at her T-shirt, and she remembered exactly what he'd been doing. Her already taut nipples were throbbing with anticipation and a little sigh of pleasure escaped her parted lips. The shirt was over her head and tossed aside before she could take a deep breath.

"Yeow!" Gordon hissed indignantly, and she knew it had landed on him.

It was warm in front of the fire, but goose bumps prickled across her skin as his eyes scoured her body.

"Allie, you have no idea what you do to me."

Even faster than he'd removed her T-shirt, he had the bra off and her breasts were exposed to the warmth of the fire. And his eyes. She should have been embarrassed, yet she wasn't. Instead she felt utterly beautiful and desired.

One hand traced a line across the tops of her breasts, his fingers skimming lightly over her skin. His hand dropped lower, deliberately skirting the soft mounds and ignoring the nipples that ached for his touch.

He kept teasing her, running his hands over her torso, but not touching her where she needed it the most. Finally, she said, "Touch me."

For a second he smiled at her, a slow grin spreading over his face. He vaulted to his feet, saying, "Hold that thought. I'll be right back."

He was out the door before she could question him. Allie stared at the dancing shadows cast on the ceiling by the fire. *I'm falling in love with him,* she thought. *What am I going to do?*

Kyle dashed back inside. "It's raining cats bigger than Gordo."

She rolled onto her side, concealing her half-bare state with her arms. He was soaked, water dripping from his hair. He grabbed the towel she'd used on Gordon and swiped at his head a few times. Then he shrugged out of his shirt and dropped it on the floor in the entry.

Oh, my. Moisture sheened his biceps, the powerful muscles defined by each movement. A sprinkling of hair emphasized the breadth of his chest and ribcage. Beneath his stomach was flat, the navel surrounded by wisps of dark hair that arrowed under the waistband of his jeans.

She hadn't noticed how his well-worn jeans gloved powerful thighs. Well, she'd *noticed,* but she hadn't truly appreciated. The jeans outlined precisely every masculine contour of his lower body, leaving no doubt about his sexual intentions. She moistened her lips in anticipation, heat surging through her.

His magnificent body had distracted her. Now she noticed the Valentine Delights bag in his hand. She sat bolt upright, covering her breasts with crossed arms. "Kyle, you wouldn't dare use that stuff."

He pulled out a jar of Chocolate Body Paint and advanced on her, twirling the brush. "That's the difference between you and me, Allie. When you pulled this off the shelf, you only *thought* about painting my body with it. I *promised* myself that I would taste this—" he dropped to his knees beside her "—on you."

He nudged her arms away from her breasts and whisked the clean, soft brush across her taut nipples.

A shudder went through her, bringing with it a sigh and a fresh wave of goose bumps.

"Do I get my turn?" she asked, her voice more than a little breathless.

He unsnapped the first button on his jeans, revealing more skin dusted with dark hair. "I'm counting on it, angel."

With a flick of his strong wrist, he opened the jar. Hovering over her, a mischievous grin on his face, he dipped the brush into the chocolate. "I love chocolate," he told her, "but I haven't had any in years."

"Years?" she echoed, unable to concentrate with every fiber in her body aching for his touch. "People die without chocolate."

"No, they don't. They stay thin."

He whisked a bit of chocolate onto one breast. The mixture felt thick, heavy and cool, making her nipple contract even more. A swish of the brush put an equal amount of chocolate on the other breast.

"Okay, those happy parts are covered." Kyle lowered his head, the fire highlighting the sensual sparks in his eyes. And the glint of humor.

He flicked his tongue over one breast, slowly licking the chocolate off the raised peak. She moaned, reaching for him and circling her arms around his incredible shoulders. His tongue swirled around her nipple, then sucked it hard into the warm cove of his mouth where he played with it, tugging gently at the sensitive nub.

"Don't stop," she heard herself demanding.

He transferred his attentions to her other breast, removing the chocolate coating so leisurely that she thought she would die of frustration before he finished. She writhed in his arms, pushing herself upward, offering herself to him.

Suddenly his lips were on hers, bringing with them the sweet taste of chocolate. Through the searing kiss, he continued to caress her with light, teasing strokes until she arched her hips off the floor.

"This is certainly my chocolate fantasy," he said.

Then he unbuttoned her faded jeans and had them off even faster than he'd removed the rest of her clothes. She gazed up at him and found his eyes were hot with desire. He stroked her bare skin, fanning his hand across her breasts and down her tummy. Her pulse staggered as his fingers brushed her intimately.

He took a hard, sharp breath, his eyes narrowing, but his fingers kept slowly moving. She gasped with pleasure. They were still staring at each other as if hypnotized, and she knew that she would never forget this moment or the look on his face.

"Touch me, Allie," he whispered, his voice raw with need.

He was stretched out beside her, the top button of his jeans undone. She unzipped them and slipped her hand under the waistband of his underwear.

"You don't know how good that feels."

"Just wait until I get my turn with the brush." She was trying to be funny, but her voice sounded too gritty.

He pulled away and peeled down his underwear. Her gaze roved across his bare torso, the firelight casting golden light on the rippling muscles. The flames were reflected in his eyes, too. They were heavy-lidded but still sparkled blue.

He fumbled with his jeans and brought a small foil packet out of one pocket. He had its contents on in a second and was looming over her, parting her legs. He guided himself into place as she arched upward, unable to wait any longer. She froze, startled out of her sensual haze by the thrusting pressure.

He stopped, half-way, whispering, "Am I hurting you?"

Unable to speak, she shook her head.

He nudged forward. "I'll take it slow and easy."

Chapter Ten

"I'M CRAZY ABOUT YOU," Kyle murmured, desperately needing to tell Allie how he felt.

"Oh, Kyle," she moaned, a smile playing across her lips.

His hips flexed and she quivered beneath him, her nails scoring his bare back. He struggled for control, his body straining with the effort, determined not to let himself go until Allie was ready. Her hands were on his shoulders now, digging in, and her hips churned beneath him. He concentrated, his eyes squeezed shut, loving the feel of being inside her.

"Yes, o-o-oh—yes!" she finally cried, her eyes squeezed shut as she reached orgasm.

Breathing like a racehorse, every pore in his body throbbing with pleasure, he climaxed. Pitching forward, he remembered just in time to take the force of his weight with his forearms or he would crush Allie.

"Where have you been all my life?" he asked. Gathering her in his arms, he rolled onto his side.

"I never knew it could be like this," she whispered.

His blood was pounding in his temples so hard that it took a minute for him to realize what she meant. "It's always going to be like this," he said, knowing her jerk of a boyfriend had been selfish in more ways than one.

Kyle couldn't remember being this happy. For years now, he'd thought success would make him content, but it hadn't. Every new venture was a challenge he enjoyed, yet something was always missing. Now he knew what it was. He wanted to share his life with someone. With Allie.

"You know," he said, turning to face her, and admiring the peachy glow of her skin in the firelight and her tousled hair. "This was the first day that I've taken off in years. I had fun—just being with you."

"Really?" She seemed truly surprised.

"Yeah. I have what I want—a fleet of catering trucks, hamburger stands, cafés and now, Reflections, my ultimate goal." He gazed at her, finally ready to say what he hadn't been able to tell another woman. "I'm glad I discussed the past with you. It helped me put things in perspective. I've been pushing hard with each new restaurant to prove I'm not the fat kid who'd caused his father's death anymore."

Allie smiled at him and brushed her fingertips across his cheek. "I'm glad I was able to help."

He kissed the tip of her nose. "You've shown me that I don't have to keep proving myself. Now I can be happy."

NOW I CAN BE HAPPY. Allie was wondering if she could be happy, too. She wanted to give their relationship a chance. All she had to do was confess that she was Restaurant Rita.

Simple. Just tell Kyle. But not tonight, she decided as he adjusted his arm so that she could rest her head more comfortably. *Let me have tonight. Is that too much to ask?*

Once she'd believed she'd known Drew Porter. But he'd played her along, pretending he wanted to marry her. All the while, he'd been romancing the owner's daughter. Her experiences with Kyle were limited, and they'd happened with amazing quickness. She didn't know him and had no idea what he might be like when things weren't going his way. He was a complicated man with a troubled past. Who could predict how he would react if she told him the truth?

Granted, he was a good man. He'd stepped forward to keep a woman he didn't know from being taken hostage. But even the best of men would find it difficult to forgive someone who'd shattered his dreams. Reflections was a goal Kyle had been pursuing for years and the negative review she'd written just might ruin the restaurant.

"Once Reflections is running smoothly, I'm going to kick back instead of going ahead with another project," Kyle told her. "My dream was to have a five-star restaurant. Now I do."

She silently prayed that her assessment of Reflections was wrong. She desperately wanted Kyle to be successful. He'd worked so hard, pulling himself up

from nowhere. And he gave people like Marie an opportunity to realize their dreams. This time she didn't
want to be right.

"I'm going to cut back on the time I spend at
work," he said, his hand caressing her bare thigh.
"We can spend evenings together."

Now was the perfect time to confess, but she
couldn't. Instead, they talked for hours in front of the
fire. Finally, they fell asleep on her chocolate-stained
sheets, Gordon snuggled up to Kyle, purring like a
diesel.

TOO SOON, MORNING CAME and Kyle left to check on
his two cafés that specialized in breakfast. Allie waved
goodbye, barely hearing his promise to come back as
soon as he could. She knew the *Tribune* must have
circulated through the small town. She couldn't put
off telling him much longer.

"I did the right thing, didn't I?" she asked out loud.

Naturally, Gordon didn't have an answer. He trotted into the kitchen and rubbed against the refrigerator, reminding her that it was mealtime. Allie filled his
dish and the cat did an immediate face plant in the
fishy-smelling food.

The firm knock on the door an hour later meant
Kyle had returned. She almost didn't answer it. How
could she tell him?

"You're not going to believe this," Kyle said when
she let him in. He waved a copy of the "Around Ce-

dar Ridge" section of the *Tribune*. "Restaurant Rita gave Reflections one lousy star and fried the place. Now I'm going to lose all the money I invested. I'll be forced to fire a bunch of really great people."

"Kyle, I—"

"Listen to this." He cut her off, pointing to the column. "Restaurant Rambo says the decor sucks. You thought it was beautiful, didn't you?"

"Well, I—"

"Check this. 'A delicious piece of cod was smothered in a sauce that claimed to be mustard-basil, but looked and tasted like pond scum.' Great."

She gulped, noticing the lively twinkle in his eyes had been replaced by cold fury. This was a new person, a man she didn't know. And she remembered how Drew had changed—in a heartbeat—from a man she'd known for years into a self-absorbed monster.

She didn't know Kyle at all. Everything had happened so fast. Too fast. Dared she admit that she was Restaurant Rita? Maybe she should just keep quiet. But if she didn't tell him, they couldn't have a relationship. She couldn't hide the truth forever.

"The paper hit the streets late yesterday while we were here. People canceled reservations, leaving Reflections with exactly two couples last night. Dakota quit. He won't work in a town where people don't appreciate gourmet food."

"You could get someone else," she said, stalling.

He savagely raked his fingers through his hair. "Even if I do get another chef, Cedar Ridge believes every word Rambo writes."

"Kyle, doesn't the review say anything good?" she asked, trying to find something positive so she could ease into her confession.

"Yeah. The desserts are 'to die for.' What a crock! Reviewers always say *something* nice. Look at this. 'There was enough garlic in the garlic-mashed potatoes to wipe out the entire vampire population of the Western Hemisphere.' Is that the all-time put-down, or what?"

At the time she'd written the line, she'd thought it was clever; but now, hearing Kyle, it sounded mean and silly.

"Vampires... garlic. That's so off-the-wall," he said, blinking at her and slowing down for the first time.

She opened her mouth, set to tell him the truth, but nothing came out. He was so upset, so angry. She didn't want his anger directed at her. She wanted him sweet and loving, the way he'd been last night.

"You mentioned the garlic, too."

"Yes, I..." she responded, not knowing where to begin. He was furious, his whole demeanor taking on a new dimension that alarmed her.

"The wigs in your closet..." He paused.

"Kyle, I..."

A swift shadow of recognition swept across his face. "The offbeat way you write instructions to assemble the toys..."

His words hung in the air like a deadly vapor. Now she knew Charlotte Keats was right. She did not want this man to know she was Restaurant Rita. No telling what he might do.

"Garlic...vampires...disguises," he said slowly, disbelief reflected in his deep blue eyes. He stared at her for a second that seemed to stretch into eternity. "You're Restaurant Rita, aren't you? The wigs aren't for the theater. You sneak into restaurants wearing different wigs. You write the column the way you write directions—with an attitude."

"Yes," she admitted. "I'm Restaurant Rita."

After a minute of astonished silence, he chuckled—a harsh sound that ricocheted through the small apartment. "Why didn't you tell me? It wasn't as if you didn't have plenty of time. Just when were you planning on telling me?"

"I wanted to tell you. I should have told you, but—"

"But nothing. You're a coward. You never would have told me, if I hadn't been smart enough to figure it out."

"You're wrong. I would have told you. I knew you'd be upset, so—"

"Upset?" He flung his hands in the air, his eyes blazing with anger. "No. I just *live* to get involved with women hell-bent on ruining me. It took me years to build up my business. This will wipe me out.''

''I wasn't trying to ruin you. I was just doing my job. I—''

''You lied to me. You claimed you loved Reflections.''

''No. You heard what you wanted to hear. I said the fish was good and the desserts were fabulous. The lemon grass tasted like sour lawn clippings. The snapper was too delicate for lemon grass.''

His cold eyes skewered at her, and his jaw jutted out at a stubborn angle. For a moment he said nothing. When he did speak, his voice held nothing but contempt. ''Henry did recognize you, didn't he? You wore the same lavender dress, but had on a blond wig the night you reviewed Reflections.''

''Yes, I had on that dress—''

''So who was the old dude? Did you pull the same stunt you did with me? Did you bring him back here and sleep with him, too?''

Anger mushroomed inside her, building so quickly that her breath burned in her lungs. It took a few seconds to muster a response that wasn't a slap in the face. This man was more like Drew than she'd suspected. ''Papa Valentine came with me.''

''You're lying. I helped Papa Valentine open Valentine Delights. He'd never turn on me like this.''

''Papa Valentine was sworn to secrecy. Don't blame him. I wrote the review.''

"You know," he said, walking over to the kitchen table, "I thought you were the perfect woman. I was wrong." He picked up the last jar of Chocolate Body Paint. "You want to open a coffee bar, but you haven't got the guts to do it. It's easier to hide in your apartment and write cutesy instructions and attack other people as Restaurant Rita."

He turned and hurled the jar of chocolate. It hit the fireplace and shattered, showering chocolate over the hearth.

"Boys to men," she said, every syllable etched with anger. "A small leap. I've had enough of your tantrum. Get out."

Chapter Eleven

"KYLE PAXTON CAN JUST go straight to hell."

Like a mantra, Allie kept repeating those words while she wiped chocolate off the fireplace. The sound echoed through the room, silent except for the rain pecking at the window. Gordon sat nearby, licking chocolate off his paws, not paying any attention to her.

"I thought Kyle was a good man. Boy, was I wrong. The jerk has a bad temper."

Anger burned, hot and raw, as she remembered how he'd implied she was a cheap slut who jumped into bed at the drop of a hat. Wasn't that just like a man? They press and press, then they turn on you.

You brought it on yourself, whispered a little voice. The choice had been hers. She could have—and should have—gotten to know Kyle better before allowing him to make love to her. She'd dated Drew for almost a year before she'd become intimate with him.

Why hadn't she waited with Kyle? Because there was something about him that drew her like a moth to a flame. She couldn't resist him. Even now, her pulse accelerated as she thought about making love to him. Quickly, she swept the image out of her mind.

She cursed Kyle for the childish way he'd behaved as she wiped off the last of the chocolate. But there was a kernel of truth in what he'd said. She hid behind the printed word. It was easy to write clever instructions or produce a restaurant review. It was a lot harder to put yourself on the line.

The *latte* bar she'd dreamed about was just that—a dream. She'd saved money, telling herself it was for BrewHaHa. Yet she'd never seriously pursued the idea.

"Do I have the guts to go out on my own?"

She sank down onto the hearth and looked around. This wasn't the life she wanted for herself. Before she knew it, she would be eighty years old and still home alone, talking to her cat.

"I like people. I want to be with people. That's why I have such fun hanging out at Valentine Delights." Gordon trotted over and rubbed against her legs. "What I want, Gordon, is a business of my own. But do I have what it takes?"

She agonized the rest of the day, each hour crawling by as she prowled around the lonely apartment. By nightfall, the rain had finally stopped, and she peered out at the sky, praying to see her mother's star to give her guidance. She whispered the little rhyme she'd made up the night her mother had died.

"Star light, star bright,
Wink at me with all your might.

Please, oh, please, I need to see,
That Mom is watching over me."

It sounded silly and a little childish, but the words usually comforted her. Not tonight.

The sky was overcast, making it impossible to see a single star, let alone one that winked. She'd never felt more alone. She began to cry silent, lonely tears filled with pride.

KYLE WALKED THROUGH the rain-soaked streets. He'd been wandering around the entire day, and now it was evening. Of all the people on earth to be Restaurant Rita, why did it have to be his Allie?

His shoulders were hunched forward, his fists rammed into the pockets of his jeans. Every inch of his body was taut with fury. Yet that same body longed for her, remembering the sweet taste of chocolate on her lips.

"Forget it! Don't be dragged through life by your hormones. Allie should have told you. After all, you saved her from being taken hostage. So how did she repay you? Dumps all over Reflections without even a hint of a warning."

He passed an elderly couple who were looking at him as if he were speaking in tongues. What did he expect? He was talking to himself.

What was wrong with him? He didn't need her. He needed to concentrate on saving Reflections. That was what counted. He'd borrowed heavily to build the restaurant.

But it wasn't just the money that bothered him. He'd believed that he'd forged an emotional bond with Allie. He'd trusted her with his secrets—things he'd been unable to confide in any other woman.

"A bond? Yeah, right," he said to himself. "You're the one who bonded. She told you just enough for you to feel sorry for her. But she never trusted you."

The ache in his heart was so intense that it felt like real pain. He was more lonely now than he could ever remember being in a lifetime of loneliness. His sense of loss and pain was so overwhelming that it went beyond tears.

THE FOLLOWING AFTERNOON Allie went into Valentine Delights and found Papa alone in the shop. He saw her and beamed his usual welcoming smile. She couldn't muster a smile in return.

"You told him," Papa said.

"Kyle figured it out. He went ballistic."

"Let's have a Papaccino and talk about it," he said.

He served her a mug of his special cappuccino and topped it with enough whipped cream to rival Mount Everest. Then he drizzled chocolate over the top.

"Kyle was furious. Well, I'm not surprised," Papa said as they sat at a small table. "I tried to warn him that Reflections was too far-out for Cedar Ridge, but he wouldn't listen."

"Did you agree with my review?" Allie took a spoonful of chocolate-coated whipped cream. Usually, it tasted delicious, but today it could have been shaving cream and she wouldn't have noticed the difference.

"Absolutely. The desserts were great, but most of the entrées were those strange concoctions Dakota invented that were downright awful."

"I really thought the restaurant had problems," she told him, "but I didn't have to be so sarcastic. 'Pond scum' and 'enough garlic to wipe out the entire vampire population' was too cruel. I've said things in other columns like that, too. I thought they were witty and clever, but..."

"Your columns were funny," Papa assured her. "At times they had a little edge, but, hey, the public adores shock jocks."

"Well, I don't want to be like that. I can't hurt anyone again. I—"

A customer came in and Papa went to help him. Allie waited while Papa served the man. She'd been awake all night thinking. She had told herself that moving to Cedar Ridge was going to change her life. She'd wanted to put Drew and his betrayal behind her.

Instead, what she had done was isolate herself. It had been almost a year since she had moved to Cedar Ridge. The only friend she'd made was Papa Valentine. She'd spent hours alone in her apartment, talking to her cat.

Get a life.

"I'm giving up writing," she informed Papa when he returned.

"Really? I know you're upset, but I wouldn't do anything without really thinking about it."

"I have thought about it. I want to open Brew-HaHa immediately. I'm not writing any more clever toy instructions, and I'm certainly not going to assassinate anyone in print. When you get to know people, and see how much it means to them, you feel differently. I just can't do it again."

"I understand," Papa said.

"I called a real-estate agent this morning. There are several office buildings with space available for a coffee bar. I'm seeing them first thing in the morning."

Papa nodded his approval. "If you need any help, let me know."

Allie forced herself to sip the Papaccino that he'd made especially for her. "Kyle knows you were with me when I reviewed Reflections. I told him not to blame you, but he has quite a temper."

"Kyle Paxton is a double-edged sword." Papa's expression was earnest, concerned. "What makes him a success—his ability to put everything on the line—can come back to haunt him. He rolled the dice with Reflections. If you hadn't panned it, the public would have. If he wants to be angry with me, there's nothing I can do about it."

"I didn't mean to cause problems for you."

"Kyle's temper flares at times, but he'll come 'round. His problem is that he has yet to experience failure. Over half of all new restaurants fail. He had a string of winners. Now comes the real test."

Half of all new restaurants fail, she thought. Opening BrewHaHa was going to be a challenge. She barely had enough start-up money, but she was heading in the right direction now. Kyle was wrong; she did have the guts to make her dream come true.

Chapter Twelve

IT WAS A FIREFLY NIGHT, the kind of early-summer evening that reminded Allie of the stories of the South that her mother had once told her. But tonight she was too weary to truly appreciate it. BrewHaHa had been open for three months now. Nothing she'd ever done had prepared her for such a grueling experience.

She opened at seven in the morning, which meant she had to be there at five to get ready. She closed at four, but it took her another two hours to clean up and prepare for the next day. She didn't mind the nonstop hard work because it kept her from thinking about Kyle.

The difficult part was the constant threat of financial disaster. She'd spent every dime she had saved. Her credit cards were maxed out. The cost of the lease and the equipment necessary to open a coffee bar astounded her.

It took guts, all right. She was proud of herself for doing as well as she was. BrewHaHa wasn't showing a profit yet, but it was doing a little better each month.

She opened the door to her apartment and Gordon rushed up to greet her.

"Miss me?" she asked.

Gordon rubbed against her bare legs, purring loudly. The apartment was a bit stuffy after being shut all day. She opened the windows and fed Gordon, then she noticed the blinking light on her answering machine. For a second her pulse accelerated.

"Get a grip. Kyle isn't going to call."

She hadn't seen him since he'd flung the chocolate across the room. And she didn't want to, she reminded herself. Who needed a jerk with a temper like his? Still, she couldn't help remembering that lone-dimple smile. Or the feel of his lips on hers. Or the way he'd shared his own heartache with her.

"Come on, Allie. Don't think about him."

Angry with herself because she couldn't quite forgive him—or forget him—she punched the message button, and a man's voice said, "Ms. Evans, this is Sergeant Young. We have a suspect in the Valentine Delights robbery. Contact us immediately, so we can arrange a lineup."

Allie jotted down his number, inwardly shivering as she remembered the creep with the gun. She called the station and agreed to participate in the lineup they had arranged for that evening.

"Kyle must be coming, too," she said aloud, a nervous flutter erupting in her stomach. "He and I are the only ones who saw the robber."

ALLIE WALKED THE FEW short blocks to the station. She needed the time to calm her nerves. Sooner or later she was bound to run into Kyle. It was a small town; she couldn't avoid him forever. But she didn't feel up to seeing him tonight. *Look the other way. Pretend you don't know him.*

"No," she muttered under her breath. "Don't be a coward." After all, Kyle had kept her from being taken hostage by the creep. For that, she would always be grateful.

And she was grateful to him on another level, as well. He'd behaved outrageously and said ugly things, yet he had forced her to take a closer look at herself. Now she was on the right course. Yes, she was drop-dead weary from work. But she loved it. There was something so special about knowing you had built a business all by yourself.

She shouldered her way through the glass doors of the Cedar Ridge Police Station and gave her name to the desk officer. Another officer escorted her down a nearby corridor. Kyle emerged from one of the rooms and was walking toward her.

He had recently cut his hair, she thought. It made him look young and boyish. He was wearing a blue polo shirt, which emphasized the breadth of his shoulders and made his eyes seem even bluer. Until this moment she hadn't realized how much she'd missed him despite the way he'd behaved.

He was talking to a policeman and didn't see her. *It's up to you to say something,* Allie decided. She refused to behave childishly and ignore a man who'd come to her rescue. A man she'd spent an unforgettable Valentine's Day with. A man who had made love to her.

Suddenly, he looked her way. He seemed surprised to see her, then he frowned.

"Hello, Kyle—"

"Don't speak to the other witness," said the policeman escorting Allie. "You can talk after you've seen the lineup." He smiled apologetically. "You know how it is with the courts these days. Lawyers will use anything to get clients off. We don't want them saying the witnesses compared notes."

While the policeman told her this, Kyle passed her without saying a word. When he'd drawn near, Allie's pulse had accelerated. She cursed herself under her breath. Why couldn't she get over him?

Obviously, she hadn't meant that much to him. In the three months since Valentine's Day, he'd made no attempt to contact her. He'd talked with Papa Valentine, and didn't blame his older friend for not warning him about the devastating review. But he hadn't called Allie.

She'd expected him to call and gloat about Reflections' success. Kyle had managed to salvage the restaurant. It was doing well and gaining a reputation as the place to go for that "special" dinner.

The policeman led her into a small room and gave her instructions, taking her mind off Kyle. She listened carefully and looked at the one-way mirror. In the room on the other side would be six suspects. It was up to her to identify the man who had robbed Valentine Delights.

The lights came on in the large room on the other side of the one-way mirror. In walked six men, each holding a number. She immediately spotted the robber and flinched.

"Don't worry, miss. They can't see or hear you. This room is soundproof."

"They're so close," she whispered. She could have reached out and touched the man, if not for the mirror. She shivered at the thought.

The men were standing in a row now, facing her. The robber seemed to be staring straight at her. He still had that wild, feral look about him. What would have happened had he taken her hostage? No matter how badly Kyle had behaved, he had come to her rescue. He could walk by her without a word, if he wanted, but she wasn't going to act so childishly. She was going to thank him—tonight.

"Can you positively identify any of these men as the one who robbed you while you were working at Valentine Delights?"

"Number four," Allie said. "He's the man. No doubt about it."

KYLE WAITED OUTSIDE the police station. What was taking so long? In two seconds he had pointed out the jerk who had robbed them. He was impatient to see

Allie. He hadn't expected to run into her. The police had told him that they hadn't been able to reach her.

Unexpectedly, there she was, walking toward him. Looking even more beautiful than he'd remembered. He'd started to call her a dozen times, but he'd stopped, not knowing what to say. Okay, the time had come.

He looked up at the blaze of stars in the sky and the lovers' moon gleaming the way it had on Valentine's night. He smiled to himself, thinking about the Chocolate Body Paint and "happy parts." What could he possibly say to Allie that would make up for the way he'd behaved?

The doors to the station swung open and Allie walked out. She was down the steps before she noticed him standing in the shadows. They stared at each other for a moment.

"How did it go?" he asked, not knowing what else to say.

"It was him," she said, her voice pitched low. "Number four."

"He was carrying number six for my lineup," Kyle said. "They probably switched numbers."

"Probably."

The word hung there as they gazed at each other. Allie's green eyes were wide, her expression solemn. *Say something,* he told himself.

He opened his mouth but Allie spoke first. "Kyle, seeing that scary man again reminded me of what you did. Thank—"

"Don't thank me." He put his hand on her shoulder. "I acted like a real jerk. I'm sorry. Hell, if you never spoke to me again, I wouldn't blame you. I don't want you to thank me—just forgive me."

"You have some temper. I thought I knew you, but I didn't."

"I'm sorry. I don't usually act like that. I was so proud of Reflections, and I thought you really liked it. When I found out you were Restaurant Rita and hadn't told me—what can I say—I just lost it."

"I know it was wrong to deceive you like that. I'm sorry, too. I wanted to tell you, but I was having such a good time. I couldn't bear to ruin it." She offered him a suggestion of a smile. "I saw how much Reflections meant to you, and I didn't want to be the one—"

"To tell me the truth." He shook his head, pleased that she'd cared so much about his feelings, but disgusted with himself. "People like Papa Valentine and my mother tried to warn me, but I was too stubborn to listen."

"You proved everyone wrong, though. Reflections has become Cedar Ridge's best restaurant."

He shrugged off the compliment. Reflections wasn't nearly as important as his relationship with Allie. He knew that now. But could he get her to see it?

"Why don't we go over to Valentine Delights and have a couple of Papaccinos?" he suggested. "I want you to tell me all about BrewHaHa. I hear it's a real winner."

ALLIE VENTURED A LOOK at Kyle as they walked into Valentine Delights. He'd been so earnest that it was impossible to doubt his sincerity. She had to admit that she wanted to forgive him.

Papa Valentine was behind the counter. If he was surprised to see them together, he didn't show it. They made small talk while he brewed them two Papaccinos. Naturally, Kyle took his without the fattening whipped cream, while Allie had a mountain on hers. They took a small table at the rear of the crowded shop.

"Okay," Kyle said. "Tell me about BrewHaHa."

She ate a spoonful of whipped creamed drizzled with chocolate. "I have you to thank for it. BrewHaHa was only a dream. I might never have opened it. You said some pretty awful things that night, but you were right about me hiding behind the printed word."

"I was wrong to be so nasty. You have real talent."

She pushed the Papaccino aside. "I never realized how devastating a review could be until I met you. Then it became real to me. I couldn't do it any longer. I had several reviews that I'd already done. Since they weren't negative, I submitted them to Charlotte. Then I stopped reviewing.''

"I noticed. The byline still says 'Restaurant Rita,' but the style's different. It isn't nearly as funny or as good." He smiled the one-dimple smile she'd missed so much.

"Thanks, but I like what I'm doing now much better. You know, I found out how much hard work goes into a restaurant. Just my little *latte* bar takes all my time.''

"I hear you have great scones and croissants.''

"I took a page out of your book," she confessed. "I put a small ad in the Help Wanted column, asking for someone to bake part-time. I found a single mother, like Marie. She gets up at three each morning to bake for the shop. Soon I hope I can afford her full-time.''

"You're on the right track. It just takes time and hard work." He reached across the table and took her hand. "I'm proud of you.''

"Thanks," she said as he squeezed her hand. Hearing him say it meant so much to her. Not only did she want to prove to herself that she could do it, she wanted to share her accomplishments with him.

"I'm proud of you, too," she told him. "You proved Restaurant Rita was wrong. Reflections is the place to go.''

He squeezed her hand again and smiled. "It took a lot of work. I revamped the entire menu with the help of the new chef. I got Mom to supervise the redecorating. Now it's not so L.A. that people expect a drive-by shooting.''

Heat crept up her neck as she recalled the brutal way she'd described the decor. ''I'm sorry. That was—''

''Don't be sorry. You were right.'' He gazed at her, his expression earnest. ''After I threw the chocolate and you tossed me out, I did a lot of thinking. On Valentine's night, when we were having dinner, you tried to subtly point out what I'd done wrong. But I heard only what I wanted to hear.''

''I was trying to say I'd loved your other restaurants. You had unique ideas,'' she told him. This time she squeezed his hand.

He scooted his chair closer to hers. ''You saw what I couldn't see. I'd given control to others—something I hadn't done before. That's what got me in trouble. I would never have put nouvelle Cajun tofu on a menu I designed.''

''People rave about the new menu at Reflections.''

He moved his chair even closer until his leg was touching hers. ''It took a hell of a lot of hard work to save Reflections. I spent a fortune at the *Tribune* for ads. I gave away free dinners. Finally, word of mouth kicked in. We're doing well now.''

''You proved me wrong.''

He put his arm around her and stared into her eyes. ''I had to prove to myself I could do it. Reflections was my dream, and now it's coming true. It's not quite there, but it will be soon."

"Dreams do come true," she whispered. At her words, a sensuous light sparked in his eyes.

"No," he said, a husky undertone in his voice. "Dreams are meant to be shared. That's what Papa Valentine always says, and he's right. Having Reflections doesn't mean anything without you."

His words were spoken with such heartfelt emotion that tears came to her eyes. "Not one day went by that I didn't wish you could see BrewHaHa. I wanted to share the realization of my dream with you."

"It's not too late. I know I behaved obnoxiously, but I learned my lesson. These months without you, I've been miserable. Give me another chance, Allie."

In some secret corner of her mind, she'd always hoped he would say this. She wanted to give their relationship another chance more than she'd ever wanted anything. Before that fateful—and wonderful—Valentine's Day, she would have been afraid, a prisoner of past mistakes. Not anymore.

"We've both made mistakes," she whispered. "Let's start over and take it slowly."

He gently pulled her into his arms. Their kiss was sweet compared to some of their more passionate embraces, but it must have looked hot to the people in Valentine Delights. When their lips parted everyone was clapping, and Papa Valentine was standing beside the espresso machine giving them the thumbs-up sign.

Allie felt a blush heat her cheeks, but Kyle grinned, then stood and took a bow. "Let's get out of here," he said.

"Yeah, I think we've made enough of a spectacle of ourselves."

"I want you to meet my mother," he told her as they crossed the room with his arm around her. "She knows all about you."

Allie waved goodbye to Papa Valentine. "Was she upset by my review?"

"No. She said she laughed at the garlic-and-vampires bit." He stopped and pulled her closer.

"You're not going to kiss me again, are you? These people have already had quite a show."

He flashed the one-dimple grin. "I don't think we ought to leave without a few jars of Chocolate Body Paint."

"You're incorrigible," she said with a laugh. "I thought we were taking this slowly."

"No, I'm not incorrigible. I'm in love."

Epilogue

"I CAN'T BELIEVE IT'S Valentine's Day again. Where did the year go?" Allie asked as Kyle held open the door to Valentine Delights.

It was early evening, and most people were home getting ready to celebrate, but there were a few couples at the tables. Papa Valentine welcomed them with a broad smile.

"Kyle, I'm surprised to see you. I thought you'd be at Reflections, getting ready for the Valentine's crowd."

Allie smiled as Kyle put his arm around her and gave her a little squeeze, saying, "Not tonight. This is a special day—the day we met. We're celebrating at my place. I'm making a dinner. Candlelight, red roses, the works."

"We just came by to pick up the Death by Chocolate Torte," Allie said. "I ordered it this morning from Rudy. I hope he set one aside."

"I have it in a box ready to go," Papa assured her. "Kyle, I've got the chocolates, too. Do you have time for a Papaccino?"

Kyle glanced at Allie, who nodded. "Sure. My usual. Nonfat milk and no whipped cream."

"Give me his whipped cream and extra chocolate on top, please."

They took their drinks to a table at the back. Kyle scooted his chair close to hers. Papa Valentine came up and deposited two boxes on their table. One was the gray matte-finish dessert box. The other was a ten-pound silver-foil box with Valentine Delights written in stylized burgundy script. Allie remembered last Valentine's Day when Kyle had bought the same size box for his mother.

Papa Valentine pulled out a chair and joined them. "I'm proud of you two. What you've accomplished in a year—amazing."

"Kyle achieved his dream," Allie told Papa Valentine. "He has a five-star restaurant. Half the people in Atlanta come to Reflections."

"Allie's doing so well that she's opening Brew-HaHa II," Kyle said.

"Dreams do come true, don't they?" Papa Valentine beamed at them.

"A dream isn't worth anything if you don't have someone to share it with." Kyle's voice had an undercurrent of emotion that took Allie by surprise. "Isn't that what you always say, Papa Valentine?"

"True, true," he agreed, but before he could continue, a customer came into the shop and Papa got up to help him.

Kyle's expression was so serious that Allie didn't know what to say. After an awkward silence, she asked, "Shouldn't we run those chocolates over to your mother?"

"I took her a box already. Those are for you."

"Me?" She was so touched she hardly knew what to say. Last year, her secret fantasy had been to get a beautiful box of chocolates from a handsome man. Kyle had been wonderful, bringing her gifts and flowers, but this was special.

"Why don't you open them? You'll find plenty of Chocolate Midnight Fantasies in there. I handpicked and arranged the box myself."

"How sweet," she said and he rewarded her with that lone-dimple smile she loved so much. "I'm going to save them. I don't want to spoil dinner—"

"Just one," he coaxed.

"Okay, a small one." She lifted the lid and saw the dozens of mouthwatering, sinfully delicious chocolates arranged in silver foil. Right in the center was a red velvet box. A very small box.

"Darling, aren't you going to open it?" Kyle asked.

She set the chocolates on the table, then reached for the velvet box. It snapped open to reveal a breathtaking diamond.

"Papa Valentine is right," Kyle said, a husky undertone to his voice. "Dreams are meant to be shared. I love you, Allie. Let's share our dreams and our lives."

Allie slipped the ring on her finger and it winked at her, reminding her of a twinkling star, and all the times she'd looked up at the night sky, seeking solace from the mother she'd lost. Now that comfort was on her finger, a shining reminder of the power of love—and a very special man.

"I love you, Kyle. I'd be thrilled to marry you."

He put his arm around her and kissed her, hugging her tightly. When he pulled away, he whispered, "You're the perfect valentine."

HIS SECRET VALENTINE

Kate Hoffmann

Dear Reader,

How much better could it get? Romance and chocolate! And the chance to write a story about two people who have loved each other for years—but haven't been able to admit it.

I've always enjoyed stories of unrequited love, especially when that love is finally "requited." So when the Harlequin editors asked me to participate in this anthology, I was thrilled that I'd get a chance to tell Sam and Charlotte's story, and give them a happily-ever-after ending. It also gave me a chance to work with two terrific authors, Meryl Sawyer and Gina Wilkins.

I hope you enjoy my contribution to *Valentine Delights* and that *your* Secret Valentine makes this Valentine's Day special!

Best wishes,

Kate Hoffmann

PAPA'S SINFUL CHOCOLATE TOFFEE CHEESECAKE

¼ cup water
8 oz semisweet chocolate
¼ cup melted butter or margarine
1 cup (approx. 20) chocolate wafers, crushed
   (or substitute graham crackers)
3 (8 oz) packages of cream cheese
1 cup sugar
2 eggs
1 cup sour cream
1 tsp vanilla
1 cup toffee bits
chocolate syrup

Preheat oven to 350°F. Melt chocolate with water in microwave or in pan on top of stove. Cool. Combine crushed wafers and melted butter and press into bottom of 9" springform pan. With mixer, cream the cream cheese at medium speed until light. Add sugar and eggs. Beat until smooth. Add melted chocolate and mix well. Then add sour cream and vanilla and mix until smooth. Pour batter into pan. Sprinkle top with toffee bits. Bake for 55-60 minutes. Sides will be puffed and center soft. Cool for several hours before removing from pan. To serve, drizzle chocolate syrup on dessert plate. Sprinkle plate with toffee bits and put a slice of cheesecake on top. Enjoy!

To my sister, Eileen, who has always
loved a good love story.

Chapter One

TEARS FLOODED CHARLOTTE Keats's eyes and spilled down her cheeks. She brushed at them with her fingers, then grabbed a tissue from her desk and blew her runny nose with all the delicacy she could muster.

"Old Yeller," she said, her voice catching. "The ending always gets me. When he has to...to..." She groaned, unable to finish. "I still have the copy of the book my father gave me years ago and it has big tear splotches on the pages."

"Oh, stop! I can't take this anymore." Laurie cried, waving her hand, a fresh surge of tears filling her own eyes. "Any animal story does it to me. Lassie was the worst." She drew a ragged breath. "Oh, I've got another one. That dolphin. What was his name?"

"Flipper?"

"Oh, Flipper! Even he got to me. And then there was that movie about the two dogs and the cat that trek across the country to find their masters. I wept for three hours after I watched it."

"And those phone-company commercials," Charlotte added. "Where the son calls the mother and... Oh, you know." This tortuous game of comparing what made them cry had all started with a teary reading of Laurie's latest story, and now they couldn't stop.

"Greeting-card commercials are much worse," Laurie countered, dabbing at her nose with a crumpled tissue. "Especially the one with the kid and the teacher."

"How about *The Wizard of Oz?* When Dorothy has to go home? Ten hankies, at least. Every time I see it, it takes me a day to recover."

"*Casablanca.* When they say goodbye at the airport. Don't you just want to slap Ingrid Bergman silly?"

"The Olympics when they play the national anthem at the medal ceremony and the flag goes up." Charlotte rocked back in her chair and flung out her arms. "Build an ark, Noah, and open the floodgates."

Laurie held her hand up and shook her head, fighting back another surge of tears. "The—the Road Runner," she said in between two hiccups.

Charlotte straightened and looked at Laurie in bewilderment. A laugh burst from her lips. "What?"

"You know, that cartoon. The bird with the long legs."

"The Road Runner makes you cry? How can the Road Runner make you cry?"

Laurie sniffled. "Well, he's got such a miserable life, living out in the desert, that coyote chasing after him all the time. And there's no Mrs. Road Runner, is there? I mean, who would be there to mourn if that anvil really did fall on his head? Or if the dynamite actually detonated at the right time?''

They stared at each other for a long moment, then burst out in gales of laughter, their hysterics causing another round of tears. Charlotte laughed until her sides ached, until she couldn't catch her breath and her cheeks hurt. And then she looked at Laurie and the hysteria started all over again.

Laurie hiccuped, then covered her face with her hands. "I'm such a sap," she mumbled through her fingers.

"*You* are? What about me?" Charlotte picked up her copy of the story Laurie had just turned in and shoved it at her. "You knew exactly how I'd react to your story. You knew I'd get misty-eyed. You are so manipulative, it's pitiful."

Laurie smiled smugly. "That's what you pay me for," she said. "Human-interest features that push all the right buttons with your readers."

Charlotte sighed. "And with your editor. You know I'm a hopeless romantic and you don't think twice about taking advantage of me."

Hearing a noise, they both looked up and watched as Sam Harper, the publisher of the *Cedar Ridge Tribune,* strode in. He was dressed in his usual impeccably tailored suit and Charlotte watched as Laurie gave him an appreciative once-over. She turned to

Charlotte and wiggled her eyebrows, then resumed her blatant perusal.

Charlotte had seen it all before. Sam Harper had that effect on women—the innate ability to cause heads to turn and hearts to skip a beat. Most men with good looks like his were intolerably self-absorbed. But Sam was so smooth, he managed to act as if he hadn't a clue how attractive he was.

His gaze was fixed on the sheaf of computer print-outs in his hands. "Gus, I was looking at these advertising figures and we've got a big problem. We've got to—" He glanced up, then froze three steps into the room, staring at them both, a wary look in his blue eyes. He looked furtively at his papers, then back at the door, frowned and shifted on his feet.

Charlotte sniffled, her temper rising at his use of that awful childhood nickname he'd given her when she was ten. She couldn't count the number of times she'd asked him to call her Charlotte, or Ms. Keats, especially in front of her staff, but he took perverse delight in calling her "Gus" or "Gussie"—short for Augusta, her middle name.

Pushing aside a sharp comeback, she wiped a tear from her cheek, then folded her hands primly in front of her on her desk. "Hello, Harper. I didn't hear you knock."

He glanced back at the door again. "I never knock," he said.

"My point exactly."

"But maybe I should have, this time," he added under his breath.

"Was there something you wanted?"

He studied her for a long moment, his gaze shrewdly taking in her puffy eyes and damp cheeks. "Is everything all right?"

Charlotte blinked in surprise. His furrowed brow was the closest thing she'd seen to genuine concern from Sam Harper in the almost thirty-four years she'd known him. Even after he'd pushed her into Myrtle Lake and ruined her thirteenth birthday party—his response to her mortifying mistake of telling him she had a crush on him. Even after *that*, he hadn't been able to muster up more than a halfhearted shrug and a mumbled apology.

"Everything is fine—just fine," she said.

"It's just... You look like you've been..." He shuffled the papers in his hands. "Crying."

"I said, I'm fine."

Slowly, he regained his customary composure.

Still, for all his self-assurance, Charlotte found it quite amusing that two weeping women could rattle him so thoroughly. "What was it that you wanted, Harper?"

Charlotte glanced at Laurie, then bit her bottom lip to keep from smiling, relishing the sweet sense of satisfaction at Sam's obvious discomfort. Lord, she loved those rare occasions when she could rattle Sam Harper. He was so unflappable, with an arrogance that grated on her like fingernails on a chalkboard, and an irritating disdain for anything that resembled sentimentality.

Many of his employees considered Sam a bit aloof and somewhat humorless. But Charlotte knew better. She found him downright unbearable. Those buttoned-down suits he wore that managed to make his perfectly buff body look even buffer. And that thick dark hair that always seemed to stay in place even in the midst of hurricane-force winds. Damn, even his eyelashes were gorgeous—long and spiky, the color of soot, a perfect complement to his brilliant blue eyes.

It wasn't as if she were jealous. What did she have to be jealous about? Just because she always managed to look like she'd just tumbled out of bed fully clothed? Or that her hair was nothing more than an unruly riot of curls? Or that the last time her thighs were buff, she was still a tomboy with a mouthful of braces. No, she wasn't jealous of Sam Harper.

He just...irritated her. They'd known each other since they were toddlers, thrown together by their parents as soon as Charlotte took her first steps. He'd been like the older brother she'd never had—nagging, intractable, overbearing.

From the day she'd turned thirteen, she had thought she'd been in love with him. She'd carried a secret torch for him all through her teens. But by the time their fathers had retired and left them to run the newspaper together, she'd known there would never be anything between them.

The truth be told, after nine years of working together, there were days when she could barely tolerate being in the same office. He ran the *Cedar Ridge Tribune* with brilliant aplomb and coldhearted efficiency, she would give him that. But it was the *way* he did it—without a care for the heart and the soul of the newspaper—that annoyed her.

To Sam, the *Tribune* was simply ink on newsprint, a product to be sold. To Charlotte the paper was a living, breathing part of the community, an opportunity to enlighten and inform and entertain.

So Sam, as publisher, deftly handled the financial side of the business and doled out instructions as to how to make it successful. In turn, as editor-in-chief, she ran the editorial department—but was expected to heed all Sam's comments and criticisms. He took great delight in tormenting her with circulation figures and advertising revenues and the relationship between *her* editorial content and *his* readership. She suspected that was what had brought him barging into her office now.

"I—" He glanced at Laurie who was staring up at him, a dreamy smile on her face, then back at Charlotte. "I needed to talk to you about the Valentine's Day issue. I just looked at the board and I noticed that you bumped the story on Ed Calhoun's new paint-mixing system."

Laurie popped out of her chair and gathered her things. "Before you assign me that journalistic gem, I think I'll be going. Charlotte, give me a call if you need any revisions on the story. I'll call Kip and send him over for a photo or two. Sam, it was nice seeing you again." She held out her hand and he took it. "I'll see you...soon."

Laurie pulled the door shut behind her, leaving Charlotte and Sam in silence.

"Well?" he finally said.

"If you date her, I'll kill you," Charlotte warned. "She's a good writer and I don't want to risk losing her. So stay away."

Sam gave her a long-suffering look. "I have no interest in dating her. But I would like an explanation for why you spiked the story on Ed's Paints. He's been a loyal advertiser for years." He tossed the report on her desk. "Fifty thousand in advertising last year. And this new computerized system he has is interesting news."

Charlotte yawned dramatically, waving her hand in front of her mouth. "It's not news, Harper, it's puff. Worse yet, it's boring puff. I'm trying to put together a decent Valentine's Day issue here. Ed's new paint-mixing machine does not rank high on the human-interest scale in Cedar Ridge."

He regarded her cynically. "People don't paint their homes in Cedar Ridge?"

She grabbed the report and tossed it back across her desk. "All the time. But it's not front-page news."

"He's running a color supplement in Sunday's paper."

She shook her head adamantly. "It's a boring story."

"Four pages of full color."

She pushed out of her chair. "The story doesn't need to run on Valentine's Day, Harper. In my opinion, it never needs to run at all."

"Do you realize how much money we get for a four-color supplement?"

Charlotte leaned over her desk and looked directly into his stubborn gaze. "It's an obvious attempt to pander to an advertiser. And if that isn't bad enough, there's no angle."

Sam cursed under his breath. "So make up an angle. You're the editorial wizard. It's Valentine's Day. This paint-mixing system can formulate 256 different and distinct shades of red. I told Ed we'd run the story."

Charlotte clenched her fists and bit back a curse of her own, her temper now blazing out of control. "Well, you can *un*tell him. It wasn't your decision to make. Besides, I have another story that is much more interesting and more appropriate to Valentine's Day than red latex paint."

"What could possibly be more important than making one of our biggest advertisers happy?"

"Laurie Simpson just brought me a story. It's wonderfully romantic. About a couple who met and fell in love but were torn apart at the end of World War II. He was an American soldier and she was a beautiful young Italian girl. As if it were fate, they met again, right here on the streets of Cedar Ridge, fifty years after they parted. And they're going to be married this Valentine's Day."

Sam raked his fingers through his hair. "That is so incredibly maudlin."

"And it is exactly what our readers want to read on Valentine's Day," Charlotte countered. "Just because you don't have a romantic bone in your body, doesn't mean the rest of the world is as unfeeling."

"Listen, I'm just as romantic as the next guy, Gus, but this is—"

Charlotte laughed. "What, you? Romantic? Where in the world did you get that idea?"

"I'm romantic," he said in a defensive tone. "Just ask any of the women I've dated. They'll tell you."

"Well, then, why don't we do that? Let's start with Kimberly. Isn't she the one who dumped you after you forgot her birthday—twice? And then there was Vanessa. I believe she dumped you when she found out you were dating her roommate at the same time you were dating her. And then there was that awful incident with the perfume and Bambi—wasn't that her name? You gave her a bottle of perfume three days *after* last Valentine's Day, a bottle meant for another woman, forgetting, of course that Bambi was highly allergic to perfume. I'm sorry, Harper, but I misspoke. You *are* the last of the red-hot romantics.''

He gave her an aggravated look. "I don't care what you think about me. But I do care about this paper. Our fathers founded the *Cedar Ridge Tribune* and I'm not about to jeopardize our future because you're feeling sentimental. Find a place for Ed's story. And don't even consider burying it in the back." He straightened his perfectly-knotted tie, then turned and strode to the door.

"I'll run it when I want to run it, Sam Harper!" she shouted, throwing the computer report after him. It hit him on the backside, then dropped to the floor behind him.

He turned and looked at her. "You'll run it because I told you to run it."

With that he yanked open the door and walked out. Charlotte stared after him, watching as he made his way through the editorial department to his office at the opposite corner of the building.

"And to think I once believed I was in love with that man," she muttered.

She flopped down in her chair, braced her elbow on her desk and cupped her chin in her palm. Maybe it was all for the better that Sam Harper rubbed her the wrong way. It had made it easier to stop loving him. And she had managed to put all her feelings for him aside and go on with her life.

Still, there were times when she couldn't help but wonder what might have been between them, had they been more compatible. Her mind wandered back to the night she'd realized he would never see her as anything more than good old "Gus." It had been the night before she left for college at Northwestern. She'd walked over to Sam's house to say goodbye to him and his parents. She had decided to tell him how she felt, the same way she had that night on her thirteenth birthday.

But she'd arrived to find Sam busy with one of his many girlfriends. He'd barely glanced at her as he walked out of the house with his sorority-house sweetheart, a pretty blond sophomore from his class at Tulane. Charlotte had called goodbye to them both and in the same breath had vowed to forget him. Four years of college and another three at the *Washington Post* had done their job. By the time she returned to Cedar Ridge to take over as editor, she had put Sam out of her heart for good.

She yanked her desk drawer open and pulled out a silver-foil box of chocolates, then popped one in her mouth and munched methodically. *God, he could be so exasperating!* She would give anything to hold a mirror up to Sam Harper's face, to show him that he was about as romantic as an old stump.

And at the same time, she would reassure herself, once again, that he was a man completely unworthy of *any* woman's affection—including hers.

SAM STRODE THROUGH the offices and headed back to the pressroom. As he stepped through the double doors, the clatter of the presses and the smell of ink filled his senses. He remembered the first time his father had taken him into the pressroom, the joy with which Jack Harper had described the workings of the printing presses. He'd shown his son how they turned the pasted-up version of the paper into plates and then into the newspaper that appeared on the doorstep of nearly every home in Cedar Ridge.

Back then, Cedar Ridge had been a quaint little town—a throwback to the turn of the century, nearly an hour's drive from Atlanta. But the urban sprawl of the city had been relentless. With the new expressways, the time to downtown Atlanta had been cut in half and Cedar Ridge had become a bedroom suburb.

Charlotte had never really understood the difficulties of keeping a small-town newspaper afloat. It had become even worse since the two major Atlanta papers had merged. The *Atlanta Journal-Constitution* had invaded every retail outlet in town and increased their home delivery efforts, as well.

Sam sighed. Sometimes he felt like David against Goliath. When his father and Charlotte's had founded the paper in the fifties, it only had to compete with radio and primitive televisions. But now their loyal readers had more choices to make, as did their advertisers. And he had employees to worry about. Charlotte would have to learn to understand that.

He wasn't being unreasonable, was he? All he was asking for was a little support for one of his most important advertisers. Yet she had taken no more than a few seconds to consider the idea before she killed the story. To make matters worse, she'd managed to offer up a critical review of his social life at the same time. So maybe he wasn't the most romantic guy in the world, but he certainly wasn't going to take Charlotte Keats's word for it.

It seemed as if they'd been at odds their entire lives. From the time she could walk, she'd been a constant bother, tagging along after him like an irksome little sister. She'd even developed a silly teenage crush on him. And now, she'd become a permanent fixture in his life and his own personal thorn-in-the-side.

He shoved his hands into his trouser pockets. To think he'd even loved her once—for a night. His mind flashed instantly back to that time. It had been the summer she came home after graduating from college. There had been a family picnic at their cottage up at Myrtle Lake and he'd seen her for the first time in four years. The gawky girl had become a beautiful woman.

Her once-unruly curls now framed a perfect face, an upturned nose sprinkled with freckles, green eyes, and a mouth made to be kissed. And her voice, so husky and boyish as a child, now seemed tantalizing, like the brush of raw silk against skin.

And the way she'd dressed, he mused. In bright, flowing fabrics that clung to her slender limbs, a wardrobe that seemed to speak volumes for both her self-confidence and her feminine guile.

He had watched her from the shadows that night, losing himself in the simple movements of her hands and the warmth of her sweet smile, and he was confident that he could make her love him again. He could rekindle that childhood crush. And he had expected to do this when she came back to Cedar Ridge, to take the job her father offered at the paper, as he had.

But then she'd made her announcement. She'd taken a job at the *Washington Post*. She wouldn't be coming back to Cedar Ridge after all.

It had taken him a long time to forget that night, but he had, writing it off as a momentary lapse in judgment. When she'd returned to take the job as editor three years later, she'd been different—distant, and wary of him. So they had settled into a professional relationship, a relationship that put them at odds for most of the working day.

He stood next to the press and watched as it gobbled paper from the large roll, pressing ink into the newsprint in a blur of speed and efficiency. Glancing up, he caught sight of Big John, his head pressman, approaching. Big John had worked for the paper for as long as Sam could remember. He'd been a good friend to both the Keats and Harper families.

He wore an ink-stained work apron and his white hair stood on end. A smudge of ink had found its usual place on the end of his nose and a broad smile split his face. "She's workin' fine now, boss!" he shouted, patting the press. "Nothing to worry about."

A breakdown on their main press had delayed the paper's run last night and Sam had been worried that the balky old machine was breathing its last breath. They barely had the money to repair the press, much less purchase a new one. "How far behind are we?" Sam asked.

"We're fine," John said over the clamor. "They're plating the second section right now. We'll be on press with the main by midnight. Everyone will have their paper to read with their morning coffee."

Sam nodded. "Good work," he said, patting John on the shoulder.

Big John smiled and turned to walk down the line, but at the last moment, Sam shouted his name. "You want to get a cup of coffee?" he asked.

The pressman smiled and nodded, then led Sam back to his small office at the rear of the shop. Sam sat down while Big John poured him a cup of coffee. Then Big John settled himself into his chair and cleared his throat. "So what's she done now?"

Sam frowned. "She?"

"Whenever you come back here looking for coffee, you've usually got somethin' stuck in your craw.

And nine times out of ten, that somethin' is Miss Charlotte Keats. So what's she done now?''

Sam slowly sipped at his coffee, watching Big John over the rim of his cup. "Do you think I'm a romantic guy?''

Big John grunted, then chuckled. "You're askin' *me* if you're romantic?''

"I don't have anyone else to ask," Sam said. "Charlotte seems to think I'm some kind of cold-hearted jerk. And I don't think I am. I've always thought I was a nice guy.''

Big John considered his reply for a long moment before speaking. "I wouldn't call you coldhearted. You're a little opinionated, just like your old man. You're stubborn, especially where the paper's concerned. And you like to get your own way. Some people might think you're a little arrogant and self-centered.''

"But that doesn't mean I'm heartless. I can be as romantic as the next arrogant, self-centered guy.''

Big John held out his hands. "Hey, I'm not the one you should be asking. And I'm not about to mediate another fight between you and Charlotte. You'd think after nine years of workin' together, you kids would have learned to get along. Sometimes I don't think you two have grown a lick since you were in diapers.''

"She thinks she knows me," Sam said. "But she doesn't know me at all.''

"And I'd venture you don't really know her, either," Big John countered.

Sam pushed out of his chair and raked his fingers through his hair. "Well, I don't even want to try to get inside that head of hers. Even though I've known her for years, the woman is still a complete mystery to me."

"Don't try too hard to figure her out," Big John advised. "I've learned that women have a real knack for changin' course. Once you think you've got 'em pegged, they head off in the opposite direction."

Sam nodded slowly. "Or they sneak up behind you and knock your feet out from under you. That's Charlotte, all right. She never walks away from an argument. If she's got a point to prove, she won't let go until she proves it."

"Then I guess you'd better watch your back," Big John said.

"That's exactly what I intend to do," Sam replied. "I'm the publisher of this paper and I'm not about to let her get the upper hand."

CHARLOTTE PUSHED OPEN the front door of Valentine Delights, a cozy coffee and sweet shop located in the center of Cedar Ridge's picturesque downtown. The smell of freshly ground coffee and handmade chocolates teased at her nose and she drew a deep breath.

The confectionery, located in a pretty brick Victorian storefront, had become a popular gathering place, owing to its early opening and late closing times. Besides hand-dipped chocolates, Papa had recently added luscious desserts to his menu, making the shop a pleasant place to sit, chat, and indulge in some sinful sweets.

Charlotte stopped by nearly every morning at eight for a Papaccino—a mix of espresso, steamed milk, and chocolate—with her own twist—a shot of raspberry syrup. The newspaper office was located just around the corner from Valentine Delights and Papa's had become a regular stop for most of its employees. As she stepped up to the counter to place her order, Papa looked up and gave her a bright smile.

"Hey, Charlotte. What's news?"

"Good morning, Papa." She dug in her purse for her wallet. "I don't have much news to tell. Luella Crenshaw's cat got stuck in a tree yesterday afternoon and the fire department got to use their new ladder truck. I heard Chip Watkins scored thirty-five points in the high-school basketball game last night and there was a scout from Arkansas State there to see him do it. And the mayor decided to postpone the referendum on the new parking lot."

Papa chuckled as he prepared her coffee. "I'm sure glad you stop by every morning to give me the news," he said. "Gives me something to gossip about all day long."

"Well, don't gossip too much. With the number of customers you've got in here, you're reaching more people than CNN. You might just put the *Tribune* right out of business."

"Not much chance of that," Papa said. "Not with the way your Sam runs that paper."

Charlotte frowned. "He's not *my* Sam," she retorted.

Papa's eyebrow shot up. "You know what I meant." He gazed at her for a long moment. "What's wrong? You and Sam have another fight?"

Charlotte shook her head. "Not anything more than usual. We can't seem to agree on anything lately. I don't remember it ever being this bad between us. In fact, it was so bad yesterday I ate that whole box of hazelnut truffles you sold me." She grabbed her coffee. "I'll take a croissant, too, please. And I'll need another box of truffles. A dozen. That should last me for another day. I swear, if Sam Harper doesn't lighten up, I'm going to turn into a blimp."

"Hey, if that happens, you could always work out at the Bad Dog Gym," Papa said. "Sam's down there two or three times a week."

"I think I'll pass," she said. "I get plenty of Harper at work."

She followed Papa to the pastry case and he pulled a croissant from a basket on top and dropped it into a bag. Then he moved to the glass candy case and slid the door open.

"I suppose business has been pretty brisk lately, with Valentine's Day coming up," she commented.

Papa nodded. "Everyone's been picking up sweets for their sweeties," he said. "Lots of folks responding to that ad I ran last week. Sam told me it would pay off. And he's the one who suggested the coupon. He sure knows his readers."

Charlotte watched as he plucked a dozen truffles from the tray, then carefully weighed them and placed them, one by one, in a silver-foil box embossed with the name of the shop. He handed the box over the counter to her.

"What about you?" he asked. "Can I show you anything for your sweetheart?"

Charlotte shook her head as she handed him the money, then paused. An idea slowly coalesced in her mind and she smiled.

It would be the perfect plan, an irrefutable way to prove her point. A way to hold a mirror up to Sam Harper and make him see the man he really was. "In fact, you *can* get me something," she said. "Pack up another six of those truffles in one of your special little boxes with the burgundy ribbon. And I need a gift card to go with it."

She quickly paid for her purchases, tucked them beneath her arm and bade Papa goodbye. As she stepped out onto the sidewalk, she smiled smugly.

"Watch out, Sam Harper. I'm mad and I'm heavily armed with chocolate."

If he really thought he had an ounce of romance in his soul, she was about to prove him wrong.

Chapter Two

CHARLOTTE PLACED THE beribboned box of candy in the center of Sam's desk, then stepped back to study it. A momentary twinge of conscience pricked her, but she quickly pushed it aside and hurried from Sam's office. She glanced at her watch and let out a tightly held breath. She would only have to wait two minutes. Sam arrived precisely at eight-thirty every morning, rain or shine.

She searched for a place from which she would be able to see into his office, and chose to loiter in front of the bank of file cabinets outside his office door. She yanked a drawer open and idly flipped through the photo file. Always predictable, Sam arrived right on time.

"Morning, Gus," he muttered as he passed by her, not even giving her a second glance, his mind undoubtedly already preoccupied with the day ahead.

Charlotte looked up and schooled her smile of anticipation into one of indifference. "Good morning, Harper."

She sidled around the open top drawer of the cabinet and faced his office, watching him as he pulled off his coat and hung it on the rack beside the door. She held her breath as he crossed his office to his desk.

A shiver skittered down her spine as her gaze came to rest on his broad shoulders and flat belly. Lord, the man knew how to wear a suit. Most of the other employees chose a more casual style of dress, but Sam preferred a suit and tie. She suspected it gave him a sense of power and authority, especially when matched against her own flamboyant style. Or perhaps it was simply a reflection of his buttoned-down personality.

His hair, still slightly damp from his morning shower, brushed the collar of his crisply starched shirt. Her gaze lingered for a moment longer as her thoughts wandered. What might it feel like to run her fingers through his hair? Or to let her hands slide down along his shoulders? Or maybe over his broad, finely-muscled chest? Or—

She sucked in a sharp breath and clenched her fingers into fists, trying to rid herself of the tingle that seemed to numb her fingertips. What was she doing? Fantasizing about the man was not what this plan was all about! This whole thing was about proving that she knew exactly the kind of man he was—a man with a heart chiseled from pure stone. Sure, his heart was surrounded by a warm body, but that was *not* the point.

She watched him surreptitiously as he flipped open his briefcase. When he reached for the phone without noticing the silver-foil box, she could barely contain her nerves.

And then he paused, his hand halfway to the phone. Slowly, he reached for the box instead and lowered himself into his chair. He plucked at the gift card, then opened the tiny envelope and withdrew it.

"'From Your Secret Valentine,'" she said softly, repeating the words she'd written. Now he would toss the card aside and laugh. Or perhaps he would crumple it and throw it in the trash. She waited and watched. A lazy smile curled his lips as he continued to stare at it.

"All right," she murmured. "Get to it. You have no patience for this romantic foolishness. A secret valentine? Not for me, Mr. Indifferent. Come on, throw it out, Harper."

But he didn't. Instead he picked up the box and untied the ribbon, then opened it. His grin widened and she cursed softly. "I can't believe you're actually enjoying this. You hate chocolate."

When he pulled a truffle from the box and bit into it, she decided it was time to push the issue a little further. Shoving the file drawer closed, she stepped toward his office.

He glanced up then and noticed her approach. In one smooth movement, he tucked the card into the breast pocket of his jacket and slipped the small box of chocolates into his desk drawer. If she hadn't been watching him so closely, she would have missed it, for he removed the evidence with an amazing sleight of hand.

"Well, Gus," he said as she stepped through the door. "On the warpath early, I see."

She ground her teeth in frustration. If the box of candy had been in plain sight, she could have asked him about it. But if she questioned him now, he would know she'd been spying. "I just wanted to check on the press problem. Did we have any delay last night?"

"Since when do you worry about the presses, Gus?"

"My name is Charlotte," she said, bristling. "I wish you would learn to call me that. And I have every right to check on the status of our printing equipment. This business *is* half mine."

He grinned. "All right, *Charlotte*. The press is working fine. The paper got out on time. All's well with the world."

She shifted uneasily, then tipped her chin up. "Good. I'm glad to hear that."

"Was there something else?" he asked, arching his eyebrow in sarcastic curiosity.

"No."

"Then hop on your broom and get out of here. I've got work to do."

Stymied, Charlotte headed to the door, but his voice stopped her.

"By the way, I had a chance to look at Laurie's feature for the Valentine's Day issue. I noticed it had been set on the system already so I ran a hard copy and read it last night."

Charlotte stopped and turned back to him, her hands braced on her hips. "I told you, I'm not going to pull that story for Ed's Paints."

He held up his hand to stop any further complaint. "I don't want you to. Actually, you were right about the story. It's very...well reported. I think it's perfect for Valentine's Day. In fact, if I might make a suggestion, I think we ought to send a photographer to the wedding and maybe do a follow-up. You know—a happily-ever-after angle would probably sell a lot of papers."

Charlotte stared at him, then snapped her mouth shut when she realized it was hanging open. What was he up to now? Did he think this would square everything between them? "Just because you've acknowledged the appropriateness of that story does not mean I've changed my opinion of you," she said. "I still think you are far too cynical about real human emotions."

He watched her, nodding slowly, as if he were actually considering what she said. After a long moment, he drew a deep breath. "Well, I still disagree with that assessment," he said. "I think I'm a warm and lovable guy. A real romantic at heart." He patted his chest, right over the spot where he'd placed the card in his pocket. "And I'm sure there are lots of women out there who think so, too."

Charlotte laughed dryly, trying to ignore his oblique reference to the Secret Valentine. "Where are they all?

I don't see them breaking down your door to get to you," she countered.

He leaned back in his chair and linked his arms behind his head. "I could ask the same of you," he said. "You may be bursting with romantic sentiment, Gus, but I don't see you cozied up to that special someone. Valentine's Day is coming up and I'd hazard a guess that you'll spend the night at home with your nose in a book." He grinned and arched a sardonic eyebrow. "You can talk the talk, Gus, but sooner or later you've got to walk the walk."

Her eyes narrowed and she glared at him. "I don't know what ever possessed me to come back to Cedar Ridge and work with you. You have got to be the most egotistical, overbearing, arrogant—"

"Yeah, yeah. You can stop there," he said. "I've heard it all before. Now I've got to get back to work. Would you close the door on your way out?"

With a frustrated little scream, she spun on her heel and stalked out of his office, slamming the door behind her.

Damn, that man drove her absolutely, stark-raving mad! So much for *her* plan to take Sam down a peg or two. How had he managed to turn this whole argument around on her? This was about the lack of romance in *his* soul, not the lack of romance in *her* life!

She clenched her fists and cursed beneath her breath. So maybe she hadn't had a date in longer than she cared to remember. But that didn't mean she wasn't open to the idea of a little romance. She just hadn't met the right man. Heck, she hadn't even managed to meet the *wrong* man.

"Well, I'm not about to let him have the last word on this one," she muttered. "Sam Harper wouldn't know real romance if it dropped out of the sky and hit him over the head."

HE FOUND THE FLOWER on his desk when he arrived that morning. A yellow rose with an accompanying card signed as the last three had been—"Your Secret Valentine." If he'd been a real over-the-top romantic, he probably would have known the significance of a yellow rose. But for him it was just a flower and another in a line of gifts from his mysterious Secret Valentine.

There had been the little box of chocolates the first day. The next day had brought a fancy greeting card. The day after that, a jar of brightly colored jelly beans. And now, a flower.

Sam smiled to himself, then sat down. How could she possibly think she was fooling him? He'd known the moment he opened the box of chocolates—no, *before* he'd opened the box—that Gus had sent them. Sam had seen her eating those very same truffles on more occasions than he could count. And she'd even tried to disguise the signature on the card.

But he'd studied her writing for nearly ten years, on memos and articles, at the bottom of the paychecks they both signed. He hadn't realized that he'd subconsciously absorbed the unique flourishes, the passionate way she wrote her name, the odd way she formed the letter *S*.

Sam picked up the card that came with the rose and ran his thumb over the scrawled signature—"Your Secret Valentine." Funny how he could know her handwriting so intimately, like a husband might know a wife's, yet they shared nothing deeper than a business relationship.

He knew Charlotte Keats better than he'd known any other woman in his life. He could sense her moods, predict her responses, identify her perfume in the air. He could point to the articles in the *Tribune* that she had written just by reading the lead paragraph. He knew which movies she would like and which books she would hate. Hell, he could probably shop for her wardrobe in a pinch, he was so familiar with her favorite colors and fabrics.

Yet, even though he knew all those things that a lover might, there were pieces missing. He didn't know how her mouth tasted, or what her hair would feel like between his fingers. Or how her body might respond to his hands. He didn't know what his name might sound like on her lips in the midst of passion.

He frowned, then held the rose up to his nose and drew a deep breath. He'd experienced all those things with other women, yet he'd never really known them—not the way he knew Charlotte Keats.

What he *did* know was that she would stop at nothing to make a point. Gus was probably the most pigheaded woman he'd ever known. And she had a point to make with this Secret Valentine charade. She wanted him to react, to blow the whole thing off, to reveal himself as some unromantic slob who couldn't even be charmed by the notion of a secret admirer.

But now that he knew the game was on, he wasn't about to let her win—at least, not before he had a little fun. He snipped off the stem of the yellow rose and tossed it aside, then slipped the flower into the buttonhole on his lapel.

He found her in the composition and pasteup department, bent over the computer layout for tomorrow morning's "Home and Garden" section. The Friday edition featured "Home and Garden," Wednesday was "On the Town," and Monday's paper included a section for both businessmen and concerned consumers called "Marketplace." The special sections had been Charlotte's idea—a concept that would help the paper compete for readership with the *Atlanta Journal-Constitution*. She had lobbied hard for the extra budget and in the end, he had found the money for the project.

It had been no surprise that she'd made a resounding success of the concept. The special sections were intricately planned and wonderfully entertaining. How she and her small staff of writers had been able to dig up such terrific stories in a small town like Cedar Ridge had been beyond him. But she'd done it.

And now she wanted more money, to add special sections to the Tuesday and Thursday editions. His advertising sales staff had worked day and night to come up with the commitments needed to test the new sections, but it was going to take a little longer before they would be financially ready to go on press with them.

"Give me a smaller point size on the head and add a kicker," she said. "The Beauty of Bulbs."

The layout artist typed in a few commands on the keyboard and she studied the results. "I like that better," she said. "When you're all finished run me a hard copy and bring it by my office."

"No problem, Ms. Keats," he said.

She turned to leave, then stopped when she saw Sam watching her. Her gaze drifted down to the yellow rose he wore in his lapel, then snapped back up to his face.

"Were you looking for me?" she asked, her eyes darting back and forth between his face and the rose.

If she'd tried to fool anyone else, she might have succeeded. But knowing her game made her sudden interest in his lapel flower all the more satisfying. She wanted him to mention the rose, to explain it. But he wasn't about to give her the satisfaction.

"I wanted to discuss the supplements you proposed for the Tuesday and Thursday editions," he said. "I've had a chance to review the figures from the sales department and it looks like we'll be able to go ahead with them, starting next month.''

She gave the rose one last look, then nodded curtly and walked past him. "Good."

He followed after her. "Is that all you have to say?"

She headed toward her office, grabbing a stack of galley proofs from the basket along the way. "What do you want me to say? It's a brilliant idea. You would have been a fool not to see that.''

"Not even a little gratitude? We worked our butts off scraping together enough advertisers to support the cost. You could at least say thanks.''

She sat down at her desk and looked up at him. "Thanks. Now, I'm really busy. Jessica Patterson's first-grade class is coming in for a tour this afternoon and I've got three articles to edit before then.''

He sat down in a chair in front of her desk and leaned back, stretching his legs out in front of him. "Do you ever wonder why we're always at odds, Gus?"

Charlotte blinked, as if startled by his blunt question. She shrugged. "Probably because you do everything in your power to drive me crazy?''

"I don't do it deliberately," Sam replied. "I mean, I don't come to work thinking about how I'm going to make Charlotte Keats miserable.''

An odd expression crossed her face—one that looked a bit like regret. She sighed. "You don't make me miserable. You just make life difficult some-times.''

''We really should try to get along a little better,'' Sam said.

She smiled grudgingly. ''We've known each other for over thirty years, Harper. And we've never gotten along. You've always been a pain.''

''We're kind of like siblings,'' he said. ''If we hadn't grown up together, we'd probably get along just fine. I guess we could blame all this on our parents.''

She picked up a pencil and twisted it through her fingers. ''Maybe. But maybe we're a *little* to blame.''

Sam leaned forward in his chair. ''I know it may be too late, Gus, but I was thinking we could call a truce. A cease-fire. If we both put a little effort into it, we might be able to get along better. After all, we're probably going to be working together for another thirty years.'' He held his hand out over her desk. ''Truce?''

Hesitantly, she reached out. ''All right,'' she said. ''If you try, I'll try. And you can start by calling me Charlotte. I hate it when you call me Gus.''

Sam grinned at her and she forced a reluctant smile of her own. ''All right, Charlotte. Here's to a new be-ginning.'' He took her fingers in his and shook her hand, realizing that this was the first time since they were kids that he had touched her.

He glanced down at her delicate fingers, surprised by how fragile her hand seemed in his. He'd never really noticed before, but he'd just assumed she would have ordinary, capable hands. But her fingers were long and slender, her nails perfectly manicured. For an instant, he wondered what those hands would feel like, skimming over his skin, touching him intimately.

Halting his runaway thoughts, he cleared his throat and dropped her hand, then stood to leave. "I'd better go."

"Nice rose," she said, almost as an afterthought.

He bent to sniff at it, then shot her a wide smile. "It *is* nice, isn't it." With that, he turned and walked out of her office.

But when he sat down at his desk, he couldn't seem to focus on work. Instead, his mind constantly returned to the feel of her fingers in his.

At first, the suggestion of a truce was just another move in this secret game they played. But, now, as he considered an improvement in their relations, he realized that it wasn't such a bad idea.

Especially if it gave him another opportunity to touch her.

CHARLOTTE RUBBED HER eyes, then stifled a yawn. The office was dark; the lights turned off as soon as the paper was put to bed at six. The faint sound of the presses drifted from the lower floor of the building, a steady rhythm that seemed to work on her like a tranquilizer.

"Are you still here?"

She glanced up to find Sam standing in the doorway of her office. His tie was unknotted and the first few buttons of his shirt were undone. His jacket, hooked on one finger, was tossed over his shoulder.

Charlotte shook her head. "I was just getting ready to go home." She grabbed a stack of edited copy and tossed it in her Out basket. "Was there something you—"

"No," he said, "there's nothing I wanted. I just stopped by to say good-night. Part of the peace treaty we agreed on."

"Well, good night, then," Charlotte said, watching him warily.

He turned to leave, then changed his mind. "Actually, there *is* something I'd like to talk to you about. Why don't I walk you home? We can talk about it on the way."

Although her house was only a fifteen-minute walk from work, she wasn't sure she wanted to spend even that much time alone with him outside the office. Since she'd started this Secret Valentine game five days ago, her thoughts seemed to lean toward fantasies when it came to Sam, and the prospect of saying good-night on her front porch made her very uncomfortable. "That's not necessary," Charlotte replied. "If it's business, we can discuss it here."

He grabbed her coat from the rack behind her door. "It's not business."

Her curiosity piqued, she stood and rounded her desk, then reached out to take her coat. But instead, he held it up to help her put it on. She turned and slipped her arms into the sleeves, a tremor fluttering through her when his hands rested for a moment on her shoulders. Then she grabbed her purse, ignoring the work she'd stacked up to take home with her. No doubt she would have plenty to occupy her mind once she was alone at home.

They descended the stairs from the second-floor offices and headed for the front door. He pulled it open for her, then took her keys from her fumbling fingers and locked it behind them. The February night chilled her as they walked down the street. Pulling her collar up around her neck, she gave him a sideways glance, unable to read his expression. He looked . . . happy. And she couldn't recall ever seeing Sam Harper so relaxed, especially in her presence.

They rounded the corner and she finally decided to break the silence that hung between them. "What was it you wanted to talk about?"

"Would you like to get a cup of coffee? We could stop at Papa's," he suggested, pointing to the shop ahead of them.

"All right," she said. "But just for a quick cup. I have to get home."

Once again, he hurried to open the door for her, then followed her inside. Papa waved at them from behind the counter as they looked for an empty table.

When they found one, Sam pulled out her chair, then helped her out of her coat—a continuing study in perfect gallantry.

"What would you like?" he asked.

When she made a move to get up, he stopped her, his hand coming to rest on her arm. "I'll get it."

Charlotte cleared her throat, her gaze drifting down to where his hand still touched her. "I—I'll have a Papaccino, decaf...with skim. Raspberry flavoring. No whipped cream and—" She paused. "Maybe I should get it."

"No," he insisted. "I've got it." He repeated her order.

"And a little shaved chocolate on the top," she added lamely, rubbing the place where his fingers had been on her arm and trying to ignore the tingle that remained.

He returned a few minutes later with a small tray holding their coffees and two of Papa's famous desserts. "I thought you might be hungry. I noticed you didn't send out for dinner."

She quickly grabbed her coffee and took a sip, hiding her confusion behind the huge ceramic cup. Had he been watching her? They worked late at the office together nearly every night, but he'd never taken notice of her activities before.

Charlotte drew a slow breath. The fragrant brew warmed her blood and relaxed her, but once again, a silence had developed between them. She reached for one of the desserts he'd brought—a sinful chocolate toffee cheesecake—and methodically devoured it in an effort to keep her hands busy and her mind off his intense gaze.

When she'd finished, she looked up to find him smiling at her. "I was hungry," she said.

"I can see that."

Slowly, he reached across the table. She stared at his hand and jumped when he brushed his thumb along the corner of her mouth. He pulled back. "You had a little chocolate there," he explained, holding up his thumb as proof. She watched him with wide eyes as he licked his thumb, savoring the bit of chocolate.

Her hand fluttered to her mouth and the brand that his fingers had left there. She rubbed at it with her napkin as if that might make it go away. "What did you want to talk about?" she asked, placing the napkin neatly beside her plate.

"I was hoping you might be able to help me."

"With what?"

He smiled with what looked suspiciously like embarrassment. "I've been receiving little gifts lately. Candy, flowers, cards."

She swallowed hard, the cheesecake now sitting in her stomach like a lump of lead, then braced herself for his anger. Somehow he had figured out what she was up to and now he was about to lower the boom. And leave it to him to catch her unawares, plying her with coffee and sweets, pretending to be nice to her, playing the well-mannered gentleman.

"The gifts always come with a card signed 'Your Secret Valentine.' I was hoping you might know who the gifts are coming from."

Charlotte groaned inwardly. So he was going to draw this out, tease her, like a cat toying with a mouse, making her think she might just get away before he pounced again.

"I think I know who's sending them," he continued before she could answer, "and I thought maybe you could tell me if I'm right. It's Laurie, isn't it?"

Charlotte gasped and stared at him. "Laurie?"

"Yeah, Laurie. That free-lance writer you work with. I mean, I'm pretty sure we made a connection that day in your office. A woman just doesn't look at a man like that without...wanting him. I think it's her. Am I right?"

"I—I don't know," Charlotte said, dumbfounded at the bizarre turn in the conversation.

"You mean, she hasn't confided in you? I thought she was your friend."

"No. I mean, I don't think it's her, Harper."

"Sam," he said distractedly. "If I call you Charlotte, you have to call me Sam." He took a quick sip of his coffee, scowling. "Gee, I thought for sure it was Laurie. Maybe it's that Allie woman. You know, the one who does the restaurant reviews. What's that name she uses?"

"Restaurant Rita?" Charlotte shook her head. "No, I'm sure it's not Alexis Evans. She only stops by once a week to turn in her review. And you've been getting gifts every—" She froze, her mind scrambling to remember exactly what he'd told her. "Day. I—I mean, you did say you'd received a gift every day this week, didn't you?"

He nodded. "It has been every day," he said, not noticing her obvious blunder. "You're right. It would have to be someone who is in the office regularly. Unless my Secret Valentine has an accomplice on the inside."

"Maybe you should wait until your Secret Valentine is ready to reveal herself. She could be keeping her identity a secret for a reason."

He leaned back in his chair and considered her comment, then shook his head. "What possible reason could she have? I'm a nice guy. I don't know what she's afraid of."

"Perhaps she thinks you wouldn't want to go out with her," Charlotte suggested.

"But I would," he replied as if the notion were completely unfounded.

"You would?" she croaked, choking on a swallow of her coffee. She coughed, then grabbed her napkin and pressed it to her mouth, her eyes watering.

He smiled and, for a instant, she thought she detected a hint of smugness there. What was going on? He was completely captivated by the notion of a secret admirer! And he had every intention of pursuing this woman! This was not part of her plan.

Charlotte twisted her napkin around her fingers. She would have to do something about this strange turn of events. But what? Should she admit to him right now that his "secret admirer" was sitting across from him at this very moment? Or should she keep quiet?

She couldn't have been wrong about him. Sam Harper didn't have a romantic bone in his body. Yet he was acting like a man with a serious crush—a crush on someone he'd never met, someone who didn't even exist.

"I would like to meet her and go out. Since you and I had our little discussion, I've been thinking about what you said. And maybe I'm not the most romantic guy in the world. But that doesn't mean I can't change."

"Then you're admitting I was right?" Charlotte asked.

He met her gaze for a long moment and she felt as if he could see to her very soul, as if he knew about the deception. "Only if you promise not to rub it in," he said, his voice low and seductive.

She drew a sharp breath, trying to sort out the whirlwind of confusion that had overtaken her mind. "I should get going," she said, turning in her chair to tug her on coat.

"I'll walk you home," he said, standing.

"No!" she cried. Her sharp reply seemed to echo through the quiet atmosphere of Valentine Delights. She glanced nervously around to find most of the patrons and Papa looking her way. "I can find my own way home," she said. "Have a nice weekend."

Charlotte hurried to the door, panicked that he might decide to follow her. But to her relief, he didn't. Once she reached the sidewalk, she took a long, steadying breath of the crisp evening air.

"You've done it now, Charlotte Keats," she murmured. "How are you going to get yourself out of this one?"

Chapter Three

"YOU HAVE MAIL!"

Sam glanced up from the Monday-morning reports spread over the surface of his desk and stared at his computer, the source of the impersonal announcement. They'd installed a computerized phone and mail system six months ago, but he rarely received E-mail. Most people who had something to tell him preferred to stop by his office and talk, or ring him on the phone.

Frowning, he reached out and typed in a few commands. An instant later, a letter appeared on the screen.

TO: SamHarper
FROM: YrSecretVal
Dear Sam,
Though I've wanted to speak to you for so very long, it seems that I can't bring myself to take that step. This letter is the very closest we will ever come to exchanging words. We cannot meet. Please understand that you will always have a place in my heart. Just not a place in my life. I must always remain Your Secret Valentine

He chuckled softly. "Clever move, Gus. But don't think this is the end of it. If you think you can blow me off, hiding in cyberspace, you're kidding yourself.''

He quickly hit the Print command, then tapped his foot impatiently as he waited for a hard copy of the letter to roll out of his printer. When it did, he snatched it up and headed toward her office.

He found her, staring at her computer, completely absorbed in editing a story. She looked so pretty this morning, her long, curly hair pulled back with a brightly-colored scarf. An outrageously large pair of earrings dangled from her ears and her bright yellow blouse reminded him of the color of daffodils. Her perfume hung in the air and he savored the scent for a moment before he spoke.

"We have to talk," he said.

His words made her jump and she clapped her hand to her chest and slowly turned his way. "Don't ever sneak up on me like that again! Couldn't you have at least knocked?"

Sam grinned and watched the color rise in her cheeks. Lord, she *was* pretty. How could he have ignored her beauty for such a long time? "I never knock," he teased. "Besides, this is important." He waved the letter under her nose. "Read this."

She sent him a leery expression, then reluctantly did as she was asked. Sam watched her face for some trace of surprise or nerves—anything that might indicate that she had been the one to write the letter. But she managed to keep her expression cool and unreadable.

"I'm sorry," she said, placing the paper on her desk. "I know how much you wanted to meet this woman. And now, you never will."

Sam sat down and leaned forward, bracing his elbows on her desk. "I'm not about to give up. Not yet. The way I figure, it's got to be someone in this office." He paused. "But then, my E-mail address is on my business card. Maybe it's Claudia, that pretty blonde in pasteup. Or Diana, that sales rep from the paper company."

This time she did look surprised, her gaze darting between him and the letter. "It doesn't matter who she is, Sam. She doesn't want to meet you."

"Yes, she does," he replied. "She just doesn't know it yet."

She cleared her throat uneasily, then met his gaze. "Sam, I think you'd better let this one go. Besides, you can't force her to reveal her identity if she doesn't want to."

He put on a properly stubborn demeanor and shook his head. "I'm not going to give up!"

Charlotte pushed out of her chair and began to pace the room, all the while avoiding his gaze. "Why are you so upset?" she finally asked. "Women dump you all the time."

"This woman is . . . special. She's different."

"'Different' is not always a good thing. Any woman who hides her identity behind gifts and electronic mail probably has more than her fair share of neuroses."

Sam reached out and grabbed her hand, bringing an end to her restless pacing. "You've got to help me, Charlotte. You have to write a letter to her—from me. Convince her to meet me."

Charlotte snatched her hand away and rubbed her fingers as if she'd been burned. "No! I'm not going to play Cyrano for you, Sam. If you want to write to her, do it yourself."

"But I'm not the writer, you are," he said, looking up at her with a pleading expression. "Nobody can put words together like you do. You'd be able to convince her."

An odd look crossed her face—a flush of embarrassment and then a hesitant smile—and he suddenly realized that this was the first time he'd ever expressed an opinion about her writing. Sure, he'd voiced his complaints about the subjects she chose to write about. But he'd never told her that he thought she was a brilliant writer. He should have—long ago. Maybe she would have graced him with that heart-stoppingly sweet smile.

He marshaled his thoughts and tried to remember that it was Charlotte who had started this whole silly charade. "I'm going to ask her to the Valentine's Ball," Sam said.

Her smile faded. "If she's afraid to meet you, there's no way she'll ever agree to go to the Valentine's Ball. That's one of the biggest social events in this town. Besides it's only four days away. You can't ask so late."

"It's never too late for love," he said. "It'll be perfect." He grabbed the letter from her desk and flipped it over, then handed her a pen. "Start writing."

She shook her head adamantly. "No."

"Write," he said. "You're the only one who can make this work. Come on, Charlotte. Do this one favor for me."

She bit her bottom lip and shook her head again. "I can't. This is something...personal. Between you and—" she swallowed hard "—her."

"If you write this letter, I promise to say 'yes' to the very next thing you ask me for. Whatever it is."

Charlotte picked up the pen and twisted it through her fingers, then groaned softly. "All right. I'll write your letter. But only this once. If it doesn't work, I'm not going to write another."

Sam smiled with what he hoped looked like intense gratitude. Playing the lovesick fool was a lot easier than he'd thought it would be. And the more besotted he acted, the more uneasy she got. He had expected her to confess by now, but she'd remained silent.

He reached out and gave her hand a squeeze, allowing his fingers to rest below her wrist. She stared down at his hand, the pen clutched in her other one so tightly her knuckles had turned white.

He fought the sudden temptation to weave his fingers through hers, to pull her hand up to his mouth and press a kiss along the inside of her wrist. Lately, he'd found himself taking every opportunity to touch her, to brush against her, to place his hand on her back as she walked through a door. He couldn't understand it. Maybe the little game he was playing with her had brought out the devil in him. Even now, he didn't want to let her hand go, but he did. After all, he was a man in love with another woman.

"Thank you," he said. He grabbed the paper and pen. "Why don't you just type it into the computer? This is her E-mail address. Now, what are you going to write?"

She turned to her computer. "Dear Secret Valentine," she said as she typed.

"My *dearest* Secret Valentine," he amended.

She typed in the correction. "Thank you for your recent note," she continued.

"Your note was a ray of sunshine on a gloomy day," he said.

Charlotte quirked an eyebrow up. "That's a little clichéd, don't you think?"

He grinned. "I like it. It's kind of romantic." Pausing, he rubbed his chin in mock seriousness. "You have left me yearning to—"

"Yearning?" Charlotte asked.

He nodded, trying to keep from laughing out loud at the edge in her voice. She sounded jealous, but he knew better than that. "It means 'desiring.' Or 'lusting.'"

She sighed impatiently. "I *know* what it means."

"Then type it. Yearning to look into your beautiful eyes."

"How do you even know she has beautiful eyes?" Charlotte muttered, sending him a sideways glance.

"I just know," Sam replied. "Please say that you'll give me the chance."

"I thought I was supposed to be writing this," she complained. "I'd never write drivel like this."

"Don't interrupt me. I'm on a roll. My heart will not beat again until you agree to meet me at the Valentine's Ball."

Charlotte rolled her eyes, but kept typing. "Oh, brother."

"Love."

"Love?" she asked.

"*Love,* Sam. Make that, your devoted Sam. Now, send it."

Frowning, she quickly typed the last sentence, then hit the Send command. He imagined the letter racing through cyberspace and arriving at her home computer seconds later. No doubt, he would receive his answer tomorrow morning, earlier if she went home for lunch.

He jumped up and grabbed the copy of the letter from her desk, then carefully folded it and tucked it into his breast pocket. "Thanks, Charlotte. I appreciate your help. And I'll let you know when she writes back.''

He turned and walked out of her office, leaving her to stare after him. No doubt he'd left her completely confused. But sooner or later she would have to make another move, write another letter, send another gift. And he would be waiting.

THE DRESS SHOP WAS QUIET as Charlotte stepped inside. She'd been on her way home when she had passed the pretty designer boutique just a few doors down from Valentine Delights. After another tension-filled day at the office, waiting for another run-in with Sam's Secret Valentine, she had intended to stop at Papa's for a very large box of chocolates. But a dress in the window of the shop caught her eye and she forgot about her taste for truffles.

''May I help you?''

Charlotte smiled at the saleswoman and shook her head, wandering toward a rack of evening dresses. ''I'm just looking.''

''For the Valentine's Ball?''

She opened her mouth to say ''No,'' but something made her stop. As she fingered a beaded cocktail dress, she considered the possibility. Why not use her invitation? She could cover the event for the paper, she could socialize with some of Cedar Ridge's most important citizens and she could—

She cursed silently. Why did she really want to go? So she could be there when Sam's date didn't show up? So she could provide the proverbial shoulder to cry on? Heck, she was the one responsible for this whole miserable mess!

She thought it would have been over by now. She had typed the letter for him and he had waited patiently for a response. And when he didn't receive one after two days, she had assumed he'd given up on the woman. But he'd stopped by her office this morning with a garment bag, eager to show her the tux he'd purchased in Atlanta. She even had to help him pick out flowers for the "date" he was certain would change her mind before the big event tomorrow night.

Guilt stabbed at her heart. After all this, it would serve her right if he hated her forever. He would swear off romance for good. It was *her* fault his heart would be crushed. It was her fault he wouldn't have anyone to dance with tomorrow night.

Her mind flashed an image of the two of them dancing together, he in his perfectly-tailored tux and she in a gorgeous evening gown. He would pull her into his arms and slowly they would begin to move, swaying with the music, his lean body warm and hard against hers. Then perhaps he would lean over and whisper some—

"All of our dresses are one of a kind," the saleswoman interrupted. "So you won't have to worry about someone else showing up in your dress."

The fantasy dissolved in the blink of an eye and Charlotte berated herself inwardly. Since she'd written the note for Sam, she'd felt anxious, upset. At first she had just thought it was the tension created by her deception. But what she felt was closer to envy. She was becoming jealous of his "Secret Valentine."

This "phantom" woman had captured Sam's attention, had brought out a side of him she'd never known existed. She'd been wrong about him. He could be romantic if he really wanted. And when it came to his "Secret Valentine," he wanted to be.

But there was no "Secret Valentine," she reminded herself. And what started out as no more than a practical joke had turned into a situation that could conceivably hurt him. How would he feel, left alone—and "yearning"—at the ball?

"I was thinking about going," she said, idly examining a price tag. "But I don't have anything to wear."

The saleswoman smiled. "You've come to the right place. Why don't you let me choose some gowns for you to try on. There's a fitting room in the back. It will just take me a few moments."

With nothing better to do with her evening, Charlotte walked back to the large room lined with mirrors, and stepped inside. She looked at her reflection for a long moment, then turned to leave.

What was she doing? She wasn't the type to attend a formal ball. She'd never worn anything much fancier than what she wore to work—a flowing skirt, a pretty blouse, some artsy jewelry. Even business suits were too formal for her. She preferred comfort over image.

The saleswoman stepped into the fitting room, three gowns tossed over her arm. "My name is Anne. I thought we'd start with this one." She held out a strapless gown the color of emeralds. It was cinched in tight at the waist, then flowed out into a wide skirt. "This would look absolutely stunning with your hair."

She left Charlotte alone until she had slipped into the gown, then magically reappeared to help zip it up. Gazing into the mirror, Charlotte ran her hands over her hips, amazed at how tiny her waist looked in the dress, how voluptuous her merely average chest had become. "It's beautiful," she murmured.

"Not many people can wear this color. But with your green eyes and ivory skin, and the hints of auburn in your hair, it's perfect. And only a tall, willowy figure can carry off the wide skirt."

Charlotte plucked at the skirt with her fingers. "I'm not sure I'd call my figure willowy."

"In that dress, your figure looks flawless. Let me get some shoes. There's also a matching wrap. And I think we have a lovely pair of gloves dyed to match. What size for the shoes?"

"Eight," Charlotte said distractedly. She sighed and stared at herself in the mirror, fluffing up the skirt, then smoothing it down. She didn't look at all like herself. She looked like a gawky girl dressed up in her mother's pretty evening finery. Closing her eyes, she tried to imagine herself at the ball, a staff photographer at her side, snapping photos, a cassette recorder in her hand catching all the comments and quotes. But her mind kept flashing back to the image of her dancing with Sam and no matter how hard she tried, she couldn't make it go away.

She was going to the ball to work, *not* to be with Sam. She would be there alone, without a date. Everyone would assume she had come to cover the event, ever the efficient and responsible journalist. And although Sam might be surprised at her appearance, she certainly wouldn't be forced to make any explanations. They might not even have time to talk, much less share a dance.

The saleswoman returned with shoes and gloves and also a pretty bracelet and a faux emerald-and-pearl choker. Charlotte slipped on the gloves, smoothing them along her arms and above her elbows, telling herself she couldn't possibly go. But by the time Anne fastened the choker around her neck she'd changed her mind.

"You have gorgeous hair," she said.

Charlotte smiled hesitantly. "I always thought it was a little . . . unruly. There are mornings it takes me a half hour to get a comb through it."

The saleswoman pulled it back and twisted it once, then gently pulled soft tendrils out to frame her face. "If I were you, I'd make an appointment at Etienne's to have your hair done. Tell him Anne from Panache sent you. And if he doesn't have time to do you, be sure to ask for Arnaud. I'm sure he'll be able to fit you in. He'll do your makeup, too."

Drawing a deep breath, Charlotte took one last lingering look at herself. She couldn't really do this, could she? What would she say, how would she act? And would Sam actually believe that she'd come as a reporter? If she were smart, she would stay home.

She took a deep breath and let it out slowly. "I'll take it," she said, pushing every doubt she had aside.

"The dress?"

"The whole thing. The dress, the shoes, the accessories. Everything." It would cost her a bundle, but if she was going to do it, she might as well do it right.

Anne smiled. "Your escort is a lucky man. He's going to spend the evening dancing with the most beautiful woman at the Valentine's Ball."

Charlotte forced a smile. "I hope so," she said softly. "I really hope so."

How grimly ironic, she thought. She hoped to be the woman to make Sam forget his Secret Valentine—who just happened to be herself.

CHARLOTTE GLANCED AT HER watch, then quickly made a few more edits on Restaurant Rita's latest review before typing in the command that would send the page back to composition for the Sunday edition. It was nearly six and the Valentine's Ball started at eight. She had just enough time to get to the hairdresser before she rushed home and changed.

The Valentine's Ball was sponsored by the Cedar Ridge Historical Society, a group of well-organized matrons who had dedicated themselves to the preservation of the community's genteel past. They held the ball every year on Valentine's Day eve in the Taggert Mansion, a huge antebellum plantation home that sat on the edge of town.

At one time, before the War Between the States, all of the land in and around Cedar Ridge had been owned by the Taggerts. They raised cotton and shipped it to Atlanta. But the Taggerts were an industrious family and saw the profit to be made in textiles. They built their first cotton warehouse after the war ended, and then two or three textile mills, and soon a town had sprung up where once there had been fields.

The *Cedar Ridge Tribune* was housed in one of the Taggerts' old textile mills, the printing presses laid out on the ground floor where the owners had once stored bales of cotton and operated a cotton gin. The second floor, which used to house the looms, now held the editorial, advertising, production and circulation departments of the newspaper.

As owners of one of Cedar Ridge's "historical treasures," Charlotte and Sam had been invited to every Valentine's Ball since they'd taken over at the

paper. But like Charlotte, Sam had never been one for
formal occasions—until now.

"Burning the midnight oil?"

Her heart fluttered at the sound of his voice and
Charlotte looked up to find Sam standing in the
doorway of her office as he had so many times over
the past few days. His shoulder was braced on the
doorjamb, his arms crossed over his chest. He was
dressed in the tux she'd seen this morning, only it
looked much better on his finely muscled body than it
did on the hanger. A crisp, white pleated-front shirt
with a wing collar and onyx studs provided a startling
contrast to his dark hair and tanned skin.

He held out his hands and turned in a slow circle.
"So, how do I look?"

She swallowed hard, then opened her mouth to
speak, but her voice cracked. "You—you look fine.
Very handsome."

"I'm ready. I have to pick up Diana in an hour. She
lives in Buckhead."

"Diana?"

He looked momentarily surprised, then smiled.
"Didn't I tell you? I can't believe I forgot to tell you.
She's my Secret Valentine. The sales rep from the pa-
per company."

Charlotte gasped, then quickly tried to hide her
confusion. "That can't be."

"It *is*," he insisted. "I couldn't believe it, either.
You see, I thought it might be her so I called her up

and asked her. She admitted to the whole thing—the gifts, the cards, the letter. She's always seemed so self-confident. I mean, look at her. She's gorgeous. I didn't think she'd be the type to be shy about her feelings."

"But she can't be your Secret Valentine," Charlotte protested.

He gave her a worried look. "Why not?"

Charlotte opened her mouth, then snapped it shut. She shrugged, avoiding his inquiring gaze. "I— It's just that— I was thinking it was Sarah in accounting."

"Well, it's not," Sam said. "It's Diana. I really think it was the note you helped me write that changed her mind about going to the Valentine's Ball with me."

"You're the one who wrote it," Charlotte said.

"But you helped," he replied. "I guess I owe this all to you."

Charlotte forced a smile. Oh, this was going too far. "You really are excited about this, aren't you?" she murmured.

"Why shouldn't I be?"

"Well, you really don't know much about this woman, Sam. For all you know, she could be a...a pathological liar. Don't you think you should take this slowly?"

He took a seat in one of her guest chairs. "A dull, coldhearted, unsentimental man would take it slowly," he said in a solemn tone. Then he grinned. "I've decided to be more romantic, more spontaneous. I'm going to jump in, headfirst. Hell, if tonight goes well, I may be married by tomorrow morning!''

Her breath stopped in her chest. Now this had gone way too far! She had to tell him. She had no choice. "Sam, before you get carried away here, there's something I have to—"

He held out his hand to stop her. "Don't worry, I've got that covered."

She blinked in confusion. "Got what covered?"

"You know," Sam said, lowering his voice. He leaned forward. "Protection."

"That's not what I meant!" Charlotte cried. "And furthermore, I don't think you should be having sex with a woman you've just met!"

He arched his eyebrow and grinned. "And who *should* I be having sex with?"

"A woman you've spent time with, a woman you know well. Someone you care about, someone you respect."

He thought for a moment, then nodded. "Someone kind of like you. Only not you," he added quickly, "because we work together, and that would be a major, *major* mistake." He jumped up out of his chair and rubbed his hands together. "All right, I think I've got this straight. I've got to get going if I'm going to pick up Diana on time." He circled her desk, then bent down and kissed her on the top of her head, an innocuous gesture that seemed to paralyze every nerve in her body. "Thanks for your help, Charlotte. I really do appreciate it. You're a real friend."

With that, he strode out of the office. The moment he was out of her line of vision, she sank back into her chair, exhausted from their conversation and all that had passed between them.

She groaned. A friend? A *friend?* She didn't want to be his friend! Hell, she had been happier when they were enemies. At least then she had known where she stood with him. Now, all she really knew was that she shouldn't want him the way she did.

And yet she couldn't seem to help herself. Against every shred of common sense and self-preservation, she'd fallen in love with him all over again. Just like she had when she was thirteen and like she had every year after that, until she'd gone away to college.

Hadn't the past taught her anything? No matter how much she wanted him, he wasn't the man for her. Nine times out of ten, he didn't even notice she was in the room. And when he did, he looked at her with what could barely pass as indifference.

But that had changed. In very subtle ways, he'd started to break down the barriers they'd constructed between them, started to reveal himself as a man she could be attracted to. The man she'd come to know in the past week and a half was not the Sam Harper she'd loved all those years ago. This man was different.

She buried her face in her hands. Maybe it was time to let this go, to let him think that Diana really was his

Secret Valentine. Considering his track record with women, it wouldn't take long for Diana to become history. And then, finally, this would be all over. He would never need to know that *she'd* been his Secret Valentine.

She took a long breath and focused her thoughts. It might be best to skip the ball tonight, to let nature take its course between Sam and his Secret Valentine. But a strange surge of protectiveness came over her. That, and a healthy dose of journalistic curiosity.

Who was this Diana woman? And what was she really up to? If she attended the ball tonight, she might be able to find out. But she also might have to spend the entire evening watching Sam have a wonderful time with the new lady in his life.

"So what's it going to be?" she murmured. "You've got the dress and the invitation. In another hour, you'll have the hair and the makeup."

In fact, she had everything she needed—except the courage.

Chapter Four

THE TAGGERT MANSION was ablaze with lights, every salon and drawing room on the first floor bustling with guests. Sam tucked his date's hand into the crook of his elbow as they strolled through the house, the strains of a waltz filtering in from the large ballroom. The mansion had been lovingly restored to its former antebellum splendor by the Cedar Ridge Historical Society, with help from the major businesses in the area, including the *Tribune*.

Most of the guests knew Sam and they made a point of saying "Hello" and chatting for a moment or two. He was grateful for the diversion. After a half hour trapped in the car with Diana, he had gotten a little tired of dodging her rather obvious desire for him, the overly bold touches and the coy sexual innuendos. Had he been so inclined, they probably could have driven straight to a hotel and jumped directly into bed, skipping the preliminaries entirely.

"I'm really glad you brought me," Diana cooed, giving his arm a squeeze. "When can we leave?" She giggled—a sound that was already beginning to grate on his nerves.

Sam forced an indulgent smile. "We just got here. Wouldn't you like to dance?"

She ran her finger playfully down his arm. "I'm really more of a . . . private dancer."

"You know, Diana, it's really a shame we didn't get to know each other sooner." Then he would have known better than to ask her out, Sam mused. He wouldn't have to endure this too much longer. He and Diana had been seen together, so talk of his beautiful date would no doubt make its way back to Charlotte. That was what this whole thing was about, wasn't it? Making Charlotte Keats suffer for her little deception?

He'd thought she would confess the entire scheme earlier that evening at the office, especially after he'd mentioned marriage. But the sudden appearance of a flesh-and-blood Secret Valentine seemed to have rattled her so thoroughly she couldn't figure out which end was up—and which Secret Valentine was real.

He smiled to himself. She probably thought the whole thing would just disappear. She hadn't bothered to answer the E-mail note they had sent, so he had been forced to go to his contingency plan. He'd called Diana, pretending he thought *she'd* been sending him gifts and notes, and asked her to the ball.

Calculating and cunning, Diana had been too shrewd to spoil a good opportunity when it presented itself. She'd admitted that, yes, she was indeed his Secret Valentine. And yes, she would be thrilled to accompany him to the Valentine's Ball.

As he walked through the crowd, he looked for the photographer from the *Tribune*. The paper covered the ball every year and he was certain this year would be no exception. Perhaps a photo of him and Diana might be in order, as long as a copy found its way onto Charlotte's desk.

"Oh, look!" Diana said, pointing across the salon into the foyer. "There's a photographer." She patted her perfectly-styled hair and smiled. "If someone's going to take my picture, I'd better make a quick trip to the little girls' room and check my lipstick." She pursed her lips and pressed herself up against him. "That little kiss in the car really took its toll—on my lipstick and my body."

"I'll be here when you get back," Sam said, peeling her fingers from his arm. He watched her walk away, her hips swaying seductively in the skintight red dress. "Unless I decide to throw myself off the roof first," he muttered.

He turned to look for the *Tribune* photographer, then stopped short as his gaze fell on a woman standing nearby. Like him, many of the other guests had turned their attention her way, whispering to each other as she moved through the crowd.

"Gus," he breathed, his attention completely captivated by a vision in emerald silk. The gown fitted her perfectly, hugging a waist that he was certain he could span with his hands and leaving her chest, shoulders and arms bare. Her hair, a riot of mahogany curls, was piled on top of her head, with tendrils falling around her face and shoulders, caressing her neck.

Mesmerized, he slowly pushed through the crowd until he reached her side. She was deep in conversation with the president of the historical society. He gently touched her arm. "Hello, Charlotte," he said.

She turned, as if startled by the sound of his voice, then smiled nervously and excused herself from her conversation. "Hi, Sam."

"What are you doing here?" he asked, bending his head close to hers to be heard over the chatter of voices.

"I'm covering the ball for the paper." She glanced around. "Where's your date?"

"She went to the powder room," he said, unable to drag his gaze away from her face. Lord, her beauty took his breath away. It was like he'd never really seen her before tonight. Perhaps it was the sophisticated dress or the elegant surroundings, but he was looking at her through new eyes—and she looked incredible. "Would you like to dance?" he asked.

"You want to dance with me?"

He held his hand out. "I can't think of anything else I'd like to do more." He took her fingers in his and led her into the ballroom. The small band switched from a waltz to a slow Gershwin ballad and Sam gently pulled her into his arms and began to move with the music.

At first she seemed stiff and uneasy, but slowly, he felt her body grow pliant beneath his touch, until it seemed as if they'd been dancing together for years. "You look beautiful," he said, leaning close and murmuring in her ear.

She turned her head and her nose bumped against his cheek. He pulled back and smiled down at her. A blush crept up her cheeks and her eyes glittered, reflecting the light from the crystal chandeliers. "I—I'm not much of a dancer," she said. "And this dress even makes walking more difficult."

He ran his hand up and down her back, feeling her warmth through the fabric of her gown. "I didn't know you planned to come," he said.

"Oh, yes," Charlotte replied. "I've planned to come since I got the invitation."

"Why didn't you say something at the office earlier?"

She attempted a nonchalant shrug, but he could see right through it. She'd kept it from him on purpose. "I guess I didn't think it was important. You were so excited about meeting your Secret Valentine and I was...excited for you." She took a deep breath, then smiled more brightly. "So how are things going? Are you having a good time?"

"A very good time," he said. "Now that you're here," he added beneath his breath.

As they danced, he made a quick search of the room for Diana, knowing that she would be back sooner or later. When he caught sight of her red dress near the entrance to the ballroom, he stopped dancing and grabbed Charlotte's hand.

"Let's go," he said.

"Where?" she gasped.

"Just come with me. We need to talk."

He pulled her in the opposite direction from the one Diana had taken, steering her through the open French doors and into the cool night air. It had rained earlier in the day and the air was damp and sweet-smelling. A few other couples strolled the wide veranda, nodding as they passed.

A frown marred her perfect features. She rubbed her arms with her hands and looked up at him. "What is it?"

Sam slipped out of his jacket and reached around her to drape it over her shoulders. He let his hands rest there, his thumbs softly stroking the silken skin at the base of her neck as he stared down into her eyes. Feeling as if he couldn't fight the temptation any longer, he slowly bent his head and brushed his mouth against hers.

As he pulled away, he felt her breath, quick and shallow, against his skin. She stood frozen, looking up at him with wide eyes. And then, drawn by the need to have more, he kissed her again, this time more deeply, his tongue gently parting her lips and invading her mouth. She moaned softly but made no move to pull away.

At that instant he realized he wanted her—all of her, heart and soul and body. He wanted Charlotte Keats more than he'd ever wanted a woman in his life. He murmured her name against her mouth.

The sound of his own name on her lips, soft and pleading, slowly drew him back to reality and suddenly the spell that had descended over them evaporated and his powers of reasoning returned. He cupped her face in his hands and looked down at her closed eyes and moist lips. Drawing a long, deep breath, he fought the urge to taste her again, ignoring his growing desire.

What the hell was he doing? More to the point, what the hell was he *thinking?* Charlotte Keats was his business partner and a woman who had the capacity to drive him crazy. They'd fought their way through more than thirty years of life together and now he was acting like—like he was in love with her.

He should know better than this. All this "Secret Valentine" romance business had addled his brain—so much so, that he'd come to believe she really wanted them to be more than just business associates.

She'd begun the whole deception to prove a point, to get back at him for their argument over her choice of stories. She didn't have any feelings for him and he was a fool to imagine that she did.

Gently, he dropped his hands from her face and pushed her away. She opened her eyes, then blinked, as surprised as he was at what had happened between them.

His mind slowly settled on a way out of this mess he'd made. "Was that all right?" he asked softly.

She nodded.

"And how did it make you feel?"

"It made me feel . . . good." Her last word was said almost breathlessly.

He clenched his jaw and tried not to think about how beautiful she looked, how much he still wanted her. "Then you think Diana will be pleased?"

She swallowed hard. "Diana?"

He nodded. "Yes. I've been trying to decide whether I kiss in a romantic way, the way a woman might appreciate. What do you think? Do you think Diana will like the way I kiss?"

"I don't understand."

"Well, you've been so helpful with this Secret Valentine thing. Writing the letter, choosing the flowers, giving me such good advice. I knew you'd be able to help me with this, as well."

Pain flashed through her eyes and he felt an unbidden rush of regret. She couldn't have actually *wanted* him to kiss her, could she? He pushed the ridiculous notion aside. No, all she wanted from him was to prove her point, to make him look the fool.

"Well, I'd better go find Diana," he said.

She looked down at her hands, avoiding his gaze, then hesitantly removed his jacket from around her shoulders and held it out to him. "I think that would be best. And I'd better get back to work."

"Good night, Charlotte."

She looked up at him, meeting his gaze. "Good night, Sam."

It took all his willpower to walk away from her, to keep himself from dragging her back into his arms and kissing her senseless. But she was the one who had started this game between them and she was the one who would have to put an end to it.

CHARLOTTE'S KNEES wobbled beneath her tulle petticoats and silk-taffeta skirts. She reached for the veranda railing and when she finally grasped it, she leaned back and drew a steadying breath of crisp night air.

With a shaky hand, she reached up and touched her lips. They were still numb with the aftereffects of his kiss—the same effects that had sent her mind reeling and her pulse pounding.

There was no use trying to deny it. That kiss only proved what she'd been trying so hard to ignore. She *was* in love with Sam Harper. Again. That was why she had come here tonight, dressed in a beautiful gown. Not to cover the event, but to be with Sam.

In reality, she'd hoped she might stir his desire a bit, maybe even enough to make him forget his so-called Secret Valentine. But she'd never expected to be a guinea pig for his romantic overtures.

Why couldn't she just put all this in perspective and let it go? Sam had no interest in her, no desire to pursue a romantic relationship. In his mind, she would always be good old Gus, the gawky tomboy who had tagged along after him like some lovesick puppy dog.

Well, she wasn't that goofy-looking girl with the braces and the skinned knees anymore. She was a woman now, a woman who could control her desires, who was in charge of her own destiny. And Sam Harper was not part of her great cosmic plan!

But would she be able to maintain her resolve when faced with seeing him nearly every day? Or would being around him only cause her to fall more deeply in love?

Charlotte placed her palms on her flushed cheeks. "What am I going to do?" she murmured.

It wouldn't be so bad if he hadn't gotten himself involved with a profligate liar like Diana. Sooner or later he would have to find out that Diana hadn't sent the gifts. He would be angry at her deceit, perhaps angry enough to send her packing.

And then, maybe, after it ended, she and Sam could—

She stopped herself, cursing softly at her runaway thoughts. It would take some time, but she *could* put this whole unfortunate incident behind her. She could see Sam at the office without the memory of their kiss rushing back full force. She could even be happy for him when he finally found the right woman.

Charlotte tipped her head back and drew another deep breath. Gathering up the last shreds of her composure, she smoothed her skirt and headed back inside. If she was lucky, her staff photographer would have finished snapping shots of all the important guests and she would be able to make a gracious and badly needed exit.

But as soon as she stepped back into the ballroom, her gaze was caught by a couple dancing very close near the edge of the dance floor. She stepped behind a potted palm and peered through the fronds at Sam and his date.

A rush of jealousy stole her breath away. The woman was gorgeous, voluptuous, and clinging to Sam so closely that he probably had no doubt what she had stuffed into that red dress.

The music came to an end and Charlotte watched as Diana wrapped her arms around Sam's neck and gave him a less-than-chaste kiss. Then she whispered something in his ear and turned to make her way through the crowd—alone. Sam gave her a long look, then shook his head and headed in the opposite direction.

Charlotte smiled. Now was her chance. She would corner Diana and find out what the manipulative hussy was really up to. Charlotte was a journalist, after all, and a formidable interviewer. If she couldn't get Diana to spill her guts, no one could.

Charlotte grabbed her skirts and started through the crowd, keeping an eye on the red dress. Diana walked into the small ladies' room just off the ballroom and Charlotte didn't hesitate to follow her inside.

She found Diana in front of the mirror, studying her face as she carefully applied fresh lip liner to her smudged mouth. Charlotte stepped up beside her and tried to affect the same vapid expression as she toyed with her hair. "I just love your dress," Charlotte gushed.

Diana gave her a sideways glance. "Thanks," she said in a haughty tone. "Yours is nice, too. Although, you wouldn't catch me dead in that color."

"Find me a coffin and I could remedy that," Charlotte muttered.

"What?" Diana asked.

"I was just saying that I saw you dancing with Sam Harper." Charlotte clucked her tongue and put on an envious expression. "He's quite a catch."

Diana tossed the lip liner aside and began to carefully apply bright red lipstick, astounding Charlotte with her skill. Whenever Charlotte had attempted lipstick that color, she'd ended up looking like a reject from clown school.

"Hmm," Diana said, studying her work carefully. She replaced the cap on the lipstick and dropped it back into her purse, then shrugged. "He's all right. Handsome enough, but he doesn't have a lot of money. He runs that puny little newspaper. There can't be much future in that.''

"No," Charlotte said. "I wouldn't think so. How did you two meet?"

Diana turned to her and leaned a bit closer, as if she were about to relay a bit of juicy gossip. "It's really a funny story. You see, someone had been sending him little gifts at work—cards and candy. A Secret Valentine. Well, Sam thought it was me. When he called to ask me if it was, what could I say? I've wanted to get my hands on that incredible body of his for months now. I saw my chance and I took it."

"But what if the real Secret Valentine shows up?"

"I'll deal with her if and when I have to. Until then, I'll just make sure Sam is interested in only one woman—and that's me." Diana finished powdering her nose, then gave herself one last look. "Perfect," she said.

Charlotte nodded, then stared more closely at Diana's reflection in the mirror. She wrinkled her nose. "What is that on your neck?"

Diana tipped her chin up. "Where?"

"Right there. It looks like . . . a pimple."

Diana craned her neck and ran her fingers along her jawline. "Where?"

"Right there." Charlotte pointed to a spot in the general area of her ear.

"Show me," Diana whined.

Charlotte shrugged. "Sorry, I've got to go. Have a really nice evening. And don't worry about that pimple. Once you get outside in the dark, nobody will ever notice it."

Smiling smugly, Charlotte turned and walked out of the ladies' room, leaving Diana in the midst of a full-blown cosmetic crisis. She rounded a corner only to see Sam with his back against a pillar, his arms crossed over his chest, a drink in his hand. He was staring out at the dancers with an enigmatic expression.

She glanced both ways. She had two choices—to return to the bathroom and listen to Diana moan about her complexion, or to make a long circle around the ballroom to the exit. Gathering her skirts and her courage, she decided to head for the door.

A few minutes later, safely outside the range of Sam Harper, she gave the photographer instructions to leave, then collected her wrap and purse, and walked through the front door and out onto the wide veranda. The cool night air cleared her mind and she felt a surge of relief wash over her as she started toward the front steps of the Taggert Mansion. She'd made it through the evening in one piece and for that she should be grateful.

But just as she was about to make her escape, a voice stopped her.

"Charlotte!"

She froze, fighting the instinct to run like a frightened child. Pasting a smile on her face, she turned slowly. "Sam," she replied, trying to keep her voice even.

He crossed the veranda. "Are you leaving already?"

She nodded and drew her wrap more tightly around her, as if it might offer protection against his presence. "We've got all the photos we need. And I've got an early day tomorrow. I'm tired. And my feet hurt."

He gently touched her arm. "Let me walk you to your car."

Charlotte evaded his touch, and his gaze. "That's not necessary. I came alone, I can find my way home on my own. I'll see you tomorrow morning, bright and early." Although she tried to sound cheerful, she suspected she had failed miserably. Did he suspect how his kisses had made her feel? Or had she been able to hide her reactions beneath a facade of indifference?

"I want to walk you to your car," Sam insisted. He took her elbow again and walked with her down the front steps.

"What about your date?" she asked.

He shrugged. "The last time I saw her she was headed toward the ladies' room. She seems to be obsessed with her own face." The last was said with a healthy dose of irritation.

"Don't you think she's going to wonder where you've gone to?"

"I don't care. I wanted to talk to you about what happened before, on the veranda."

Charlotte held up her hand and shook her head. "There's no need. I understand."

His jaw tensed. "But I want to explain. Just keep quiet and let me—"

"Sam, I know you didn't mean anything by that kiss and I didn't—"

With one sure movement, he grabbed her by the shoulders and turned her to face him. Charlotte's words stopped in her throat as she met his gaze, his blue eyes intense and passionate. And then, he brought his mouth down on hers and kissed her, like he had before—only not like he had before.

This time it was different. His kiss was urgent, demanding, almost angry, as if he had something to prove. She felt herself losing control again and willed her mind to clear. Placing her palms on his chest, she shoved him back. "Don't," she murmured, the one word a warning. Her knees went weak and she found herself afraid to move, afraid that if she took one step she would crumple into an emotional mess at his feet.

Sam's expression softened and he reached out and placed his palm on her cheek. "Why not?"

"You know why," Charlotte replied evenly.

His jaw tightened and he slowly shook his head. "No," he countered. "I don't. Why don't you tell me, Charlotte? Tell me why I shouldn't kiss you. Because at this very moment, I'm not even sure myself." His hands slid down to clutch her shoulders, giving her no chance to escape. "Tell me."

She fought against his hold, but he wouldn't let her go. "Why are you doing this to me?" she asked, her voice trembling with frustration and confusion. "Why can't you just leave me alone?"

"Is that what you really want?" he demanded. "Because I don't think it is."

She tried again to twist away from him. "It is! I don't want you to kiss me and I don't want to hear about your evening with your Secret Valentine. We're business associates, Sam Harper. Nothing you do outside the office interests me in the least."

Sam smiled at her, a humorless smile filled with an unmistakable challenge. "But I think it does," he said. "In fact, I'd venture to guess you'd like very much to know what I'm thinking right now."

With one concentrated effort, she struck out against his arms and broke his grip. Hauling her skirts up with her hands, she backed away from him. "Do you want me to admit that I was wrong? Is that what this is all about? All right, I was wrong. You *are* romantic. You're handsome and sexy and a man any woman would be thrilled to have in her bed. There it is. That's what you wanted. Now leave me alone," she warned.

He took a step toward her. "I can't, Gus."

"I'm not Gus! I'm not that stupid little girl anymore, that girl who kept falling in love with you. Not anymore, Sam. And never again."

"You're lying."

She shook her head, watching him warily, feeling like a small animal facing a powerful predator. "Let me go," she said. "I don't want to play these games with you. I can't."

He laughed. "But you started this whole thing. And now *you* don't want to play? Sorry, Gus, that's not good enough."

"*You're* the one who kissed *me!* I didn't start anything. This isn't my fault."

"Is that what you believe?"

"Leave me alone! Just let me go! I don't want to talk to you anymore." Drawing a deep breath, she spun on her heel and stumbled down the cobblestone drive.

"Go ahead!" he shouted after her. "Run away, Gus. Run as far and as fast as you can. But nothing is going to change. Sooner or later you're going to have to face up to this. Sooner or later you're going to have to admit that this whole thing was your fault."

She looked over her shoulder once to see him standing in the middle of the drive, illuminated by the spill of light from the house, his hands shoved into his pockets, his expression unreadable.

By the time she reached her car, she was out of breath and out of resolve. Tears pushed at the corners of her eyes and a painful stitch twisted in her side like a knife. Her hands trembled as she searched her purse for her keys. She dropped them twice before she managed to push the key into the lock.

As soon as she gained the relative safety of her car, she bent her head and let the tears course down her cheeks. She gripped the steering wheel with white-knuckled hands and cursed herself.

"I don't love him," she murmured. "I don't. I don't love Sam Harper."

But no matter how many times she said it, no matter how many ways she found to deny it, she knew the truth. And to her utter mortification, she feared that he did, too.

Chapter Five

CHARLOTTE GRABBED a tissue from the box on her desk and wiped the smudged mascara from under her eyes. She sniffled, then tossed the crumpled tissue on her desk and turned back to her computer.

Still dressed in her evening gown, she'd come directly to the office to write the story on the Valentine's Ball. The dark silent surroundings seemed like an oasis in the midst of her suddenly chaotic life, a soothing balm to her shaken emotions. Below her, the printing presses churned out the last pages of the Valentine's Day edition, the rhythm lulling her into a sense of security.

Valentine's Day. She would be glad when the next twenty-four hours had passed and they could move on to a more innocuous holiday like Presidents' Day or Saint Patrick's Day—a day that couldn't possibly make a mess of a woman's life. Valentine's Day was just another opportunity for raised hopes and dashed desires. If she could have her way, she would outlaw the holiday altogether.

Her ride to the office had been tearful, although she wasn't quite sure why. She'd been angry and frustrated and confused. And above it all, she'd been shaken to the core by Sam's kisses and his touch. Perhaps, after all that, she had realized how difficult it would be to go back to the way it was between them.

Drawing a shaky breath, she continued typing, eager to finish the story, as if writing might purge the whole event from her memory. She was tired and she wanted to sleep, to close her eyes and forget everything that had transpired over the last two weeks. It had all started with Valentine's Day and their argument two weeks ago over the story on Ed and his amazing new paint-mixing system. Why couldn't she have just shut her mouth and agreed to run the damn story? After all, 256 shades of red could be interesting to some readers. Why did she always have to fight him at every turn?

He had been right. This *was* all her fault. In the past, they'd maintained a cautious distance, a distance from which her feelings toward him were unfaltering. But since the appearance of his Secret Valentine, they'd grown steadily closer. And in that closeness, he had somehow sensed the attraction growing inside her, the emotions she had tried so hard to deny. And he'd used those feelings against her.

Her mind flashed back over the events of the past couple of weeks, over the changes she'd seen in him. How often had she secretly wished that she were the recipient of his newly awakened romanticism? How many times had she wanted *her* eyes to be the ones he "yearned" for? She'd waited years for him to turn into the kind of man she could love, and now he had.

But his transformation had been built on the false foundation of her deception—and would soon come tumbling down.

Perhaps, in some subconscious way, she had willed this to happen, to finally force the issue between them after years of silence. And maybe, deep down inside, she had hoped that he would find out who was really sending the gifts and that he would take them not as a deliberate deception, but as a sign of the feelings she'd kept hidden so long.

She bit her bottom lip and fought another surge of emotion. But that wasn't what had happened. Instead, what had started out as just another volley in their ongoing battle had deteriorated into a full-scale military disaster. And now she was left to pick up the pieces and face him tomorrow morning at the office as if nothing had passed between them.

What would happen when they saw each other the next time? Would he smile at her, or would his expression be cold and distant? Would she ever be able to look him in the eye and not think about the kisses they had shared? The way she felt at this very moment, the prospect didn't seem likely. But, perhaps, if she was lucky—and resolute—her feelings for him would dissipate as they had years before.

She sighed and closed her eyes, tipping her head back. Spending endless hours thinking about what might have been and what had yet to happen was not going to make her feel any better. Work would be her salvation and that was where she would hide.

Charlotte looked down at her computer, then typed in a final closing paragraph to her story. She hit the command to send the text back to composition and pasteup so that it could be dropped into Saturday morning's edition, along with a photo or two. Then she glanced at the clock on her desk.

It was nearly 1:00 a.m. and suddenly she felt utterly exhausted, as if just one more errant thought about Sam Harper would render her unconscious. She straightened the papers on her desk, then turned to grab her keys, purse and wrap from where she'd tossed them on her credenza.

"I stopped by your house," a voice said, echoing through the silence of her office.

She spun around in her chair to find Sam standing in her office doorway. His bow tie was draped around his neck and the top two buttons of his shirt were undone. His hands were jammed into his trouser pockets and he looked the picture of casual indifference.

"I should have known I'd find you here," he continued.

Charlotte drew a deep breath, steeling herself against his penetrating gaze and consciously placing the first brick in the wall that would soon rise between them. She sighed, then stood. "Go home, Harper," she said, drawing her wrap around her shoulders. "Go to bed and try to forget everything that happened between us tonight. I plan to. And to-morrow morning, when I wake up, things will be back to normal. I'll detest you and you'll have nothing but contempt for me."

"I don't think that's going to happen," he said softly.

"And why not? If I can do it, you certainly can."

He pushed away from the doorjamb and took a step into her office. "I don't think you can," he countered. "Admit it, Gus. You'll never forget that kiss."

She felt her temper rise at the challenging tone of his voice. Oh, this was typical! He'd detected some reciprocation in her kiss, some chink in her armor, and now he thought he could exploit it. Always looking for control, always searching for a way to get under her skin. Of all the egotistical, manipulative, perverse—

A rush of righteous indignation fueled her temper and in that instant, she realized the battle between them had begun again. Perhaps it had never ended. She shook her head and sent him a look dripping with condescension. "Let me make something perfectly clear," she said, surprised at the resolve in her voice. "You kissed me, Harper. I didn't ask you to, nor did I give you any indication that I wanted to be kissed. I merely stood there and let it happen. It was a stupid thing to do and I should have stopped you."

"Are you saying it didn't mean anything to you?"

She raised her eyebrow and smiled smugly. "That's exactly what I'm saying."

He laughed, shaking his head at her audacity. "I don't believe that. You kissed me back and don't try to deny it. I felt you go soft in my arms, Charlotte. I wasn't imagining that."

She adjusted her wrap around her shoulders and smoothed her skirt. "Believe me, Sam, you would have known if I was an equal participant."

He arched an eyebrow. "Oh, really. I think you were. In fact, I think you wanted me to kiss you."

"I didn't," she said in an even voice.

"Prove it."

Clenching her fists, she tried to remain cool and composed. Another course in the wall went up. She slipped out from behind her desk and slowly strolled across the office, her eyes locked with his, her skirts rustling around her feet. She stopped in front of him, letting her gaze run up and down the length of his body.

Then, in one swift movement, she reached up, grabbed his face between her hands and yanked him down until they were only inches apart. "I'd be happy to," she said. She pressed her mouth to his, then snaked her arms around his neck and furrowed her fingers through his hair.

The kiss was deep and passionate, and so startlingly powerful that she surprised even herself. It was a perfect assault on his senses, her body pressing against the length of his, her lips and tongue making the possession total and undeniable.

At first, he deliberately tried not to react, but his restraint only made her more determined to prove her point. She ran her hands over his chest, then grabbed his shirt and pulled it open, scattering his onyx studs all over her office floor. Rubbing her hands through the soft sprinkling of hair on his chest, she deepened the kiss until she finally felt him losing the grip on his self-control.

And then, knowing that she'd won, she stepped back and looked up at him, giving him a self-satisfied smile. A gentle shove against his bare chest was all it took to send him stumbling back and out her office door. "If I was an equal participant, that's what it would have felt like. Sleep tight, Harper," she said.

She gave him a little wave, then grabbed her office door and slammed it in his face, so hard that the pictures on her wall rattled. A smile slowly curved her lips and she felt a welcome rush of power.

After all that had happened between them, it seemed that she still had the will to stand up to him. She still knew how to push Sam Harper's buttons. Now if she could just keep his hands off of *her* buttons, she would be all right.

SAM STARED AT THE closed door of Charlotte's office. The sound of it slamming still rang in his ears, and his mouth was still moist from her kiss. He cursed softly, then ran his fingers through his hair and pressed the heels of his hands against his temples.

His pulse pounded in his head and he didn't care to think about the other obvious signs of his desire, especially what was happening right below his cummerbund. What the hell had she done to him? He'd thought their earlier kisses had bordered on perfection, but he'd never felt anything quite like Charlotte Keats when she decided to "participate."

He cursed again and turned away from the door, determined to put as much distance as he could between himself and Charlotte. But he took only three steps before turning around and heading back to her office door. It was about time he settled this thing between them once and for all. He yanked his shirtfront together, then clenched his fingers into a fist and pounded on the door.

"Go home, Harper," she called from inside.

"I'm not going anywhere." He tried the door, but found it locked. "Let me in, Charlotte. We're going to put an end to this little charade once and for all."

"I have nothing more to say to you."

"Well, I have something to say to you." He drew a long breath. "I knew!" he shouted.

Sam waited for her reply, but his revelation was met with only silence.

"You hear me, Charlotte? I knew it was you sending the gifts and the notes. I knew you were my Secret Valentine."

The door swung open and Charlotte stared up at him, her eyes wide with disbelief. "You knew?" she cried, her question more an accusation than an inquiry.

Sam grinned. She'd opened the door. Maybe she wasn't as angry with him as he'd thought. "Yeah, I knew. From the very start. I recognized your favorite chocolates. And you didn't do a very good job of disguising your handwriting. I knew all along."

She sputtered. "But—but, why—"

"Why didn't I say anything?" He shrugged. "At first, I wanted to see what you were up to. And then, I decided it would be fun to catch you at your own game."

"You wanted to make a fool out of me," she countered.

Sam wanted to say yes, to confirm all her worst opinions of him. But he had grown tired of the charade between them and it was time to be brutally honest and face the consequences. "Maybe at first," he admitted. "But after a while, I guess I just started looking forward to the presents."

"Yeah, right," Charlotte said. "If you expect me to believe that, you've got to be—"

He grabbed her arms and looked down into her eyes. "If you know what's good for you, Gus, you'll shut up and listen to what I have to say."

She snapped her mouth closed and glared at him, clearly not pleased with taking orders, but overcome by her innate curiosity.

"I *did* look forward to the gifts," he said. "And the notes. And even though I knew it was probably all a big joke, I was stupid enough to hope that there might be some kind of feeling behind what you were doing. Not just another attempt to rattle my cage." He laughed and shook his head. "Can you buy that? I actually wanted to believe that you—cared."

She blinked, clearly surprised by his confession. She opened her mouth to speak but then changed her mind again at his warning look.

"So, you win, Gus. I'm the comic relief in this little drama we've staged. And I guess you got exactly what you wanted. Congratulations." He turned to leave, but she reached out and stopped him with a touch of her hand.

"Sam, wait. I didn't mean to—"

He held out his hand to keep her from going further. "Yes, you did. And you know what? I'm glad you did. Because for a while there, I thought you might be right. I thought maybe I didn't have it in me to love a woman. But I was wrong."

She gasped and her eyes went wide. "What are you saying?"

"I'm saying that I *have* loved a woman, for a long, long time. I was just too blind to see it."

"Who?" she asked in a small voice. "Who did you love, Sam?"

He laughed sharply and tipped his head back. "You won't be happy until you've twisted the knife, will you?'' He looked directly into her eyes. ''I loved you, Gus. I've loved you for... Hell, I'm not sure how long. Maybe since we were kids. Maybe since that night at your birthday party when you tried to kiss me and I pushed you in the lake. I finally admitted it to myself at the picnic for your college graduation, but then you left for Washington and that job at the *Post,* and I put it aside. By the time we started working together, it was buried so deep even I couldn't find it.''

''And now?''

''Now?'' He held his arms out and laughed sharply. ''Now, I realize why I work so damn hard to keep this paper going. Why I put on a damn suit and tie every day and why I work sixteen-hour days.''

''You—you work so hard because you love it,'' she said, as if she were stating the obvious.

He shook his head. ''No, not because I love the *Tribune.* Because I love you. As long as we had the paper, we'd be together. And deep down, in some dark corner of my soul, that's all I really wanted. I knew how much your job meant to you and I was willing to do anything to keep you happy.''

''I—I didn't know you felt this way,'' Charlotte said.

He shook his head and smiled ruefully. ''Neither did I.'' With that, he drew a deep breath and took a step back. ''And now that I've made a complete ass of myself, I'm going home. Hopefully, if you have any compassion at all, you'll forget this entire conversation and treat me the way you always have—like a person whose presence you can barely tolerate.''

With that he turned and strode through the office. He took the stairs to the street level two at a time, wanting to put as much distance as he could between them. Yet for every step he took, he felt a stronger need to return.

He had opened his heart to her. But he'd left before she'd had a chance to respond. Was it because he was afraid to hear what she had to say? Afraid that she might not feel the same way he did? He couldn't have read her wrong, could he?

His mind flashed back to a memory of that first kiss they'd shared on the veranda. He'd caught her unawares, with her defenses down. And he had felt an undeniable current pass between them, electric and alive. But was that only wishful thinking?

If she'd loved him in return, she wouldn't have let him walk out as she had. She would have stopped him, then admitted that the kiss had had as much effect on her as it had on him. He'd confessed his feelings and she'd done nothing. If that wasn't an answer, he didn't know what was.

Sam stepped out onto the street and headed for his car. But at the last minute he walked right past it. He pulled his jacket collar up and shoved his hands into his pockets. A walk would do him good; the cold crisp air might clear his head.

He wasn't sure what to do next. After all, he'd never been in love before, unless he counted that night before Charlotte left for Washington. He'd always assumed that when he finally fell in love, the feelings would be mutual. But then, he never counted on loving Charlotte Keats.

As he walked, the streets of Cedar Ridge were silent, the houses dark. A dog barked in the distance, the sound carried on the wind that rustled the trees. He walked without purpose, not sure where he was going, only sure about the need to keep walking.

Time passed, counted only by his footfalls on the empty sidewalks, not by the ticking of his watch or the rise and fall of the moon in the sky. He kept his gaze fixed a few feet in front of him. His mind spun with all that had happened. One night and she had changed his life. One kiss and she had captured his heart.

He stopped then, suddenly aware that he didn't want to walk anymore. Slowly, he looked up to find himself standing in front of Charlotte's house. He stepped into the shadows of a tree and leaned up against it, his gaze drifting up to the illuminated window on the second floor.

He'd never been inside her house, but he'd passed it a hundred, maybe even a thousand times. He tried to imagine what it was like inside. His mind wandered through the first floor, then up the stairs to her bedroom.

He would find her, lying in her bed, asleep, her hair tousled, her skin silken. He would stand over her bed and watch her, counting the slow, even breaths, listening to the soft sounds she made in slumber. He would reach out and touch her hair, brush his hand along her cheek.

And then she would wake. She would reach out to him and draw him closer, until he lay beside her, beneath her, above her. They would make love and all the walls between them would come tumbling down. She would meet his passion with desire of her own and they would begin again, putting the past behind them once and for all.

Sam took a step forward, his gaze still locked on the bedroom window. Would it happen that way? If he walked up to the front door and knocked, would she invite him into her bed? Or would she reject him again?

He pinched his eyes shut and cursed softly, then turned away from the house. He wanted to believe it could be good between them, but he also had to be practical. She didn't care for him as deeply as he cared for her. And she might never feel what he felt.

He glanced at the eastern sky, then looked down at his watch. In just five hours he would find out for sure. In five hours, he would see her again. He would look into her eyes and he would either come face-to-face with his future—or with his past.

CHARLOTTE SAT IN THE center of her bed staring at the television and sobbing. On the screen, Humphrey Bogart said goodbye to Ingrid Bergman as a well-worn tape of *Casablanca* wound to its end. Tears glimmered in Ilse's eyes as the camera focused on her in a final close-up. She turned away and slowly walked toward the waiting plane and Charlotte felt a flood of tears pushing at the corners of her own eyes.

"That's right!" she shouted to the character on the screen. She wadded up a tissue and tossed it at the television. "Run away. He's no good for you. Get on that plane and get as far away from him as you can." She grabbed a chocolate from the box on her lap and waved it at the screen. "He'll just make your life miserable."

She shoved the chocolate into her mouth, then reached for the gallon jug of milk on the nightstand. "Men are pigs," she said, after taking a huge gulp. She wiped her mouth with the back of her hand, then reached for another chocolate. "You fall in love with them, they find out, and they just run the other way. But heaven forbid if they suddenly develop feelings for you. You're just supposed to forget everything and kiss their feet. You've got it right, Ilse. Just walk away. Go off with that nice dependable Victor and save the world."

She stared at the screen as the credits began to roll, then snatched up a new tissue and blew her nose.

Grabbing her remote, she flipped off the video player and flopped back on her bed to stare up at the ceiling.

"So what are you going to do, Charlotte?" she murmured. "It's nearly sunrise and in another few hours, you're going to have to go to work."

She rubbed her eyes, then pulled the covers up to her chin. If only she could just stay in bed for the rest of her life, living on chocolates and romantic movies. She could do all her work from her home computer and she would never have to face him again. But was that what she really wanted?

"So he loves me," she murmured. "At least, Sam Harper *says* he loves me." She covered her eyes with her arm and groaned.

His words echoed in her mind, but she wasn't sure whether she'd actually heard them pass his lips or only imagined them. He loved her. But could he really have meant what he said? Or was this just another in a long line of tricks to con her. How was she supposed know whether to believe him?

She had never been able to read him in the past. Even with all the sparring that had taken place between them, she'd never really sensed where she stood with him. He'd kept his emotions locked tightly inside him. She knew him so well, but she didn't know him at all.

She tried to bring order to her chaotic thoughts as she slowly went through everything he'd said. But the words seemed to fade into the depths of her mind and she kept coming back to the kisses they'd shared.

How could she deny feelings like that? Something had happened between them in that instant they'd made physical contact. From the moment his mouth touched hers, it was as if all her doubts and fears dissolved, only to leave her with the crystal-clear knowledge that she did indeed love him.

Could it be that simple? She loved him and he loved her? But they'd spent years making each other as miserable as possible, always tense and watchful, full of mistrust for each other's motives. How were they supposed to put habits like that behind them?

She tried to picture what it might be like—to be able to talk to him about everything that was in her heart, to be able to trust him with her feelings and fears. For a brief moment, she could almost imagine it, but then every little dispute they'd had intruded on the dream, bringing all the chaos back again.

Charlotte pressed her hands over her eyes and cleared her mind. What did she know of him? He was an honorable man, of that much she was certain. He was steady and dependable. And in the past few weeks she'd had a chance to see something within him she'd never seen before—a warmth and a charm that had captivated her heart.

And above all, he was honest. She couldn't remember an instance in the entire time she'd known him that he'd deliberately lied to her—except for the past couple of weeks. He'd known all about her scheme and neglected to tell her. But then, perhaps she deserved that.

Charlotte sighed. What was she supposed to do? Every shred of self-preservation she possessed told her she should continue to build the wall around her heart. But in her heart she wanted to tear it down. How would she know when it was the right time to trust him?

She'd never thought he was a man worth loving and that had made her choices so easy. But nothing was simple anymore, for try as she might, she couldn't keep herself from loving Sam Harper.

Chapter Six

THE MORNING SUN SHONE through the wide plate-glass windows of Valentine Delights. Sitting at a table near the door, Charlotte stared into her Papaccino as if she might find a few more ounces of courage at the bottom of the cup. She'd been sitting there for nearly two hours, since seven that morning, swilling chocolate-laced coffee and trying to work up the fortitude to go into work.

She hadn't slept a wink all night and had stopped by Papa's for some badly needed caffeine. But once she had settled at a table, she couldn't bring herself to leave. Instead, she sipped at her coffee and watched as early-morning customers came and went, their last-minute Valentine's Day purchases packed in pretty silver-foil boxes by Papa and his helper, Rudy.

Today was the most romantic day of the entire year and here she was, alone, confused, and starting to get a little jittery from all the caffeine she'd imbibed. How many Valentine's Days had passed uneventfully in her life? Every single one, if she were to be honest. But this Valentine's Day would be different.

Today she would make a decision that would change her future. She would decide either to love Sam Harper, or to finally put loving him behind her for good. She took another slow sip of her coffee. She would make a decision, all right, but she just wouldn't make it this exact second.

"How long are you going to sit here taking up my table space?"

Charlotte looked up to find Papa Valentine standing over her, his arms akimbo, a teasing smile quirking his lips. "I bought this coffee and two others," she said. "Plus a croissant. If you try to kick me out of here, I'll write a nasty story about you and put it on the front page of the paper with a huge, Second Coming headline. You'll never sell chocolate in this town again."

He held out his hands in mock surrender and chuckled. "All right, all right. But that gloomy expression of yours is driving all my customers away," he replied. "It's Valentine's Day, the weather is sunny and beautiful, and everyone is supposed to be happy. Now, either put a smile on that pretty face of yours or go sit in the corner."

Charlotte grudgingly forced a smile. "Is that better?"

"Not much," Papa said, pulling out the chair beside her. He sat down and braced his arms on the table. "Do you want to tell me what's wrong? Or should I wait a few days and read it in the paper?"

She shook her head. "It has nothing to do with the paper." She paused. "I mean, it does have to do with the paper, but it's not news. It's... personal."

"Sam?" he asked.

She looked at him and blinked. "How did you know?"

"This is a small town, Charlotte, and news travels fast. It seems you two were seen in a passionate clinch outside the Taggert Mansion last night at approximately 10:16 p.m. by four ladies from the Cedar Ridge Historical Society."

Charlotte groaned and buried her face in her hands. "I thought we were alone."

"In a town this small you can't sneeze without half the population saying 'Bless you.' Besides, I figured something was up. Sam was in here last night right before we closed at midnight."

"With his date?" she asked.

Papa shook his head. "Naw, he was alone. In fact, he sat at this very table, looking pretty much the way you do, a hangdog expression on his face. Now, if I were a good investigative journalist, I'd think maybe the way *you're* feeling and the way *he* was feeling are somehow connected. Would I be right?"

"He must have left the ball right after I did," she murmured, "and driven that awful Diana woman home."

"Diana," Papa said. "She was his date, right? Lots of interesting gossip this morning about that dress she was wearing. Red with sequins, wasn't it? It created a real impression with the ladies at the historical society."

"My guess is people were just waiting for her seams to pop," Charlotte muttered. "It would have been great entertainment while the band was on a break. That dress couldn't have been any tighter—or more low-cut."

"So what were you doing kissing another woman's date?" Papa asked. "And your business partner, to boot."

Charlotte sighed. "It's a long story, but I'll have you know that it all started with a little box of chocolates from your shop. Maybe I should blame you for this whole mess."

"If you're going to blame me, then maybe you ought to tell me what I did first."

She paused and considered confiding in him. Papa did seem to know a lot about romance. And he knew Sam. Maybe he could give her a little more insight into the male point of view. "This is off the record, all right?"

He nodded.

"Sam and I have always maintained a very businesslike relationship. We've never involved ourselves in each other's personal lives and we've kept a safe distance at the office, as well. A few weeks ago, I did something that changed all that and now everything has...fallen apart."

She told Papa the whole story, from every detail about Sam's Secret Valentine to the startling kisses they'd shared the previous night. When she finished, she forced a smile. "So you see, I've made a real mess of things. And I'm afraid I can't put our relationship back to the way it used to be, no matter how hard I try."

"And why would you want to make it the way it used to be?"

"Because, I used to feel safe and sure of what I was doing. I was happy. Now I'm just confused and upset and—"

"In love?" he asked.

She blinked at him in surprise. "I— No, not—" She paused, then cursed softly. "Yes. Maybe. All right, I'll admit it. I think I'm in love with Sam Harper. This doesn't mean I welcome the prospect, but at least I can be honest with myself."

Papa nodded, silently considering what she'd told him.

"So, what do you think?" she asked. "What should I do?"

"What do you want to do?"

Charlotte shook her head dispiritedly. "I don't know. I guess I'd like to think that he loves me. But I just can't seem to get myself to believe that, even though he said it."

"Why not?"

"Because, I've loved Sam Harper nearly all my life, but never once has the feeling been reciprocated. I could be the poster child for unrequited love."

"He said he loves you. I don't see why there's any confusion."

"But why now? What suddenly changed his mind? Two weeks ago, he couldn't stand me and now he suddenly loves me?"

"Kismet?" Papa asked.

"Do you mean like fate? Or destiny?"

"All I know is that everyone in this town has been watching you two since you were kids. And we've all been waiting for this to happen. So my advice is to go with the flow. If you and Sam were meant to be together, you were meant to be together, starting now. And there's not a whole lot you can do to change that."

"So you think I should believe him?" Charlotte asked.

Papa reached out and patted her hand. "The man I saw in here last night looked like a man in love. Now, unless I've missed my guess, he wasn't mooning over that lady in the red-sequined dress. I think he had his mind occupied with the beauty in the emerald-green gown."

Charlotte arched her brow and gave him a questioning look. "Everyone's been talking about how pretty you looked last night," he explained. "The ladies of the Cedar Ridge Historical Society thought your dress was lovely."

She laughed. "Somehow I get the feeling that 'What's news?' is not our special little saying. Is there anything else you want to tell me about last night? Anything I might want to add to my article in tomorrow's paper?''

He chuckled and patted her hand. "No, but I do have a bit of advice for you, Charlotte. There's only two things you can trust in when it comes to romance,'' Papa said. "The first is good Belgian chocolates. And the second is your heart. Trust your heart and you'll never be sorry.''

She drew a deep breath. "But I've kept my feelings locked up so tight for so long, I'm not sure I can tell him exactly what's in my heart. I'm not even sure I know.''

"Well, if you can't say it yourself, you could always say it with chocolates,'' Papa teased.

A slow smile curled the corners of her mouth. Charlotte reached out and grabbed Papa's hands. "That's it! That's what I'll do.'' She jumped up from her chair and glanced around the shop. "First, I'll need a dozen of your hazelnut truffles. No, make that two dozen.''

Papa clapped his hands, then stood. "Two dozen truffles, coming up.'' He strode across the shop and stepped behind the counter, then began to arrange her chocolates in a silver-foil box. A few moments later, he returned and placed the box in front of her. He held out a gift card and a pen.

"This is perfect,'' she said as she grabbed the pen. Charlotte scribbled a quick note on the card, then handed both back to Papa. "Can you ask Rudy to deliver these to Sam's office right away?"

"You're not going to deliver them yourself?" Papa asked.

Charlotte shook her head, then rushed to the door. "I've got some other things to take care of. Just make sure Sam gets the chocolates and he reads the note."

Papa chuckled. "Valentine Delights always delivers what we promise. I'll make the delivery myself." He crossed to the door and pulled it open for her. "You have a nice Valentine's Day, Charlotte."

She paused in the doorway, then gave him a confident smile. "I'm going to do just that, Papa," she replied as she walked out into the bright sun and fresh morning air.

When she reached the sidewalk, she stopped and stared at her reflection in the plate-glass window. She could do this. She could face Sam and tell him how she felt. And then they would begin again—a clean slate, a fresh start. And what better place to begin than the place where all this had started, so many years ago?

A CHILL WIND BLEW across the surface of Myrtle Lake. Charlotte pulled her jacket more tightly around her as she stared out at the water, her skirt whipping around her legs. With a sigh of frustration, she glanced down at her watch and then turned back to the cottage.

"So much for new beginnings," she murmured. Lunchtime had come and gone and the gourmet goodies that she'd laid out on the cabin's dining-room table had long ago been put away. The champagne, still corked, had probably reached room temperature right along with the excitement she had felt.

Where was he? Had he received the chocolates and her note? Charlotte brushed her hair out of her eyes impatiently. Perhaps she should have just faced him at the office instead of asking him to drive the hour out to the cabin. But the office was for business and what she had to say to him went way beyond business.

The water lapped around the pier and her thoughts wandered back to the night of her thirteenth birthday. If the past had taught her anything, she might as well jump in now and get it over with. He'd rejected her then. And now, she had set herself up for yet another rejection. At least there weren't thirty of her very best friends around to witness her humiliation.

Maybe it was the card she'd sent with the candy. She hadn't been sure what to say and had written the first words that came into her mind, something simple and direct—or so she'd thought.

The feeling is mutual. We need to talk. Meet me at the cabin.

Sincerely,
Your Secret Valentine.

Had she been *too* direct? Or maybe too vague? *The feeling is mutual.* It wasn't the most poetic inscription in the world, but it said what she wanted to say. If he truly loved her, then she loved him. And if he didn't love her, then she didn't love him. As she ran the phrase over in her mind, she realized how wishy-washy it sounded.

But the rest of the note had been perfectly clear. So why wasn't he here? Charlotte groaned inwardly and pressed her hands to her cold ears. Maybe he regretted what had happened between them the previous night and wanted to forget his "Secret Valentine." Maybe, for him, the feeling was no longer mutual.

Charlotte glanced at her watch again. She would wait another fifteen minutes and then she would leave. She walked to the end of the dock and sat down on the weathered bench. As she watched a hawk circle lazily above the water, her mind wandered back to the summers of her youth.

They had been thrown together from the time of her earliest memories. On blistering summer days, while their fathers worked at the paper, she and Sam would travel to the cabin with their mothers, riding in the back seat of Lila Harper's blue convertible. They'd played together and sung together, and at the very beginning they'd been the best of friends.

But as they grew older, they began to grow apart, until she was certain she'd done something to make him angry. The more she tagged after him, the more angry Sam had become. He no longer wanted to climb trees and skip stones. She knew now that he'd simply outgrown her, moving into his teens two years before she had.

The summers passed and she watched him from a distance, wary and confused. And then one day, a few weeks before she turned thirteen, she realized that she had begun looking at Sam in a different way. He wasn't a buddy anymore, or the big brother she never had. He was a boy—a tall handsome boy that her girlfriends chattered and giggled and blushed over.

She'd fallen in love with Sam Harper, just as surely as she loved him to this day. But when she had tried to tell him, he'd... She closed her eyes at the memory and tipped her head back.

"Hello, Charlotte."

Her eyes snapped open and she turned to watch Sam sit down beside her. He was dressed in a bulky sweater and jeans. Her breath caught at the sight of him. He didn't look at all like the Sam Harper she encountered every day at the office. He looked... relaxed, approachable—and incredibly sexy.

"I—I didn't think you were going to come," she said softly, avoiding his gaze.

He pulled the card from his pocket and stared at it. "I had something to take care of and I got into the office late. I came as soon as I got your note."

"When you didn't come, I thought—"

"I'm here, Charlotte. And I came because I figured it was about time we got things straightened out between us."

An uneasy silence grew as they sat side by side on the bench. Charlotte tried to read his expression, but his face was emotionless, composed. She thought she would be able to see his feelings just by looking into his eyes, but she couldn't. He was as unreadable as he'd always been.

"What does this mean?" he asked, holding out the card.

She shifted nervously and crossed her arms in front of her. "I—I don't know," she replied. "What do *you* think it means?"

His jaw tightened and he sighed. Cursing beneath his breath, he stood and moved to the edge of the pier. The muscles across his back tensed and he braced his hands on his hips. She fought the temptation to reach out and touch him and instead clenched her fists and held her place.

"I don't know what the hell it means, Charlotte," he said, shaking his head, his back to her. "I couldn't begin to guess." He turned around to face her, then leaned back against a weathered piling. "You know, I think that's the problem with us. We've spent so much time bickering with each other that when it finally comes time to say something meaningful, we can't."

"Maybe we've known each other for too long," she said, clutching her icy fingers in front of her. "Most people don't know as much about each other as we do. We grew up together, we spent most of our lives arguing. Old habits are hard to break."

"And that means we shouldn't even try?"

"No," Charlotte said, a hint of defensiveness in her voice. "It just means that we'll have to try harder."

"So, what do you want to say, Charlotte? Why did you bring me here?"

She drew a deep breath and steadied her nerves, but her hands were still shaking from that morning's caffeine overdose. Biting her bottom lip, she stood and walked toward him. He stared at her for a long moment, his arms crossed over his chest.

"This is the place I first realized I loved you," she said. "Right here on this pier. On my thirteenth birthday party, when I tried to kiss you and you—"

"I remember."

She glanced up and met his gaze and caught a brief flash of emotion in his eyes. She slowly gathered her courage. It was time to take a chance. Now or never.

"I love you," she said softly, averting her gaze. She didn't want to look at him for fear of what she would see—for fear that the intense expression she'd seen last night would no longer be there.

Time seemed to stop, each moment of silence an eternity, every breath she took a knife to her heart. She kept her eyes fixed on his chest, studying the pattern in his sweater until tears blurred her vision.

But then he spoke and suddenly, she could breathe again. "And I love you, Charlotte," he said, reaching out to touch her cheek.

A sob caught in her throat and she snapped her head up to meet his eyes. "You—you do? I mean, really, you do?"

He smiled and nodded. "Yeah, I really do."

The silence between them grew again as they gazed into each other's eyes. "What are we supposed to do now?" Charlotte asked.

"I think a kiss might be in order."

Clutching her hands in front of her, she took a step toward him. Placing his hands on her shoulders, he drew her nearer. He bent his head and brushed his lips against hers, a gentle fleeting contact that left her wanting more. And then, as if that simple touch had opened a floodgate of emotion, he pulled her against his body and covered her mouth with his.

Charlotte felt her knees go weak and she wrapped her arms around his neck to keep her balance. She moaned softly and he deepened the kiss, weaving his fingers through her hair and cradling her head in his hands, moving her mouth against his until it fit perfectly. Her mind whirled and her body pulsed with a maelstrom of sensations.

Then he pulled back slightly and looked down into her eyes, a lazy smile quirking his lips. "Do you really want to start over?" he murmured.

She nodded, her gaze fixed on his.

He took a step back and then another. "Then do it," he said, grinning.

Charlotte frowned. "Do what?" she asked.

"Come on, Gus. I know that's why you brought me here. If we're going to start from the beginning you're going to have to do it." He held out his arms and took a final step to the edge of the pier. "Just give me a shove and get it over with."

Charlotte gasped. "You want me to push you into the lake?"

"That's how this all started. If we're going to begin fresh, then I think turnaround is fair play."

"It's the middle of February. The lake is freezing!"

"I know you want to," he said. "It's the only way to even the score."

She crossed her arms and shook her head. "I *don't* want to. Besides, you'll catch a cold."

"Come on, Gus."

"I hate that name," Charlotte said. "I've asked you not to call me that."

"Gus," he teased in a seductive tone. "Gus, Gus, drives a bus. Chews tobacco and likes to cuss."

She screamed in frustration at the childhood taunt, then gave him a gentle shove, hoping that it would end his teasing. But it didn't. With a satisfied smile, he stumbled back, his arms flailing dramatically. In the blink of an eye, she knew he was going in. Instinctively she reached out and grabbed his arm, but it was too late. Both of them tumbled off the edge of the pier and hit the icy water with a splat.

She felt his arms around her waist as she struggled to find the bottom with her feet. An instant later, she surfaced, sputtering and gasping at the shock of the icy water. With gentle hands, he pushed the wet hair out of her eyes. "Are you all right?"

She nodded, still coughing.

He chuckled. "I didn't mean for you to come in with me."

Charlotte pushed her hair back, then sneezed. But before she could speak, he pulled her up against him and covered her mouth with his.

His tongue teased at hers, gently coaxing, growing more passionate by degrees. A flood of warmth coursed through her body and she forgot about the icy water that lapped around them. He cupped her face in his palms and rained kisses over her. "God, I love you, Gus," he murmured.

Her teeth chattered uncontrollably, not from the cold, but from the powerful emotion that rocked her to her very soul. "And I love you," she said, brushing her lips against his. "I've always loved you."

He moaned softly, then scooped her up in his arms and slowly made his way to the shore.

Charlotte wrapped her arms around his neck, startled at the ease with which he carried her. "I didn't mean to push you, but I—"

"Shh," he said, nuzzling her neck. "We're even now. From this moment on, the past doesn't make a difference. This is a new beginning for us, sweetheart."

He carried her to the cabin, not putting her down until they stood before the dying embers of the fire she had built earlier. He lowered her onto the couch and then pulled off the leather boots and thick socks she wore. He kicked off his own tennis shoes and socks, then pulled her up to stand in front of him. He ran his hands down her arms and wove his fingers through hers, his gaze never wavering.

"You're soaked," she said softly, plucking at his sweater. "You better take that off." She grabbed the hem of his sweater and helped him pull it over his head. Beneath the sweater, a wet T-shirt clung to his torso.

Sam smiled. "What about you?" he asked. "I think you'd better take that jacket off." He tugged on the cuffs, then pushed it over her shoulders until it dropped to the floor.

She stood, staring at his chest. Hesitantly, she reached out and touched him, feeling his warmth seep through the cold fabric. "Maybe you should take off the T-shirt," she suggested, captivated by the hard muscles hidden from her eyes.

"You think so?" he asked.

She glanced up at him and he arched his eyebrow. She felt the color rise in her cheeks. "I—I wouldn't want you to catch a cold."

He twisted, pulling the T-shirt over his head, then tossed it over his shoulder. Charlotte's breath caught in her throat at the sight of his naked torso. Lord, he was gorgeous. She reached out and touched him—his smooth, warm skin, the soft hair that dusted his broad chest, the ripple of muscle across his belly.

Drawing a deep breath, she closed her eyes. She knew exactly where all these wet clothes would lead, but now that they'd admitted their love for each other, she didn't want to wait any longer. She'd been waiting for Sam Harper her entire life, whether she admitted it or not.

She reached for the front of her blouse. Her gaze locked on his as she slowly undid the buttons, one by one, and shrugged out of the damp cotton. Then she unzipped her skirt and it slid over her hips and puddled around her feet. She stood in front of him, dressed in only her silky bra and panties, vulnerable, yet not afraid.

His gaze skimmed over her body and she watched the passion smolder in his eyes. "Make love to me, Sam," she said, stepping toward him. He brushed his thumb along her jawline. A shiver skittered down her spine.

"Cold?" he murmured.

Charlotte nodded.

Stepping around her, he pulled a colorful wool blanket from the back of the sofa, then draped it over her shoulders. The fire snapped behind them, the embers nearly dead. He turned to add another piece of wood to the grate, but she reached out and stopped him.

"We don't need the fire," she said with a hesitant smile.

Groaning softly, he turned back to her and yanked her into his arms. His mouth found hers once again and, urgent and demanding, he kissed her, hard and deep, his hands roving over her body beneath the blanket.

Frantically, he stripped off his jeans and the clinging silk boxers beneath, revealing his long, muscular legs. Her heart skipped as she took in the evidence of his arousal.

With a trembling hand, she reached out and touched him there, his hardness stoking her own desire. He sucked in a sharp breath and she looked up at his expression of tightly-held control. And then the control was gone, and he closed his eyes and tipped his head back, pulling her body against him.

Suddenly her world filled with exquisite sensation and frantic longing as they explored each other's bodies. Her bra and panties were discarded with ease and he drew her to the sofa, her breath coming in short gasps as his mouth moved over hers. He pulled the blanket around them and they tumbled onto the soft cushions.

He was above her, then beneath her, then beside her, his hard, lean form bringing a gentle flood of warmth to the very tips of her limbs, his hands making her ache with desire. And through the haze of passion, she knew that this was right. This was what she'd been waiting for. This was the man who had been her destiny all along.

She whispered his name once, and then again, and then he was inside her, moving, drawing her into a primal rhythm that she could neither resist nor deny. He rocked against her until he reached her very core, touching her, then retreating; then deeper and harder, faster, until they both neared the edge.

He stopped then, stilling his movements. Holding his breath, he looked down into her eyes, his gaze intense, his control near shattering, and she knew he could see to the very depths of her soul. He could see the truth there—the love—as she could, clear and lucid in his gaze. She reached up and brushed her thumb along his lower lip, then said his name once more, soft and pleading.

At the sound of her voice, a slow shudder rocked his body and she felt his body tense in her arms. "God, I love you," he breathed, slowly burying himself again. And then, as if he could wait no longer, he began to move, fierce and frantic, relentless, driving into her until she lost all touch with reality.

They found their release together—clinging, clutching, two bodies melded into one, perched on the precipice and then crashing out of control. Sensation surged through her body, shattering every odd notion of pleasure and passion. On and on the feelings went until they could go no further; until they both collapsed in utter exhaustion, spent yet sated.

With a moan of sheer contentment, Charlotte curled up beside him, throwing her leg over his hips possessively, her head cradled on his shoulder. His heart beat strong and quick beneath her ear and she sighed, never having felt more alive than she did at this moment. As their breathing slowed, he gently stroked her temple, his touch reminding her that what they had just shared was real, and not one of her fantasies.

"I love you," he whispered. "I can't seem to stop telling you that."

She looked up at him. "And I love you," Charlotte said.

He gave her a devilish smile and pulled her nearer. "No, I love you."

She giggled at the teasing tone in his voice. "Well, I'm sorry, Harper, but *I* love *you!*"

He tipped his head back and chuckled. "I'm glad we can still argue. That hasn't changed and I hope it never will."

"But what *will* happen when we argue now?" she questioned, worry suffusing her voice.

He tipped her chin up and kissed her. "It won't change the way I feel about you, sweetheart. You're stubborn and opinionated. But I fell in love with Charlotte Keats and I knew exactly what I was getting myself into."

"And you're arrogant and egotistical and—"

"Coldhearted?" he asked.

She smiled. "I was wrong about that," Charlotte said. "In fact, I've never been more wrong about anything in my life."

"I know how you feel," Sam said, brushing his palm against her cheek. "I always thought you were a real pain, Charlotte. But I've definitely changed my opinion on that score. No more pain, just this incredible...pleasure."

She sighed. "So, what are we going to do? I mean, about work? Are we going to tell everyone?"

He considered her question for a long moment, then shrugged. "We're going to have to say something. In fact, if we don't get back to the office within the next few hours, the *Cedar Ridge Tribune* won't be delivered on time tomorrow morning."

Charlotte pushed up on her elbow and frowned in concern. "What's wrong? Is the press down again? Why didn't you tell me this? Harper, you are going to have to get over this pathological need to run the show. I'm an equal partner in—"

Sam pressed his fingers to her lips to stop her words. "The press is fine," he murmured. "They're just holding the main until I okay the copy on one bit of news."

"What news? I'm the editor and all news goes through me."

"That's why I had the pressmen wait."

"What news?" she repeated.

"An announcement. A very important announcement. Actually, an announcement of our engagement. I couldn't really run it until I checked with the editor. So what do you say? Do we tell them to run with it?"

Charlotte stared down at his smiling face. Her mouth dropped open and she tried to speak. But when nothing came out, she snapped it shut. She blinked, then shook her head. "I—oh, dear— Is—is that a proposal, Sam Harper?"

He quirked an eyebrow up. "Am I not making myself clear? I want to marry you, Charlotte. We've wasted enough time already. A good fifteen years, by my count."

"But we've hardly spent *any* time together."

"We've spent our whole lives together," he countered.

"I mean, romantically. You know, intimately."

He reached out and searched the floor with his hand until he found his wet jeans. "This is why I was late getting here," he explained as he pulled a tiny box from the back pocket. "It's a little soggy, but I think it will do. Happy Valentine's Day, Gus."

Hesitantly, she took the box from his hand and opened it. Her heart stopped when she saw the diamond ring inside. It glittered, reflecting the light that streamed through the cabin windows.

"Marry me, Charlotte."

She tore her gaze away from the ring and looked down into his eyes. "I don't know what to say."

He wove his fingers through the damp hair at the nape of her neck and pulled her closer. "Say yes," he growled.

Charlotte smiled, then laughed. "Yes!" she cried, wrapping her arms around his neck.

She kissed him then, with all the love that she'd hidden for so long and with all the love that she'd discovered inside her that day. She was in love with Sam Harper and he loved her. And what had once seemed impossible, was now inevitable.

And as he pulled her body beneath his and began to make love to her again, somehow she knew that she would never, ever look at Valentine's Day the same way again.

Epilogue

"I DON'T CARE IF HE *is* an advertiser. I'm not ordering my wedding cake from Bert's Donut Shop." Charlotte stood in the doorway of Valentine Delights and scanned the room for a table, ignoring Sam's ongoing argument.

Sam reached over her shoulder and pointed to a table near the counter, then grabbed her elbow and steered her toward it. "Bert assures me he can make a lovely cake. And don't forget, he's placed an ad in the Monday issue of the *Tribune* for twenty-seven years running."

Charlotte quickly wove through the tables, Sam hard on her heels. "We are not going to discuss this, Harper. If we decide on doughnuts for the reception, Bert can make them. But we're talking about a wedding cake, here. A finely crafted combination of white cake and butter-cream frosting."

"Chocolate," he said.

"White," she repeated. "With flowers and leaves and curlicues. And a little bride and groom on the top."

"Are you still arguing about the wedding?"

Charlotte looked up to find Papa Valentine standing beside their table, his arms crossed over his chest.

He smiled and shook his head. "Now it's the cake. Last week it was the flowers. Next week you'll be arguing about the napkins."

"We're not arguing," Charlotte replied. "We're discussing."

"We're arguing," Sam countered.

Charlotte gasped. "We are not!"

"Yes, we are," Sam said. "And we've been argu—" He stopped at Charlotte's censuring look. "*Discussing* ever since the day Charlotte said she'd marry me. We can't seem to agree on anything about the wedding. I told her to do whatever she wants, but she said I had to be involved. So I get involved and she doesn't want to hear my opinion."

Papa chuckled. "Have you set a date yet?"

Charlotte and Sam looked at each other, then at Papa, embarrassed expressions on both their faces. "We will," she said. "As soon as we get a few more details ironed out."

"Do you want my opinion?" Papa asked.

"She won't listen," Sam said.

"I will too!" Charlotte cried.

"I think you should elope," Papa said.

"Elope?" they said in tandem. They looked at each other for a long moment, then at Papa and back at each other.

"Elope," she repeated. "I don't think we've discussed that possibility."

"What do you think?" Sam asked.

Charlotte frowned. "I don't know, what do you think?"

Sam reached out and took her hand, a smile curling the corners of his mouth. "We could leave right now," he said.

"We could be married by morning," she said, her expression brightening.

"No more arguments."

"No more *discussions*."

"Husband and wife," Sam said.

"Wife and husband," Charlotte replied.

With that, they both jumped up from their chairs and started for the door. But Papa cleared his throat loudly, stopping their exit before they'd reached the middle of the shop. Slowly, they both turned around.

"Not so fast, you two," Papa said. "I give you great advice and you're leaving without a word of thanks?"

Charlotte smiled apologetically. "I'm sorry, Papa. Thank you for everything. If it weren't for the great advice you've always given us, we probably wouldn't be together today. We'll never forget all that you've done for us."

"And I'm going to do one more thing." Papa clapped his hands. "Rudy!" he called. "We need a wedding cake. Pack up that Triple Chocolate Passion Torte I just made. These two are on their way to get married, so make it snappy. They've been waiting for this day long enough!"

GIFT OF THE HEART

Gina Wilkins

Dear Reader,

This year—on February 4, 1997—my husband, John, and I celebrate our twentieth wedding anniversary. I still carry the heart-shaped key ring he gave me on our first Valentine's Day as a married couple, ten days after the wedding. Our Valentine's Day festivities since then have grown to include our very special children—Courtney, sixteen, Kerry, thirteen and David, seven. February 14 has become a day to officially express our joy in being together as a family.

Being included in the Valentine's Day anthology with Meryl and Kate was a true pleasure for me. My characters, Richard and Jessica, discover, as my own family has, that Valentine's Day is much more than a cute, greeting-card holiday. It's a celebration of love.

I hope you enjoy this story of love, romance... and chocolates!

Happy reading,

Gina Wilkins

PAPA'S DIXIE FUDGE CHESS PIE

1½ cup sugar
1 stick of butter
3 eggs (slightly beaten)
4 Tbsp cocoa
1 tsp vanilla
pinch of salt
1 unbaked pie shell

Cream together sugar and butter. Add other ingredients. Pour in unbaked pie shell. Bake at 425°F for 10 minutes. Reduce oven temperature to 350°F and bake for an additional 30 minutes.

Chill before serving. Keep refrigerated.

Hint: Serve with a scoop of vanilla ice cream.

For my special Valentines—
John, Courtney, Kerry and David.
I love you.

Chapter One

JESSICA PATTERSON stared down at the professionally-wrapped package in her lap and tried to ignore a sudden, unpleasant premonition.

"Well?" her fiancé prodded, adjusting his glasses with one finger. "Aren't you going to open it?"

She managed a weak smile and toyed with the gaily-colored bow. On her left hand, a near-flawless marquise diamond in an exquisite gold setting gleamed softly. When Richard had placed it on her finger a year ago, he'd somewhat diminished the tender moment by explaining that he'd been assured the ring was an excellent investment.

"It's...er...almost too pretty to open," she said, keeping her gaze on the rectangular box he'd presented for her birthday.

"Doesn't make much sense, does it?" He sounded genuinely puzzled. "To spend all that money on fancy papers and ribbons that will just be ripped away. Still, I know people expect that sort of thing, so I had this done at a gift-wrapping counter."

"It's lovely. Did you select the paper?" She touched an unsteady fingertip to the floral wrapping, hoping he'd put at least that much personal effort into the gesture.

He shrugged, looking a bit sheepish. "Well, no," he admitted. "You know I'm no good at that sort of thing. I just told the girl to use her best judgment."

Girl. Brilliant research scientist Dr. Richard London had never quite caught on to the subtleties of politically-correct terminology.

He shifted restlessly on the sofa beside her and she knew he was getting impatient for her to open the gift. Dramatic moments and sentimental gestures weren't really his thing.

He resorted to such behavior as rarely as possible, and then only because prevailing social customs gave him few other options. Now, for instance. It was his fiancée's birthday, and he had dutifully provided a gift, frivolously wrapped in paper and bows....

She drew a deep breath, telling herself to stop being so silly. There was no reason to believe this gift would be momentous. It wasn't as though her life were going to change when she removed the wrapping. So why was she so reluctant to do so?

She tugged briskly at the bow, and set to work on the pretty paper some other woman had chosen for her.

A moment later, she looked up blankly, two softbound books in her lap. "Computer manuals? You bought me computer manuals?"

Richard's smile was tinged with self-satisfaction. "That was the easiest part to have wrapped," he explained. "Actually, I bought you a computer. It's out in my car. I thought we'd spend the rest of the evening setting it up and studying the features."

She blinked at him for a moment, then asked the first question that popped into her head. "But...what about dinner?"

He waved a dismissive hand. "No problem. We'll order a pizza.

"Wait'll you see this computer, Jess," he continued, his voice warming with a passion that she bleakly wished was due to her. "I had my assistant order it to my specifications. It makes your old 386 seem like an abacus in comparison. Pentium microprocessor, 200 megahertz, 64 megs of RAM, two gigabytes of hard drive, eight-spin CD-ROM. More than you need, I assure you. Seventeen-inch color monitor. A 28.8 fax modem. We'll finally have you on-line. I can E-mail you whenever I'm running late, or have to cancel plans or whatever."

She stared at him, distantly noting the way his enthusiasm for computer hardware made his dark eyes sparkle behind his glasses. She couldn't believe she actually felt slightly jealous of the reaction the new computer evoked from him.

He hadn't noticed that she was wearing a new dress. It was blue—almost the same color as her eyes—and it fit her in a way that had made the plump salesclerk grimace with open envy. She'd had her auburn hair cut that afternoon into a soft bob that fluffed around her face. Richard hadn't commented on the new style since he'd arrived for their date half an hour ago.

It was Friday, February 7. Her thirtieth birthday. She'd gone out of her way to look especially attractive for him. Had foolishly, unrealistically anticipated a romantic evening of dinner and dancing. And he wanted to order a pizza. Spend the evening assembling a computer.

Her silence seemed to puzzle him. "Jess? Is something wrong?"

Four years her senior, he was a good-looking man, with slightly tousled brown hair, chocolate-colored eyes fringed with long, dark lashes, cleanly sculpted features and a firm mouth that had, occasionally, curved unexpectedly into breathtaking smiles that had almost stopped her heart. He was brilliant, successful, highly admired and respected in his field.

She'd known him for two years. After almost a year of dating, he'd proposed marriage. She had accepted his rather pragmatic offer because she had fallen in love with him sometime during the course of their first otherwise-uneventful dinner date. To this day, she couldn't say what it was, exactly, that had hooked her. Maybe it was because she'd somehow convinced herself that behind his attractive face and incisive mind was a truly gentle man capable of great love and loyalty, despite his awkwardness at expressing his emotions.

She'd spent the thirteen months since he'd proposed wearing his ring, seeing him whenever his busy schedule allowed, and waiting for him to decide on an optimal date for their wedding. It was always right after the next project was completed. Or as soon as he could make arrangements for time away from the lab.

In the meantime, her biological clock kept ticking.

And he'd bought her a computer for her birthday.

He was the only man who'd ever made her heart sing.

And now he was breaking it.

"I got a laser printer to go with it," he said a bit tentatively, as though suddenly aware that she wasn't sharing his enthusiasm for the gift.

"I think you'd better go now, Richard." The words were out of her mouth almost before she'd known she would say them.

His dark eyes widened. "Excuse me?"

She struggled to maintain her composure, telling herself she should at least make an effort to be gracious. The computer had probably cost him a fortune. He, of course, undoubtedly considered it a worthwhile investment. "Thank you for the, er, gift, but I'm not feeling very well. I need some time alone."

"You're not feeling well?" Switching instantly into doctor mode, Richard touched her forehead, then took her wrist, covering her pulse with two fingers. He looked vaguely concerned, but also relieved to have an explanation for her odd behavior. "Are you in pain? Dizzy?"

Jessica tugged her hand out of his grasp. "I just... Please go, Richard."

His expression suddenly cleared. "Oh," he murmured. "*That's* your problem."

She stood abruptly. If he *dared* . . .

He smiled with a kindly patience that set her teeth on edge. "Is there really any need for me to leave, Jess? I won't mind if you want to take a Midol and lie down with a heating pad for a while. I'll just be working on the computer, and when you feel better, we'll—"

She stalked to the door, no longer caring whether he thought she'd lost her mind. Maybe she had. Or maybe she'd lost it thirteen months ago and was just now figuring it out.

"Get out Richard," she said, opening the door. "And you can take your paper and your ribbons and your computer manuals with you."

His brows drew downward. His voice deepened, took on that I'm-a-serious-scientist don't-waste-my-valuable-time edge that he resorted to when he didn't know how else to react. "Jessica, you're being unreasonable. If I've done something to offend you, you should just say so rather than carry on like this."

"I think I'm making myself clear enough," she said, her voice as cool as his. "I want you out of my living room. What part of that statement didn't you understand, Dr. London?"

In all the time she'd known Richard, she'd never seen him lose his temper. She'd seen him annoyed, impatient, frustrated, exasperated—but never downright mad. Something in the set of his jaw told her he was close to that point now.

As entertaining as it might have been to watch him finally lose his cool, she didn't want him staying long enough to let her find out. She didn't want to risk falling apart in front of him. Not tonight.

"I don't know what this is about," he said, his face taut, "but I see no reason to continue this pointless performance. When you're ready for us to discuss this like mature adults, call me."

That did it. Her voice took on a tone of mock surprise. "Oh, yes, we *are* mature adults, aren't we, Richard?"

She was amazed to realize that she was shouting now. And even more astonished that she no longer cared whether she was making a fool of herself. "We're getting more mature by the day, in fact. Why, before long we'll be so *mature* we'll qualify for Medicare. Not that anyone would notice the difference. We'll still be conducting our endless courtship, sending each other polite little E-mail messages, and getting together occasionally for pizza to be eaten in the romantic glow of a seventeen-inch color monitor!"

He stiffened. An expression that might have been hurt flashed through his eyes, so quickly she wasn't even certain that that was, indeed, what she'd seen. It was quickly replaced by offended dignity. "Look, if you don't want the computer, you can trade it for something you like better."

"You really don't get it, do you, Richard?" she asked sadly, her anger fading into bitter regret. "It's *you* I'm trading in."

She tugged the ring off her finger and slid it into the front pocket of his dark suit jacket. "I'm sorry," she whispered. "You're an amazing man, Richard London. You'll probably find the cure for cancer someday. But I just can't go on playing Miss Adelaide to your Nathan Detroit. I need more."

He planted his hands on his slender hips and stared at her. "I haven't a clue what you're talking about."

"I know you don't," she whispered, the break in her heart opening wider. "And that's the saddest part of all. Goodbye, Richard."

He lifted a hand toward her. "You don't really mean this."

Avoiding his grasp, she opened the door. "Goodbye."

Still looking dazed, he stepped out automatically. Then turned to say something else.

Whatever it was, she didn't hear it. She'd already closed the door.

RICHARD STORMED OUT of Jessica's apartment building, still finding it hard to believe she'd thrown him out. The diamond ring felt like a fifty-pound weight in his pocket.

What on earth had possessed her to take it off her finger and return it to him that way? No forewarning, no explanation, nothing. Just, "Get out, Richard."

He could only assume she had lost her senses.

He glared up at her window. Okay, so he would give her some time to get herself together. Perhaps tomorrow they could discuss this rationally.

What part of that statement didn't you understand, Dr. London?

He winced at the sarcastic words. So unlike Jessica.

Thinking morosely of the boxes in the trunk he'd anticipated opening with her this evening, he put his hand on the door handle of his car. He really wasn't looking forward to going home alone when he'd cleared the entire evening to be with Jess. It was nearly a half-hour drive from her apartment in Cedar Ridge to his in nearby Atlanta. And he was hungry, darn it. He'd gotten tied up in the lab and had missed lunch. That pizza had sounded pretty good to him.

He was quite sure this would all be settled once Jessica calmed down.

Hormones, he told himself with a bemused shake of his head. As well as he understood their effects on the female emotional system, he still found individual reactions to them as baffling as any man did.

Had he thought Jessica was serious about breaking their engagement, he might have been more upset. As it was, he was merely annoyed that he hadn't handled her outburst a bit more carefully. Obviously, he'd missed some signals he should have identified. He would try to be more observant in the future.

He would call her tomorrow, he promised himself, climbing behind the wheel of his sensible sedan. They would have dinner, maybe at that new Thai restaurant everyone was talking about. Restaurant Rita of the *Cedar Ridge Tribune* had given it a glowing recommendation. Jessica liked fine food and a fancy atmosphere; maybe that would soften her up. Then he would make a gracious apology for whatever he'd done to offend her, she would accept—probably with a touch of embarrassment at her uncharacteristic moodiness—and everything would be fine.

Maybe they would spend tomorrow evening experimenting with her new computer. Followed by a few pleasant experiments in her bed.

As for tonight, he supposed he would have to stop at a take-out establishment for dinner. Maybe he would take the food with him to the lab. Since he had the evening free, he might as well spend it productively.

Chapter Two

RICHARD CALLED FOUR TIMES Saturday. Three more times on Sunday. Jessica didn't answer the phone, even when she heard him irritably argue with the answering machine that he *knew* she was there, and he wanted to speak to her personally.

She spent the weekend wrapped in an afghan and her misery. Wearing comfortable, oversize sweats and thick, cushiony socks, she huddled on the sofa with a box of tissues, a box of chocolate-dipped fruit from Valentine Delights, and a book she didn't bother to open.

It wasn't like her to indulge in self-pity, but she figured a woman of thirty who'd just broken a year-long engagement deserved forty-eight hours of moping and sulking. She was determined to go on with her life and put this debacle well behind her—but she would start tomorrow. Today she would nurse her broken heart and mourn her lost dreams.

He'd never even told her he loved her, she thought with a fresh wave of tears. Of course, she hadn't said the words, either. She'd been waiting for him to speak first.

He was a wonderful lover—considerate, thorough, and delightfully, rather surprisingly, creative—but he'd never spent the entire night in her bed. She'd never had the pleasure of sleeping in his arms, or waking with him.

He'd always seemed attracted to her, and he'd acted as though he respected her intelligence and was interested in whatever she had to say. He'd always been impeccably courteous to her—except, of course, for those occasions when he'd become so involved with his work that he'd forgotten dates or arrived breathless and flustered anywhere from fifteen minutes to two hours late. She'd made allowances for those lapses on the basis that brilliant scientists were known to lose track of time. It was to be expected and forgiven from someone who had the potential to make the world a better place.

Overall, their relationship was comfortable, amicable, sensible—and totally depressing for a woman of thirty who had suddenly realized what she was missing.

She deserved more, she told herself staunchly, filching a dark-chocolate-covered cherry from the half-empty silver box beside her. And she would have it.

But today, she would give herself permission to grieve for her broken heart.

HE SHOWED UP ON SUNDAY evening, rapping on her door imperiously. "Jessica, let me in," he insisted, a familiar touch of arrogance in his voice that had never really annoyed her—until now.

"Go away, Richard," she replied through the wooden door. She knew better than to open it. Richard had a way of manipulating her, giving her rather endearingly baffled smiles that always made her melt. Not this time. If she didn't see him, she wouldn't be swayed by him, she figured. She'd almost convinced herself that most of her attraction to him was purely physical. What else could it be, considering how little else he'd given her?

"Jessica, we have to talk. This is ridiculous."

"I'm sorry, but there's nothing left to say. It's over."

"But why?" Just a touch of his genuine bewilderment came through the wooden barrier. "What have I done?"

"It's what you *haven't* done," she answered, sheepishly aware how absurd it was to carry on this conversation in shouts through a door. "And if you can't understand that, then there was never any hope for us in the first place."

She knew she was being unreasonable to expect him to understand without further explanation, but she was still too hurt and too proud to beg for the affection he'd never offered. She knew he was capable of giving it, if he'd truly wanted to. Richard wasn't a stupid or insensitive man. He just refused to open up to her, for whatever his reasons. And she was fed up with it.

"Jessica, I'm worried about you," Richard said, sounding as though he were leaning very close to the door. "This isn't like you. I want to help you."

The doctor had apparently diagnosed a sudden emotional breakdown. A chemical imbalance, perhaps. Nothing that couldn't be controlled with modern medicine and a pharmaceutical miracle or two.

He knew every centimeter, every function, every feature of the human heart. So why was he having such a difficult time identifying a broken one?

"I can't talk to you now," she whispered, hoping her words carried to him. "Please go away."

"Jessica, I insist that you open this door. Talk to me. We can..."

The rest of his words faded as she moved farther from the door. She walked straight into her bedroom and closed herself in, further isolating herself from him. She distantly heard him knock a few more times, heard the irritated chime of the doorbell, and then there was merciful silence as he apparently conceded defeat.

She crawled onto the bed and curled into a fetal position. She still had twelve hours before she was to report to work the next morning, she reminded herself grimly. Twelve more hours to drown in self-pity.

She intended to make the most of every minute.

"YES, DR. LONDON, Jessica is at work today, but she's asked not to be called to the telephone. I'd be happy to take a message for you," the cheery voice at the other end of the line chirped. Although he'd never met this woman, Richard had spoken with her several times when he'd had to call Jessica at work, and he'd always thought she sounded exactly like what she was—an elementary-school secretary.

Although he was beginning to suspect that he was wasting his time, Richard sighed and said, "Please tell her I called and I would like her to call me back. As soon as possible," he added.

"Of course, Dr. London. I'll send the message to her immediately."

Richard started to hang up, but something made him ask, "Have you—er—spoken with Jessica today?"

"Why, yes. We shared a cup of coffee before school started."

"Did she seem all right to you?" he asked awkwardly, uncertain how to word the question.

The secretary seemed a bit taken aback. "I'm not sure what you mean. She seemed fine, no different than any other morning. Why? Has she been ill?" she asked in concern.

"No, no," Richard assured her hastily. "I was just, uh, checking."

"Oh." She still sounded a bit confused. "Is there anything else you want me to tell her, Dr. London?"

"No. Just tell her I called, please." He hung up the phone with the unpleasant suspicion that Jessica wouldn't be calling him back.

It took quite an effort for him to focus on his work that day. He wasn't accustomed to anything interfering with his concentration.

He wasn't sure whether to be irritated with Jessica for doing so now—or seriously concerned about her. He only wished women were as easy to comprehend as his chemical and mathematical calculations.

"YOU'VE BROKEN UP with Richard?" Jessica's friend and fellow teacher, Denise Carpenter, asked that afternoon after the final school bell rang and the children had made their grateful escape. "For real?"

Jessica began to clean off her desk, which gave her an excuse to avoid Denise's intense gaze. "Yes. For real. I gave him back his ring."

"Well, paint a white stripe down my back and call me a skunk," the irrepressible kindergarten teacher marveled.

Jessica rolled her eyes. "Was that colorful outburst supposed to convey sympathy or surprise?"

"A little of both, I guess." Denise dropped the dramatics and looked at her friend in concern. "How are you? Are you okay?"

"Yes, I'm fine. I spent the weekend indulging in an award-winning display of pouting, but now I've gotten that out of my system."

Denise propped one amply rounded hip against a corner of Jessica's desk. "I've been expecting this," she confessed.

Jessica grimaced. "You have? I wish I could say the same. To be honest, the breakup was totally impulsive on my part. There was absolutely no planning or forethought. I just snapped."

"Was it something he said or did?"

"More something he *didn't* say or do."

Denise nodded thoughtfully. "That makes sense. Especially to anyone who's met Richard."

Jessica found herself getting defensive on Richard's behalf—maybe just out of long habit. "He's a brilliant man."

"Of course he is. But I've always thought he'd make a lousy husband. Scientists generally do, I understand."

"You never said anything before."

Denise shrugged. "It was your business. If you loved him, I hoped you'd be happy with him. I just always wondered if you didn't secretly crave a bit more than you got from him. After all, you've been engaged for over a year now and I've still never heard mention of a wedding date."

"I know," Jessica muttered. "Richard never seemed to find the right time to set one."

"Maybe he didn't really want to get married." Blunt as always, Denise didn't bother presenting the possibility tactfully.

Jessica winced. "Trust me, that thought has occurred to me on several occasions lately. It just took me a while to figure it out. Which says something about *my* intelligence, doesn't it?"

Again, Denise shrugged. "Love tends to cloud a woman's judgment," she pronounced. "Trust me, you're talking to an expert on the subject. Remember Peter?"

Jessica managed not to shudder at the reference to Denise's former and utterly unlamented boyfriend. "Er—yeah. I remember."

"Weren't you the one who assured me then that anyone could make a mistake? That the best thing to do is acknowledge it and get on with your life? I'm returning that advice to you now."

Jessica nodded. "I've already decided to do just that. I just...wish it didn't hurt quite so much," she added in a small voice.

Denise touched her hand. "I know. Believe me, I know."

There was a moment of silent, feminine commiseration. And then Jessica drew a deep breath. "Well," she said, closing her desk drawer and picking up her purse. "Thanks for the support, Denise. But don't worry about me. I'll be fine."

"Hey, I know that. You're a survivor, kid. Takes one to know one. So, how would you like to meet an attractive, divorced guy with dimples to die for? He's a friend of Micky's, and he's looking to settle down again. Makes a good living at the electric plant, sings in a country-western band on weekends, dresses cowboy. He's the exact opposite of Richard. Just what you need to get over him."

It wasn't easy, but Jessica managed a smile. "He sounds...interesting, but I'm not really ready to start dating again, Denise. Not yet."

"You know what they say about being thrown off a horse. Gotta climb right back on before you forget how to ride."

"Yes, but I think I'll soak my bruises a little while before climbing back into the saddle. And that's all I can stand of *that* metaphor."

Denise grinned. "Me, too. Still, think about it, okay? You and Jake might actually get along great. He's really a nice guy."

"I'm sure he is. And if I decide I've got a hankering for a cowboy, I'll be sure and let you know, okay? In the meantime, I have to run if I'm going to have time to eat and change for the PTA meeting this evening."

Denise glanced at her watch. "Yeah, me, too. See you later."

Tucking her purse under her arm, Jessica headed for the door. "Later," she promised.

It was amazing, she thought, how much better it felt to share her pain with someone who wasn't afraid of honest emotion, who knew and understood the foibles of the heart. She still hurt—and she suspected that she would for some time to come—but it helped. And she was grateful.

Chapter Three

RICHARD SLAMMED HIS telephone receiver into its cradle late Wednesday afternoon, making the instrument jingle in startled protest. He'd just tried calling Jessica again, and he'd gotten her machine, even though he knew it was long past time for her to be home from school for the day. He suspected that she was there, listening to and ignoring his requests for her to pick up the phone and talk to him.

The situation between them was beginning to look decidedly grim. And he hadn't a clue what he was supposed to do to rectify it.

"Whoa. That sounded remarkably like a temper tantrum. Problems, Rich?"

The booming voice from the doorway made Richard look around with a scowl. He motioned the man into his office. "Come in, Dan. What can I do for you?"

Dan Heckler was an assistant administrator of the renowned Atlanta research hospital where Richard worked. A whiz at budgeting and scheduling, Dan was also able to communicate well with the sometimes-eccentric geniuses on the research staff—a skill that had served him well in his steady rise to the top of the management ladder.

He slid a thin sheaf of papers onto the remarkably cluttered desk in front of Richard. "You forgot to sign your requisitions sheets again. You know we can't do anything about them without your signature."

Richard sighed impatiently and reached for a pen. "We waste more time bothering with insignificant details," he muttered, scrawling his illegible signature across the bottom of one of the triplicate-carbon forms.

"Yeah, well, that's the government for ya. They specialize in insignificant details. So, how are things, Richard? Everything going smoothly with your staff?"

"Yes, everything's fine here at work," Richard replied glumly. "No complaints at the moment."

Dan settled into a chair and studied Richard over steepled fingers. "Anything else bothering you?" he asked casually.

Richard would normally never have responded to such an overture, but he was at his wit's end. "I'm—er—having some problems with my fiancée," he admitted.

Dan nodded in sudden comprehension. "I see. Anything I can do to help? Want to talk about it?"

Richard cleared his throat. "I think she dumped me."

Dan's eyebrows shot up. "Jessica dumped you?" he repeated in disbelief. "You think?"

Richard nodded glumly. "She gave me back my ring."

Dan winced. "That sounds suspiciously like a dump," he conceded. "What did you do?"

"What makes you automatically assume it was something I did?"

"Richard, my friend, you should know by now that the man is *always* the guilty party—at least in the viewpoint of the woman. So—what did you do?"

"Nothing," Richard insisted, lifting his hands in aggrieved bewilderment. "It was her birthday. I gave her a very nice gift. I offered to buy her dinner. And the next thing I knew, she was throwing me out of her apartment. She hasn't really spoken to me since. It's been four days."

Dan cocked his head with a frown. "There must be more to it than that."

"I swear, that's the whole story."

Leaning forward, Dan looked thoughtful. "Okay, let's take this from the beginning. I've been married for twenty-five years, you know. Got four kids—all girls. I've had some experience with the female mind. Maybe I can figure out what went wrong."

"I wish someone could," Richard said, running a hand through his dark hair.

"You said it was her birthday. *Which* birthday?"

Richard thought about it a moment. "Her thirtieth."

Dan groaned. "I see. And you had a date to mark the occasion?"

Richard nodded. "I told her I'd meet her at her apartment at seven. I was exactly on time," he added a bit self-righteously.

"Okay, so you weren't late. That's good. What was she wearing?"

Blinking, Richard stared at the other man, not quite sure he'd understood the question. "What was she wearing?"

Dan nodded. "Yeah. Was it something you'd seen before?"

"Uh—" Richard creased his brow, trying to remember. He wasn't one to pay much attention to clothing. But, come to think of it . . .

"No, I don't think I'd seen it before. It was a dress. Blue, I think. I suppose it was new."

"And you didn't mention it?"

Richard shrugged. "Jess knows I don't care much about fashion."

Dan groaned again. "Anything else different about her?"

Picturing Jessica in his mind—exactly the way she'd looked as she'd ordered him out of her apartment—Richard suddenly nodded. "Her hair was different. Shorter. How did you know?"

Another groan. "Typical thirtieth-birthday behavior. New clothes, new hairstyle. And you didn't notice."

"No, not really."

Shaking his head, Dan probed more deeply. "Okay, this gift you got her. What was it?"

"A computer," Richard answered promptly, confidently. Dan certainly couldn't criticize *that*, he thought smugly. "State-of-the-art."

He was startled to hear another deep groan. "A computer," Dan muttered. "Oh, man, you did screw up, didn't you, buddy?"

"What's wrong with a computer? The thing cost a blasted fortune. Best on the market, though God knows it'll be obsolete next week, if it isn't already, the way the industry's changing and expanding all the time. I told Jessica it was fully upgradable, and that I'd be happy to spend the evening demonstrating its functions."

Dan's head lifted abruptly. "You said you'd spend *that* evening showing her how to work the computer? What about the dinner you said you offered?"

"I suggested we order a pizza."

This time, Dan's groan was even louder.

Finally growing annoyed, Richard snapped, "Would you stop doing that? What did I do that's so bad?"

"Richard, Richard, Richard," Dan chanted in what might have been pity. "You don't have a clue, do you?"

"About what?" Richard asked defensively.

"About romance."

"What does romance have to do with this? It was her birthday. I gave her a present. Isn't that what I was expected to do?"

"It isn't what's expected of you. It's what you give voluntarily," Dan lectured. "A woman always wants romance, Richard. Especially at a sensitive time like her thirtieth birthday."

"You keep repeating her age. What does that have to do with this?"

Dan sighed deeply. "You really *are* clueless, aren't you?"

Richard growled in frustration. "I don't know what you're talking about."

Taking a deep breath, Dan launched into a careful lecture about women and what they expect from a man. Flattery, he said. Sweet gestures. Candlelit dinners.

Romance with a capital *R*.

After several more minutes of advice along those lines, Richard interrupted the oration. "You don't know Jessica very well. She isn't like that. She's much too practical and levelheaded to expect such nonsense."

"Trust me. She's a woman. She wants it all."

"Surely she knows by now that I'm not comfortable with such folderol. It's never seemed to bother her before."

"Oh, it's bothered her. She's just never mentioned it before. She was probably hoping to change you. Women just seem to love trying to change a guy. It's sort of like the pleasure they take in redecorating. They like to take credit for the improvements."

Skeptical, Richard shook his head. "That certainly doesn't sound like the Jessica I've known for two years."

"Twenty-five years of marriage, remember? And, as you know, my wife is vice president of a bank. She's no simpering bimbo, but she still expects—no, she still *demands* that sort of attention. Especially on her birthday and anniversaries. And Valentine's Day," he added. "Valentine's Day is a big one.

"Oh, hell," Dan said suddenly, glancing at his calendar watch. "It's only two days off. I'd better start shopping," he mused.

But Richard quickly put the artifically-sweetened holiday out of his mind, and asked doubtfully, "You really think that's the sort of thing Jessica expected for her birthday? Romance?"

Dan nodded solemnly. "I'd bet on it. You hurt her feelings, Rich. Women have very sensitive feelings."

Exhaling, Richard leaned back in his chair. "Romance," he repeated in a murmur. He vaguely remembered Jessica mentioning that there had been something he *hadn't* done, rather than the reverse. Maybe this was what she'd meant.

He shrugged. "I can do romance. If it's absolutely necessary."

"I think, in this case, it's absolutely necessary. If you don't want to lose Jessica, of course."

"I have no intention of losing Jessica," Richard replied flatly. "What should I do?"

"Woo her on Valentine's Day with gifts and sweet nothings. Try chocolate. Those fancy hand-dipped ones, preferably. And roses. At least a dozen. Red ones. Women simply can't resist chocolates and roses. Diamonds and perfume are always good, too. I can't tell you how many times I've gotten out of the doghouse by giving them to Betty."

"It sounds ridiculous, but if flowers and chocolates and diamonds and perfumes will patch things up with Jessica, I'll get them." Richard shook his head. "Life would be so much simpler if women thought more like men."

"Now, don't start playing Henry Higgins on me. I'm telling you, buddy, women aren't at all like men. And, on the whole, I thank God for it."

"Henry Higgins?" Richard inquired blankly.

"You know. 'Enry 'Iggins. Rex Harrison. *My Fair Lady.*"

"Oh, yes." A vague memory flitted through Richard's mind. "Theater. Based on the Pygmalion tale."

"Yeah. You might try scoring theatre tickets some night, too. Women love to dress up and go to the theater."

"You're being awfully inclusive in your evaluation of women," Richard complained. "Surely they aren't all alike."

Dan pushed himself out of his chair. "Try reading pop-psychology books sometime. According to them, women are from Venus and men are from Mars. There are whole sections in the bookstores devoted to defining the differences.''

Thoroughly perplexed, Richard rubbed his chin and decided to stop at a bookstore on his way to the jeweler and the chocolate shop. Maybe he should spend a bit more time researching this relationship thing so that he and Jessica could avoid problems like this in the future, he mused. He might not be an expert when it came to women, but if there was one thing he *was* good at, it was research.

Chapter Four

JESSICA HAD PLAYGROUND duty during lunch Thursday. Huddling into her jacket—why didn't the children ever seem to mind the nip in the breeze as they raced and tumbled so happily about her?—she tried not to think of the date or its significance. She'd been trying not to think of it all day.

She'd failed.

Her first thought that morning had been that it was February 13. That she and Richard had met exactly two years ago today, at the annual charity ball sponsored each Valentine's Day eve by the Cedar Ridge Historical Society. Neither of them had attended with an escort—both had been in the company of other friends—and they'd drifted together during the course of the evening. Richard had asked for her number before they'd parted. The next day he'd called to ask her for their first date.

They would have attended the ball again tonight, had things worked out differently on her birthday. Jessica had even bought a gorgeous red gown for the occasion, the same day she'd bought the blue dress she'd worn the night she'd ended their engagement. She wondered if she would ever want to put either of the lovely dresses on again, or if the memories associated with them would always be too painful. Maybe she should return the evening gown for a refund, since she hadn't worn it and probably never would.

"Hey, Jessie."

Roused from her melancholy reverie, Jessica turned to Denise with a forced smile. "Hey."

"How's it going?"

Jessica shrugged, keeping a close eye on two second-graders who seemed to be squaring off for a shouting-and-shoving match. She would step in to break it up if anything actually happened, but she decided to see if the boys could work the problem out themselves, first. They'd been conducting an experimental conflict-avoidance program in all classes recently, and this was a good chance to see firsthand if the kids had been paying attention.

"It's going okay," she answered her friend. "Cool today, isn't it?"

"Mmm." But Denise wasn't interested in discussing the weather. "What are you doing tonight?" she asked, instead.

"I don't know. I have no plans. Why?"

"Let's go out and do something, okay? I don't want you sitting home brooding tonight."

"I'm not going to sit home and brood."

Denise looked considerably less than reassured by Jessica's indignant denial. "Right. You're going out with me for some laughs," she said, her expression brooking no argument. "There's a new club close to my place. I've been there a couple of times. It's nice.

Good music, friendly atmosphere, no hassle from the cruisin' Romeos. Meet me there at seven, okay?''

Jessica dug her hands more deeply into her pockets. ''I appreciate this, Denise, really, but I'm not in the mood for a club tonight.''

''Tough. Consider yourself kidnapped. Meet me there or I'm comin' after ya, pal. Got that?''

Jessica couldn't help but smile at the other woman's exaggerated, tough-guy drawl. ''Oh, you are, are you?''

''You bet. And I'll bring the big guns with me to convince you, if I have to. How'd ya like me to show up with Amberly, hmm?''

Shuddering, Jessica shook her head quickly. ''Not that. Anything but that.''

Amberly Cutlip was the school counselor. She'd graduated from college a year earlier, determined to change the world to fit her homecoming-queen, sorority-girl, cheerleader-inspired ideals. Her intentions were good, but her methods were so mercilessly gung-ho, so annoyingly cheery, that many of the teachers and even some of the schoolchildren, went out of their way to avoid calling themselves to her attention. Her conversation came straight out of pop-psych textbooks, her rose-tinted optimism was cloying enough to gag a saint, and her unflagging determination would have made a steamroller proud.

Fortunately, Jessica knew Denise's threat was an empty one. Denise couldn't be with Amberly for more than a few minutes at a time without threatening to stuff her mouth with a pom-pom. Amberly thought Denise's mutterings were hysterically amusing, of course. She had no idea how serious Denise actually was.

Denise grinned at the look on Jessica's face. "So, you going to go along quietly?" she demanded, sensing victory. "Or do I slip a word to Amberly that poor Ms. Patterson is having emotional problems and could probably benefit from some concerned counseling?"

"Do that and die."

Denise laughed, then abruptly sobered. "Do this for me, okay, Jess? So I won't have to worry about you tonight. Meet me at the club and let's have some fun."

Jessica sighed and surrendered. Maybe this was a good idea, after all, she decided. She was really getting tired of sitting home and moping over Richard. And, despite her denials, she knew that was exactly what she would do tonight if she went home alone.

"All right, I'll do it," she said boldly, lifting her chin. "Seven, you said?"

Delighted, Denise nodded and gave her directions to the club.

VALENTINE DELIGHTS specialized in exotic coffees, fancy desserts and hand-dipped chocolates. Because it was close to Jessica's Cedar Ridge apartment and open until midnight, Richard and Jessica had been frequent customers. They'd lingered there over cappuccinos and dessert after many of the social functions required by his professional prominence, sharing their opinions of the events and the people who had attended them.

Richard had enjoyed those peaceful interludes in his otherwise hectic schedule. He didn't want to believe that there would be no more such evenings with Jessica. In fact, he simply refused to acknowledge the possibility.

He thought he knew what she wanted now. And he would do everything he could to have her back in his life.

She was everything he'd hoped to find in a mate. Intelligent, perceptive, committed to her career in education, a well-read and interesting conversationalist. As for her physical attractiveness—well, that was a definite bonus, as far as he was concerned.

He'd been drawn to her from the first moment they'd met, two years ago today, and he had been very pleased to quickly discover that there was much more to her than a pretty face and a nice figure. He'd known right away that they were a suitable match, and he'd characteristically wasted no time in formalizing the alliance with the traditional diamond ring.

He had no intention of letting her slip away from him now, especially over something so trivial as a lapse in communication.

From his usual position behind the counter, Papa Valentine looked up when Richard entered the coffee shop Thursday afternoon. "Dr. London," he said with a big smile of welcome. "How nice to see you."

An unconventional young man with an odd haircut and a gold ring in his left nostril bustled around the shop, serving the few customers occupying tables at this slow time of the afternoon. "Eh, what's up, Doc?" he called out in a Bugs Bunny accent. It was the way he always greeted Richard.

Rudy fancied himself a comic. He even performed quite frequently in local comedy clubs. Jessica had talked Richard into going with her to watch him one evening a few months ago. Jessica had laughed delightedly at Rudy's almost-hyperactive stream-of-consciousness absurdities. Richard had admitted that most of the humor had sailed right over his head, which had been a galling admission for a man who prided himself on his intellect.

Richard murmured appropriate responses to both greetings. He crossed the warm-wood and green-plant-decorated shop to stop in front of one of the enormous glass cases that held samplings of the many delectables available to customers. He focused his attention on the enticing display of chocolates.

Dan had assured him that women loved chocolates, and Richard remembered that Jessica had often selected a few for herself when they had dropped by. He blinked at the assortment of fillings, trying to recall which ones she'd chosen.

"May I help you, Dr. London?" Still slim and fit in his seventies, his head bald except for a fringe of snowy white hair, Papa Valentine practically exuded charm and goodwill. Jessica made no secret of her fondness for the man, and Richard admired Valentine for his dedication to his work.

Richard motioned toward the chocolates case. "I want to buy chocolates for Jessica."

Valentine's face lit with an approving smile. "Ah. A gift for Valentine's Day?"

Richard nodded, dragging his attention from what seemed to be a rather odd display of little jars that apparently held something called Chocolate Body Paint. Fancy little brushes were attached to each jar with a burgundy ribbon. *How bizarre,* he mused, trying to imagine Jessica's reaction to that particular gift. He thought he'd better stick with the more traditional offerings.

He pointed toward a display of silver-foil boxes marked in burgundy script with the store name. "I'd like them packed in one of those fancy boxes. Women like that sort of thing on this occasion, don't they?"

Valentine chuckled. "You don't exactly sound enthusiastic about Valentine's Day customs, Dr. London."

Richard shrugged. "Seems rather contrived to me. Still, if women like it . . ."

"Most of them do. If the event is celebrated sincerely, of course."

Ignoring the delicately veiled warning, Richard studied the chocolates more closely. "There are so many kinds. Do you know which ones Jess likes?"

"I believe so. She stops in every so often for a small treat. I'll pack you a nice assortment. It's a good thing you came in today. We just stocked the supplies again. Last-minute rushes tomorrow will limit my selections a bit.''

''Yes, that's what my secretary warned me. She said there's usually not much left on the big day itself, so I made a special effort to come in this afternoon. There are stores closer to my office than this one, of course, but I know Jessica has a particular fondness for your chocolates.''

Valentine beamed. ''We do take pride in our quality. I use my grandmother's secret recipes, you know.''

Richard nodded. ''You'd best make it a big box. I'm in the doghouse,'' he explained glumly, remembering Dan's wry lecture.

Valentine seemed to be fighting a smile. ''And you're hoping to redeem yourself with Valentine's Day chocolates?''

''Chocolates have long been associated with romance, of course,'' Richard commented, having done some research on the subject. ''Chocolate contains phenylethylamine, a neurochemical that simulates the endorphin release that triggers the midbrain to produce dopamine. Dopamine, as you probably know, is a natural amphetamine. It is this chemical reaction that many scientists believe may be linked to the uncomfortable physical sensations that accompany initial infatuation. Of course, as the relationship progresses, it is oxytocin that becomes more dominant.''

Looking a bit blank, Valentine frowned. "Oxy-what?"

"Oxytocin. It produces what is known as the 'cuddle reflex,' or the gentle attachment linked to mother-child bonding. Much easier on the digestion and temperament than the more forceful neurochemicals, of course."

"Uh, Dr. London, perhaps it would be best if you don't mention these clinical observations when you present Ms. Patterson with the chocolates," Valentine advised wryly.

"Of course not. That wouldn't be romantic."

Valentine gave what might have been a cross between a laugh and a cough. "No," he agreed. "I think the gift should speak for itself."

"That's not all I'm giving her," Richard confided, pleased with all he'd accomplished that day. "I had my secretary order a dozen red roses for me to pick up tomorrow, and she spent her lunch hour helping me select a diamond necklace and a perfume that's supposed to be quite popular. She assured me that any woman would forgive a man who showed up at her doorstep on Valentine's Day carrying all that."

Valentine didn't look particularly impressed, Richard noted. "Expensive gifts are nice, of course, but—"

"It's romantic," Richard interrupted to explain patiently. "A friend convinced me that I haven't been romantic enough in my courtship, so I'm going to prove that I can be as romantic as the next guy.

"I've given some thought to this Valentine's Day phenomenon and I've concluded that it's a simple formula, really. Traditional gifts for a traditional occasion. I should have realized that sooner. Though I can't imagine why Jessica didn't just tell me what she wanted, rather than expect me to find out for myself. She seemed content enough to simply go out for dinner last Valentine's Day. Apparently, there's something about a thirtieth birthday that changes a woman's expectations," he added, still bewildered by the significance of that number.

Valentine wore an expression that might have been pity—or maybe it was just masculine understanding, Richard decided. "Dr. London, Jessica is a person, not a laboratory experiment to be approached with a tried-and-true formula," he said gently. "True romance is much more than superficial gestures."

Richard smiled. "Yes, well, I'm sure this will all work out. Jessica's really a very sensible woman, and we've had an excellent relationship to this point."

"You have always seemed to be a good match," Valentine agreed slowly. "You seem to enjoy talking to each other when you come in for coffee and dessert."

"Of course we do. This is all a simple misunderstanding. I suppose it happens to every couple at some point. Now that I've realized what I've done wrong, it should be an easy enough matter to rectify the situation."

Although the older man still looked doubtful, he didn't try to dispense any further advice. He busied himself, instead, in preparing a huge, particularly elaborate box of his finest hand-dipped chocolates.

Richard didn't even blink at the outrageous price. He'd already concluded that Valentine's Day was a rather expensive occasion, particularly coming so soon after Jessica's birthday. Fortunately, he had plenty of money. And he didn't mind sharing it with the woman with whom he still fully intended to spend the rest of his life.

Tomorrow, he told himself as he left the shop with a distracted wave of farewell to Papa Valentine and Rudy, the clerk. Tomorrow he would give Jessica the best Valentine's Day she'd ever had. And then they could put this nonsense of a breakup behind them.

He glanced at her apartment building as he walked to his car. He didn't see any lights burning in the windows. Had she gone out tonight? His electronic organizer had reminded him earlier that the Valentine Ball was being held tonight. He hadn't really expected Jessica to attend without him—but perhaps she had? After all, she'd gotten the tickets, and they were still in her possession, as far as he knew. Maybe—

Maybe she'd given the extra one to another man. Another date.

His fingers tightened spasmodically around the delicate silver box of chocolates, slightly crimping one edge. He forced himself to relax them before he ruined the pretty packaging.

Jealousy wasn't his usual style, he reminded himself. He'd never considered himself a particularly possessive man.

But then, he'd taken for granted that Jessica would always be his, that there would be no other men while she wore his ring. It seemed he'd taken quite a bit for granted during the past two years.

He would be very relieved to have everything settled—to have that old feeling of security back. He'd missed her during the past week.

The thought of a lifetime without her was something he didn't even want to imagine.

Chapter Five

IT WAS LATE WHEN Jessica returned home that evening—later than she'd intended, since tomorrow was a workday.

She dragged her hand through her hair as she locked her apartment door and walked slowly toward her bedroom. She was still more than half annoyed with Denise. She had been all evening, ever since she'd arrived at the designated club expecting to spend a couple of hours alone with her friend, only to discover that she'd been set up. Denise hadn't been alone. Her boyfriend, Micky, had been there. As had Micky's friend, Jake, the singing cowboy.

Sending Denise a look that had promised retribution at the earliest opportunity, Jessica had somehow managed to be gracious. Jake was a nice guy. Attractive, in a lanky, sandy-haired way. Amusing, with his quick wit and slow drawl. Charming enough to make Jessica relax despite the awkwardness of the situation.

The whole point of the evening had been to keep her from thinking of Richard. But Denise's scheme had backfired. Although Jessica had smiled and conversed and even danced a couple of times with Jake, she'd spent the whole time comparing him to Richard and knowing that this man would never replace the one she'd sent away.

She was beginning to doubt that any man would ever fully replace Richard in her heart. She really was pathetic, she told herself half angrily. She'd broken up with Richard because she'd wanted something more, only to discover that he was all she wanted.

Oh, she still wanted more. She wanted it all. But she wanted it *with* Richard, not without him.

With some trepidation, she checked her answering machine. She expected to find at least one more querulous message from Richard. After all, he'd called her at least once a day all week, still insisting that she was being unreasonable. He seemed convinced that he could make her change her mind about ending their engagement, even though he'd offered nothing more than he'd ever given her. Obviously, he still hadn't even realized there was anything missing.

Maybe it was her secret fear that he *could* change her mind that made her continue to avoid talking to him, cowardly as her actions might seem. But there was no message on her machine this evening. Not even a hang-up.

Richard hadn't called.

She bit her lip, staring at the machine as though expecting it to explain the unexpected silence. Maybe he'd been too busy at work to call. Maybe he was giving her a bit more time to miss him before he tried again.

Or maybe he'd finally gotten the message and conceded defeat. If, as she suspected, he hadn't really wanted to get married, anyway, it was possible that he'd put his bruised pride aside and convinced himself that it was best this way.

She'd occasionally wondered if she even crossed his mind when she wasn't with him; maybe he hadn't even thought about her today. Maybe the significance of the date—their anniversary, of sorts—hadn't even occurred to him. Maybe he'd already written her off as one of his failed experiments and moved on to the next "project."

Maybe he would never call her again.

Since that was exactly what she'd convinced herself she wanted, she couldn't imagine why there were tears running down her face.

JESSICA WAS DETERMINED not to let the date get to her again on Friday. Okay, so it was February 14. Valentine's Day. Big deal. Romance could not be dictated by a calendar and a few greeting-card companies. There was no need for her to be depressed just because she no longer had anyone special with whom to share the event.

Not that she would notice much difference, she told herself glumly. Last year Richard hadn't even known it was Valentine's Day until she'd reminded him. He'd taken her out for a nice dinner, but only because they'd had a standing dinner date for Wednesday evenings, the one night when neither of them had regular commitments.

Once he'd become aware of his lapse, Richard had covered quickly by claiming the dinner had been intended all along to mark the occasion—he'd even ceremoniously bought her a rose from a woman at a sidewalk stand outside the restaurant—but Jessica had known the truth. He hadn't remembered. It simply hadn't been important to him.

So, as far as Jessica was concerned, February 14 was just another day. Nothing at all special.

Unfortunately, the rest of the world seemed to disagree with her assessment.

"Happy Valentine's Day, Ms. Patterson," her first-grade class chimed as she walked into the room that morning. Several rushed up to her desk to hand her cute little gifts and inexpensive, mass-produced "To My Teacher" valentines featuring popular cartoon characters.

She thanked them all warmly, and gently urged them back to their seats. She spent the rest of the day trying to hold their attention, when all they could think about was the party they would have that afternoon to exchange cards and enjoy the heart-shaped treats and red punch provided by the classroom mothers.

A steady stream of flowers arrived at the office during the day. Each lucky recipient made sure all the other teachers and staff had the opportunity to admire her floral tribute.

One of the sixth-grade teachers, Annie Tucker, was wearing a pair of tiny diamond earrings that her husband had given her at breakfast that morning. She seemed as pleased by the glittery specks as if they'd been massive rocks suitable for Elizabeth Taylor.

Jessica knew it wasn't the value of the earrings that had so pleased her co-worker. It was the love and consideration that had accompanied the gift. Despite her determination to remain detached, she found herself swallowing a lump in her throat when Annie went on and on during lunch about how hard her construction-worker husband had worked and saved to afford the little diamonds, and how tenderly he'd presented them.

Annie had something with her Bill that Jessica had never found with Richard, Jessica realized. Intimacy. Shared dreams. True love.

By the time the final bell rang that afternoon, Jessica had given up on trying to keep order in her classroom. Wired with the excitement of any change in the usual routine—along with a megadose of sugar from their valentine snacks—the kids practically bounced out of the room. One tiny girl with long red hair and enormous blue eyes paused in the classroom doorway, then ran over to throw her arms around Jessica's waist.

"Happy Valentine's Day, Ms. Patterson," the child said sweetly.

First graders tended to be an affectionate and demonstrative lot, so Jessica was accustomed to impulsive hugs. This one, however, almost brought tears to her eyes. Would she ever have a child of her own to cuddle?

"Thank you, Caitlin," she managed to say. "Run along, now. You'll miss your bus."

"'Kay. See you Monday."

"See you Monday," Jessica echoed, thinking of the long, lonely weekend that stretched between now and then.

Denise entered when all the children had gone. She rather nervously cleared her throat, obviously expecting a cool greeting. "Er—have you forgiven me yet?"

Jessica shrugged. "I know you meant well, Denise, but I wish you'd just told me what you had planned. It really was unfair of you to catch me off guard that way."

"I'm sorry." Denise looked genuinely contrite. "I acted on impulse. I thought once you'd met Jake, and saw how nice he was, you might give him a chance."

"Jake is very nice, Denise. I liked him. But I'm just not interested in dating him."

"Or anyone else, except Richard," Denise commented.

Jessica winced. "Okay, so I'm an idiot. I'm trying to get over that. And I will, eventually. Just don't...push me any more, okay?"

"I won't," Denise promised. "And I really am sorry about last night."

Jessica never could stay mad at Denise for long. "Apology accepted," she said lightly. "And I *did* have a nice time. I just wish he hadn't kept crooning 'Let's Fall to Pieces Together' in my ear.'' She smiled wryly. "But you were right. It was much better than sitting at home alone moping. Just don't do it again.''

Denise solemnly crossed her heart. "How're you doing?" she asked then, with the melting sympathy one would display toward the recently bereaved. "Are you okay?"

"Of course," Jessica replied briskly. "Why wouldn't I be?"

"Well, it is Valentine's Day—"

"Yes, and I've had a lovely one. Did you see the little heart-shaped satin pillow Danny Hooper's mother embroidered for me? It says 'World's Greatest Teacher.' Isn't that sweet?"

Denise still looked a bit wary after Jessica's reprimand, but couldn't seem to help saying, "I know this day can't be any easier for you than yesterday was."

Jessica shrugged. "Richard never made a fuss over Valentine's Day. I'm sure it seemed quite foolish to him."

"You'll be okay this evening?"

"Of course. There's a program on the arts-and-entertainment channel that I'd like to watch this evening, and I plan to order Chinese take-out for a lazy evening in front of the TV. I'll be fine."

"Fine. So, how about if we get together tomorrow afternoon? Just the two of us this time, I promise. We can check out some of those cute little boutiques on your street and pop into Valentine Delights for something sinful and fattening afterward. Maybe see an early movie at the discount theater."

Jessica hesitated.

"Please," Denise added. "I need to know you aren't still mad at me about last night. I want to make it up to you."

Jessica would have been a real heel to turn her down after that. She smiled. "I'd like that."

She held her smile as she watched her friend rush off to prepare for a romantic evening with Micky. It was only when she was alone that she allowed her cheerful expression to fade into an unhappy frown.

JESSICA ARRIVED HOME only a few minutes later than usual. She checked the answering machine. No messages again.

She sighed and went into her bedroom, where she stripped out of the cheery red-and-white pantsuit she'd worn for the class party. She replaced it with her baggy black sweats and white socks. It didn't really matter what she wore this evening, she thought glumly. The only person likely to see her would be the delivery person from the Chinese take-out.

On her way into the living room, she stopped by the washer to put in a load of towels. Might as well accomplish a few things during the evening, she decided, especially since she would be spending the next afternoon shopping with Denise.

Doing laundry and eating take-out in front of the TV. Alone. On Valentine's Day.

The tears she'd been holding back all day suddenly flooded her eyes and rolled down her cheeks. She was furious with herself for crying over her broken engagement again—after all, she'd spent all last weekend doing so and she'd intended that to be the end of it. But she couldn't seem to help it.

She missed Richard desperately. So much, at times, that it was tempting to call him and beg him to come back to her—to be willing to take whatever crumbs of affection he deigned to toss her way.

But, no. Remembering the glow of happiness in Annie Tucker's eyes, the rather smug satisfaction of a woman who had no doubt that she was well and truly loved, Jessica knew she could never settle for less, now that she'd identified what had been missing between herself and Richard.

She drew a deep breath, mopped determinedly at her eyes and headed for the telephone. She wasn't particularly hungry, but she was going to order all her favorite dishes, curl up beneath her afghan and have a lovely self-indulgent evening alone.

She would survive this, she told herself for at least the thousandth time. She wouldn't waste much more time moping over Richard London and futilely wishing things had been different between them.

As for Richard—well, he was probably already over her. Probably involved in a new, potentially world-changing research project. Still a bit bewildered, perhaps, about her illogical behavior, but getting on with his life.

Just as Jessica intended to do.

With another touch of bitterness, she told herself that she'd never really made much difference in his life, anyway. He hadn't allowed her to. He rarely talked about his past, never talked about his innermost feelings, gave her not even a glimpse inside him. It wouldn't take him long to find an attractive woman to accompany him to his obligatory social functions, and to be available when he wanted a bedmate.

She told herself that it wouldn't actually kill her if she ran into him with another woman on his arm. It would just *feel* like a knife had been rammed into her heart.

She was still sniffling into a tissue when her doorbell rang half an hour later. She glanced at her watch. The dinner had arrived earlier than she'd expected, considering the occasion. She snatched up the bills she'd laid on the coffee table and moved toward the door, automatically running a hand through her hair and pasting on an artificial smile. She was always very careful about confirming who was at her door before she opened it, but this time she simply forgot. Maybe because there was so much more on her mind.

"You made good time," she said brightly, opening the door. "I wasn't expecting you for another—"

Her voice died away.

Dr. Richard London stood just outside her door, impeccably dressed in a dark suit and a gorgeous tie, his thick hair, for once, immaculately combed. His arms were loaded down with a dozen red roses wrapped in green florist's paper, an enormous silver box tied with burgundy ribbon, and another gift beautifully wrapped in reds and golds.

He'd been smiling when she first opened the door, but her words had made him frown.

"You were expecting someone else?" he asked coolly.

Chapter Six

JESSICA STARED BLANKLY at Richard, speechless for a moment. She honestly hadn't expected to see him tonight. She couldn't for the life of her think of anything to say.

She belatedly remembered what he'd asked. "Er— I ordered Chinese," she explained automatically. "I thought you were the delivery guy."

Richard's frown cleared. He smiled again. "Oh. Good. You look very nice tonight, Jessica. New outfit?"

Bemused, she glanced down at the baggy black sweats. "Hardly."

"It looks nice on you, anyway. And your hair. You've cut it, haven't you? Very attractive."

She had a sudden impulse to peek behind him and see if someone was feeding him lines à la Cyrano. Richard never commented on her clothing or hairstyles. Flattery was simply not part of his conversational repertoire.

"Yes, I really like that style," he continued briskly. "It emphasizes your beautiful—" he peered at her face "—blue eyes."

She shook her head, rousing herself from the near trance she'd fallen into. "What are you doing here, Richard?"

"It's Valentine's Day," he pointed out cheerfully. "I couldn't let the occasion pass without fanfare."

She eyed him suspiciously. "You always have before."

"I won't do so again," he assured her. "May I come in?"

"Richard—"

"Only for a little while," he interrupted entreatingly. "I promise I'll leave as soon as you like, if you'll only give me a few moments of your time."

It wasn't like Richard to beg, either. He wasn't exactly doing so now, but he'd come closer than she'd ever expected. She found herself unable to shut the door in his face.

Warily, she stepped aside. "All right. But only for a few moments. I have plans for the evening."

His eyebrow lifted. "You're going out?"

It was none of his business, of course, but she shrugged and answered. "No. I have things to do here. And I'd like to get started, so say what you came to say and then go."

He almost scowled at her blunt tone, but then he seemed to catch himself and he smiled and nodded, instead. "All right. Thank you. Oh, these are for you." He thrust the sheaf of red roses into her arms.

The rich, heavy scent wafted upward, seducing her nose. "They're beautiful," she murmured, softening despite herself. "I've always loved red roses."

"Yes, I knew that," Richard said, although she had no idea of whether he was telling the truth or bluffing again.

"I'll put them in water. I don't want them to wilt."

She busied herself for the next few minutes finding a vase and carefully arranging the blooms in it. Her hands were shaking. She had to concentrate to keep from spilling the water all over herself.

Why was Richard behaving this way? Was it real or an act? Could it be that he'd finally understood what she wanted—what she needed from him? Would he finally tell her the words she'd waited so long to hear?

She found herself holding her breath as she rejoined him, carrying the crystal vase between both hands. She set the vase on the table. "They really are beautiful."

"I'm glad you like them. I specifically asked Marie to order the most perfect blooms available. Beautiful flowers for a beautiful lady," he added with a melting smile that almost made the corny line sound sincere.

Marie. His secretary. Swallowing, Jessica told herself that many men asked their secretaries to order flowers for them. Richard probably hadn't even known how to go about it.

"I have something else for you," he said, holding out the silver box. "Papa Valentine's chocolates. He personally selected your favorites."

She took the box with a murmured, "Thank you." Papa Valentine had "personally selected" her favorites. Richard, of course, probably hadn't known what her favorites were. She could feel the tension slowly building inside her again.

As soon as she set the box of chocolates on the table beside the roses, Richard handed her another gift. "I hope you like this," he said. "I've been told it's quite popular."

Told by whom? she wondered as she peeled away the paper to reveal an expensive and instantly recognizable perfume. The person he'd sent to buy it for her? "Er—thank you. Richard, I—"

He didn't give her a chance to finish her sentence. He took her into his arms before she'd realized his intention. "Happy Valentine's Day, Jessica," he said. And then he covered her mouth with his.

Jessica could literally feel her resistance melting as Richard's mouth moved against hers. He'd always been a fabulous kisser. On a physical level, they had always been entirely compatible.

He drew her closer, murmuring something that might have been her name. Oh, he was good. There was just a hint of a catch in his voice—as if he'd missed her almost as badly as she'd missed him this past week.

He kissed her again, from a new angle this time. His hands slid slowly up her body, reacquainting themselves with her shape through the thick fleece of her sweatsuit. His tongue slipped between her lips, teasing her with quick, flickering thrusts that made her ache for deeper penetration.

She kept telling herself she should stop this. Nothing had changed. A few presents and mind-blowing kisses couldn't alter the fact that he didn't love her the way she so desperately needed to be loved. Her happiness and security couldn't be bought with the most expensive gifts or the most satisfying sex.

But, oh, could he kiss. . . .

"Jessica," he murmured against her lips, sliding his hands down to cup her bottom and hold her more closely against his own rapidly hardening body. "I've missed you. I want you so badly."

She knew he wanted her. He'd never given her reason to doubt it. But being wanted was very different from being loved.

She tried to speak over the rapid hammering of her pulse in her throat. "Richard, I— We need—"

"We need to talk, I know," he interrupted, kissing her eyelids, her nose, her chin. "And we will. I understand now what I was doing wrong. And I'll change, Jess, I swear. But for now, let me just hold you a moment longer. You feel so good in my arms."

He rubbed his lips slowly across hers, the erotic friction making her shiver helplessly in reaction. "You're so beautiful," he continued. "You taste so sweet."

He was flattering her again. Did he really mean it, or were they only seductive words to him? Could he tell by looking at her that his effort was working? That he was so very close to shattering the emotional barriers she'd worked so hard to build against him?

"Oh, Richard," she murmured weakly, her fingers clenching in the luxurious fabric of his suit jacket. "What are you doing to me now?"

"Romancing you," he answered promptly, his firm mouth curving into one of those knee-and-willpower-melting smiles. "I've recently realized it's something I've too often neglected before."

Alarmed, she bit her lower lip. *Romancing* her? That was what he'd set out to do this evening? Could he possibly know how calculated it sounded when he said it like that?

"Oh, I almost forgot something." Still smiling, he set her a few inches away from him and reached inside his jacket to pull out another gift. A small, thin, square box this time, wrapped in gold foil and decorated with a heart-shaped red label inscribed with the name of a prominent Atlanta jeweler.

"Another gift?" she protested, shaking her head. "Really, Richard, you shouldn't have. This is too much."

"Open it," he urged her, looking almost boyishly eager.

Unable to resist that look, she swallowed and carefully peeled the paper away.

The diamond pendant inside was heavy and heart-shaped. Each exquisite stone caught the overhead light and reflected it in a glittering rainbow. Jessica had never seen anything more stunning.

She gasped. "Oh, my."

He leaned over to kiss her cheek. "Just a little token of my affection for you," he murmured.

Affection. The term sounded painfully tepid.

She wanted very badly to believe that Richard was offering more than a heart-shaped necklace. She hoped that what he was really giving her was his own heart. But he still hadn't said the words.

"I . . . don't know what to say," she replied.

He was watching her a bit anxiously now, obviously trying to read her expression. "Do you like it?"

"It's incredibly beautiful, of course. But—what does it mean?" she asked, taking her courage in her hands and looking straight into his eyes as she asked the question.

He seemed a bit taken aback. "What does it *mean*? Why, it's a Valentine's Day gift. Like the others."

Her heart sank. She thought she had her answer now. "Flowers, chocolates, perfume and diamonds. You didn't forget a thing, did you?"

He frowned. "I've been told that they're all traditional Valentine's Day offerings," he agreed, looking a bit wary.

Oh, yes, she understood now. He was going through the motions again, just as he'd done for her birthday. He'd considered himself obligated to acknowledge Valentine's Day, and he had done so. He'd performed a bit *too* perfectly, in fact. He'd given her a Valentine's Day cliché.

Through a thin haze of fresh tears, she looked down at the sparkling necklace. "It really is a lovely pendant. Did you find it yourself?"

"I had help, of course," he said, seeming to choose his words carefully. "Marie shopped with me. I know so little about jewelry that I thought it best to ask advice from a woman."

Jessica nodded. "And the perfume? Did she select that, as well?"

"Well, obviously I know even less about perfumes than I do jewelry. She said it was one of the most popular scents currently on the market. I trusted her judgment."

"Did you even smell it before you paid for it?" Jessica asked in a sad whisper.

He slowly shook his head, the light fading from his eyes as he sensed her displeasure. "Perfumes all smell alike to me, on the whole. Marie and the salesclerk said it smelled particularly nice, and I'm sure they're right. If you don't care for it, of course you may return it."

Roses ordered by telephone from a florist, perfume and diamonds chosen by his secretary, chocolates hand-selected by Papa Valentine. Why had he bothered to bring them himself when he could have sent a delivery person? The studied impersonality of it all hurt her deeply.

She wanted very badly to accept his gestures at face value. After all, he was trying, in his own way, and part of her—the part of her that still loved him—was touched by his efforts. But she knew the relationship was doomed to failure as long as Richard was just dutifully providing the outward illusion of romance, and not the reality.

How would she ever know if he really loved her when all he would do was mouth a script society had written for him?

She closed the hinged lid of the jewelry box. And then she picked up the bottle of expensive perfume and reached out to place both gifts in his hands.

"Thank you very much, but I can't accept these. As sweet as it was of you to buy them for me, it wouldn't be right for me to keep them now that we aren't seeing each other anymore," she said, trying desperately to sound detached and polite.

He backed away, refusing to take the items from her. "What do you mean, we aren't seeing each other anymore? Of course, we are. We're engaged. We're going to be married."

"No," she countered, her voice gentle. "We aren't. I'm sorry, Richard, but the engagement truly ended a week ago. I haven't changed my mind. And I haven't lost it, either," she added before he could make the accusation.

"If you don't like these choices, we can take them back and get something else. I know I'm lousy at that sort of thing, but I did my best."

"It's not that. I'm sure you went to a great deal of trouble to get these things for me, and I appreciate it. I really do. But it doesn't change anything."

He threw up his arms, his voice erupting in a burst of frustration. "Damn it, Jessica, why are you doing this to us? What the *hell* is going on?"

Chapter Seven

RICHARD ALMOST NEVER cursed, and she'd never heard him raise his voice. The fact that he did so now was a good indication of his state of mind.

Still clutching the jewelry and perfume boxes, Jessica took a step back from him. "I'm sorry," she repeated. "I just think it's best."

"Best for whom?" he asked, his tone bitter.

"For me," she replied honestly.

His eyes suddenly sharpened, and a muscle jerked in his jaw. "There isn't anyone else, is there? Have you met another man?"

Something else she'd never seen in him before. Jealousy. She wished she thought it meant more than instinctive masculine possessiveness.

"No," she said firmly. She saw no need to tell him that she *had* met another man—and that she'd known immediately that nothing would come of it. "There isn't another man. This has to do with us. With you, specifically."

"With me?" He seemed genuinely astonished. "What have *I* done? We've been together two years now, and you've never complained about my behavior, even when I got caught up with work and ran late. I realize I haven't been the most sentimental man in the world, but surely you can see that I'm trying to change that. If you want me to notice your clothes and your hair and give you romantic gifts, I'll—"

Jessica stiffened, angered by what she perceived as a patronizing tone. "This has nothing to do with staged romance! And it has even less to do with gifts. I don't want *things*. You can buy me computers and diamonds—the moon, for that matter—and it wouldn't change a thing. All I ever wanted you to give me was yourself. And that's the one thing you never even offered."

"I don't—"

She felt like pulling her hair in exasperation at his look of utter bafflement. "You don't even understand what I'm saying! How can a man who is so brilliant in so many ways be so dense when it comes to love?"

His eyes narrowed in response to the word. "Jess, I—"

"No," she said quickly. "I'm not asking for more platitudes from you. Don't give me more practiced lines or faked emotions tonight. I really couldn't bear any more."

He fell silent.

She sighed. "All I've ever wanted was to know that I mattered to you. At least as much as your work. I wanted your thoughts, your feelings, your hopes, your dreams, your disappointments, your fears. I wanted to know why you haven't been able to commit to a wedding date, despite your repeated assurances that you want to marry me. I wanted to know how you felt about children—*our* children. The children we'll never have now."

He'd gone very stiff, his expression so hard, so distant that he looked almost like a stranger to her then. "I've given you all I can," he muttered. "I've always thought it was enough."

"I never gave you any reason to think otherwise," she admitted with a tug of guilt at her own culpability. "I suppose I didn't realize it, myself, until recently."

"I've given all I can," he repeated, his voice strained.

"I've never thought of myself as a greedy woman," she mused softly. "But I guess I am. Not for things— nothing you could buy me would make any difference if you refuse to give your heart."

Richard seemed to flinch.

After a moment of taut silence, he reached up to carefully straighten the tie their caresses had skewed, and then he shoved both hands into his pockets. "Maybe I'd better go now," he said, his voice still oddly unfamiliar. "You seem to have made up your mind."

She'd hoped he would at least try to explain why he'd held himself back from her for so long. She'd wanted him to care enough to fight for her, to at least argue with her. To convince her that she was wrong; that he did love her and wouldn't hide from her any longer.

It broke her heart that he had given up so easily. That she'd been right, after all. He didn't love her enough, if at all.

"Yes," she whispered. "Maybe you should leave now." She saw no need to ask him not to return. This time he seemed to have finally gotten the message. He wouldn't be back.

"Richard, please. Take these with you," she said, snatching up the box of chocolates and rushing toward him with the stack of gifts.

He looked over his shoulder as he opened the door, his eyes still dark and hard. "No. I bought them for you. You can return them or give them to charity or whatever you want, but they're yours. I don't want them."

He let himself out before she could argue. The door closed behind him with a dismally final click.

Dragging her burning gaze from the door, Jessica looked down at the items clutched so tightly in her arms. The symbols of Valentine's Day, she thought. One fanciful heart covered in silver foil, another crafted of diamonds.

Neither bore the slightest resemblance to the broken heart inside her.

The Chinese food arrived only a few minutes later, the slender young man who delivered it apologizing profusely that it had taken so long. Jessica tipped him generously, then set the boxes in the refrigerator, unopened.

She'd started the evening with little appetite. Now, she had none at all.

IT WAS JUST AFTER EIGHT when Richard left Jessica's apartment building, his steps heavy, his chest tight. The traffic on the street—both vehicular and pedestrian—was especially heavy this evening, but he assumed that had something to do with the occasion. He'd left his car parked on the street; he headed toward it without enthusiasm.

There appeared to be quite a bit of activity around Valentine Delights. The popular shop was always busy on Friday evenings, of course, and with this being Valentine's Day, as well, Richard supposed they had all the customers they could handle. Trying to postpone going home, he considered stopping in for a cup of coffee.

He remembered that Papa Valentine had seemed to predict this disaster with the Valentine's Day gifts for Jessica. Richard had ignored the subtle warnings then, but now they came back to him. Maybe he should talk to Valentine again. And maybe this time he should listen.

But, no. Eyeing the milling crowd, Richard decided he was not in the mood to be around amorous lovers buying chocolates for their sweethearts on Valentine's Day.

He wouldn't mind if he never heard those two words again.

He opened his car door and slid behind the wheel. He dreaded going home alone, having to face the memory of Jessica's despondent expression as she'd accused him of things he had been unable to deny.

She'd been right, of course. It was true that he'd never offered her his heart.

He hadn't known how.

But how could he expect Jessica to understand, when it was so difficult for him to explain, even to himself, what had made him that way?

Chapter Eight

"YOU'VE GOT TO ADMIT the guy tried," Denise said the next afternoon over coffee at Valentine Delights. She and Jessica had spent the past two hours together, and it had taken her that long to ferret out the entire story of Richard's surprise visit and its unhappy outcome.

Staring glumly into her Papaccino—Papa Valentine's unique version of a cappuccino—Jessica reflected that her usual favorite-special-treat beverage was having little effect on her low spirits today. She pushed the half-empty cup away and shrugged dispiritedly.

"He tried," she agreed. "But it wasn't enough."

"Do you think he finally understood what you wanted to get across to him?"

"I think so," Jessica replied slowly. "He just didn't even attempt to do anything about it. It was obvious that he didn't want to offer anything more than he'd already given to our relationship. Apparently, he was perfectly satisfied with the pleasant, emotionally undemanding affair we had, and he saw no reason to clutter it up with sticky emotions."

"Is that what he said?" Denise asked with a frown.

Jessica shook her head. "Not in so many words. He just . . . left."

Denise tugged thoughtfully at her lower lip for a moment before speaking again. "Has it ever occurred to you that maybe Richard isn't capable of giving more? Maybe he's—I don't know—emotionally challenged, or something, the way some people are mentally disadvantaged."

"Sure, I've thought of that. But I don't believe it. I think Richard's emotional reserve is very deliberate. I don't know why he feels the need to build walls around his emotions, but he has. And he obviously had no intention of ever allowing me to go beyond them."

"He must have felt *something* for you. After all, he asked you to marry him."

Jessica made a face. She spoke with a bitterness that left a bad taste in her mouth. "You're the one who pointed out that he certainly didn't act like a man who wanted to get married, the way he was always putting off setting a wedding date. As for why he proposed—well, I suppose he found me 'suitable.' I'm reasonably intelligent, comfortable in the social situations he encounters in his work. His associates seem to like me. It isn't hard to figure out that he was looking for someone—anyone—to fill those requirements."

She knew there had been a bit more to it than that. Richard had been genuinely attracted to her. But that was just sex, again. It wouldn't be difficult for him to find another woman who stirred his testosterone.

"If that was all he saw in you, then he's not nearly as smart as I've believed all this time," Denise said in disgust. "The guy's a fool."

Jessica shrugged. "He's a very special man," she whispered, still unable to break that habit of leaping to his defense. "I just wasn't the woman who could touch his heart, apparently."

"Any sensible guy would be thrilled to have a chance with a woman like you," Denise said loyally. "Jake, for example—"

Jessica managed a smile, and lifted a hand. "Now, don't start that again."

"A good-looking, talented guy like him won't be alone forever. You really should try him out."

Jessica was almost surprised to hear herself chuckle, although it was a weak effort. "You make him sound like a used car I'm thinking of purchasing."

"Only slightly used. One previous owner. Shouldn't take too much to recondition him," Denise quipped, looking pleased that Jessica was beginning to respond to her efforts at cheering her up.

A bell chimed gaily as the glass door opened and Papa Valentine entered the shop. His mostly-bald head glistened with moisture from the steadily-falling rain, but his ever-present smile was undimmed.

He was greeted warmly by the patrons filling every available table. He made several lengthy stops on his way across the room toward the counter, where Rudy, the clerk, was patiently waiting on three elderly women who couldn't make up their minds what to order from the extensive menu of specialty coffees.

"How are you, Papa?" she asked when he approached the cozy corner table where she and Denise were sitting.

"Fine, thanks. You heard about our ordeal here yesterday?"

"Yes, I heard about it this morning," Jessica exclaimed as Denise nodded. "I could hardly believe it. We've had so little crime in this neighborhood."

Papa's face was uncharacteristically grim as he agreed. "It could have been tragic had Kyle Paxton not acted so calmly and quickly. The money loss was nothing compared to having my friends endangered."

"I hope they catch the punk who robbed you," Denise said fiercely. "Someone should lock *him* up, permanently."

Jessica tended to agree. Papa Valentine was very special to her, and to everyone else who knew him. The thought of someone callously stealing from the shop that Papa had worked so hard to establish, and that he took such pride in now, was enough to make her blood boil.

"And how are you two ladies today?" Papa inquired, deliberately changing the subject. He nodded toward the bags piled on an empty chair at the table. "Been doing some shopping?"

Denise smiled. "Mostly me," she admitted. "Jessica couldn't seem to get into the shopping spirit today."

"Must be the rain," Jessica murmured, shooting her friend a warning glance. She didn't want to get into another discussion of her broken engagement just now.

Papa was looking at her sympathetically, as if he somehow already knew about her problems. "How about a piece of my Death by Chocolate Torte to go with the coffee?" he suggested. "Surely a big slice of that will lift your dampened spirits."

She smiled. "Thanks, but I had a bite of Denise's cake. That's enough chocolate for now."

"One can never have too much chocolate," Denise intoned after swallowing a forkful of the double-chocolate cake she'd been enjoying with a café au lait. Denise never seemed particularly concerned about the extra twenty pounds she carried on her rather short frame, and they'd never interfered with her social life. Her kindergarteners thought they made her even more huggable. Jessica had always rather envied Denise's open enjoyment of life and fearless enthusiasm for new experiences. Now that Jessica was unattached, she hoped some of it would rub off on her. She could use it.

BY THE TIME JESSICA returned home later, the rain had turned into a winter downpour, which seemed fitting to her mood. Although being with Denise had cheered her somewhat, the moment she was alone in her apartment the depression returned.

It seemed so quiet. So lonely.

Maybe she needed a vacation, she mused. She should go someplace where she wouldn't be reminded of Richard everywhere she turned, the way she was here, in the apartment where they'd spent so much time together.

Spring break was only a few weeks away. Maybe she should go home, to her parents' farmhouse in rural Georgia. Spend a week being coddled and babied, smothered with sympathy and affection.

But she knew even that wouldn't help her now.

Needing to fill the silence, she slipped a CD into the player in her living-room entertainment cabinet. Vince Gill. Denise had introduced her to his music a year or so earlier, although Jessica wasn't a country fan. Yet Gill's clear, perfectly pitched voice and dazzling guitar work had appealed to her, and she'd purchased several of his CDs. Absently listening as the music filled the apartment, she unbuttoned her damp blouse and moved into the bedroom to change into lounging clothes.

When she returned, Gill was singing a melancholy tune entitled "Colder Than Winter." Jessica was quickly caught up in the mournful lyrics that described how he was freezing inside since his love had walked out the door.

Crossing her arms over her chest, Jessica shivered. She knew about being cold inside. Knew all too well the pain of losing at love. This sad song summed her feelings up much too well. She reached out quickly to turn it off.

Dashing at her wet cheeks, she sank onto the couch and huddled into her heartache, bleakly wondering how long it would be before she stopped hurting quite so badly.

She was terribly afraid the pain would never completely go away.

RICHARD SPENT THE NEXT week trying to concentrate on his work. Work had always been an easy escape for him before. It wasn't so easy now.

He had told himself repeatedly over the past few days that he should just accept Jessica's decision and let her go. Obviously, he hadn't made her happy.

And more than anything, he wanted her to be happy.

He told himself he probably wasn't the marrying kind, anyway. He was destined to be one of those scientists who spend most of their time in the laboratory, making discoveries that change other people's lives while having no personal life of their own.

Jessica, in the meantime, would surely find someone who would recognize what a fine woman she was. She would marry, have children, spend her future Valentine's Days with a man who would understand her needs and willingly, happily provide for them. That glimpse of her future was so painful and depressing that he had to forcefully push it aside to be able to work at all.

Thursday afternoon, Dan Heckler dropped by Richard's office, interrupting Richard as he dictated lab notes into a minirecorder for his secretary to transcribe later.

Richard turned off the machine. "What can I do for you, Dan?"

Dan set a steaming cup of coffee on Richard's desk. "Marie said you haven't had a break all day. Not even lunch. Thought you might need a shot of caffeine."

"Thanks." Richard took a sip of the too-strong brew, realizing only then that he was rather hungry.

When was the last time he'd eaten a real meal? He hardly remembered. It just hadn't seemed to matter.

"You aren't looking so good, Richard," Dan commented, eyeing him closely as he took a seat. "Some of your friends around here are beginning to worry about you."

Richard frowned. "Someone asked you to talk to me?" He didn't like knowing that he was the subject of workplace gossip and speculation.

"No," Dan denied quickly. "I just heard it mentioned once or twice. Thought I'd check on you, myself. You doing okay?"

Richard shrugged and took another swallow of the coffee.

"You and Jessica still split up?"

Richard nodded. "The engagement's over. I suppose that news will be out on the grapevine soon."

"Did you try the roses and chocolates?"

Scowling, Richard glared across the desk almost in accusation. "And perfume and diamonds," he replied. "They didn't sway her."

Dan looked concerned, and rather surprised. "Boy. She *must* be p.o.'d. Did she ever let you know what you did wrong?"

"Yeah, she told me. And I really don't want to talk about it now."

"You sure? I'm a good listener. And I've still got all that experience with women. Why, just last week, my oldest daughter—"

"Dan," Richard interrupted a bit curtly. "Thank you, but I really don't want to talk about it."

Dan's well-intentioned advice certainly hadn't gotten him anywhere the last time, he couldn't help adding silently. Obviously, Jessica wasn't at all like Dan's wife. Jessica wasn't like *any* other woman, as far as Richard was concerned.

Dan didn't look satisfied, but he nodded reluctantly. "All right. Just let me know if you there's anything I can do for you, okay?"

"I'm not the first guy around here to get dumped," Richard reminded him. "I won't be the last. I'll be fine."

But would he really? he couldn't help wondering as Dan left the office.

He missed Jessica so much it surprised even him. She'd been at the back of his mind every minute, and he suspected that she would always hover there, haunting him with what-might-have-beens.

Every time he thought of her dating another man, he found himself capable of a rage he'd never before felt over anything. No one had ever mattered enough to him to inspire this sort of jealousy. He didn't like it.

She'd hurt him. Badly. He hadn't realized quite how much power she'd held over him until she'd wielded it so abruptly.

"Dr. London?" Marie's voice from the doorway brought his head up.

He tried to shake off the dark mood he'd fallen into again. "Yes, Marie?"

"I'm leaving for the day. Unless there's anything else you need?"

"No, that's all for now. I'll have this dictation on your desk in the morning."

"Fine. Er—are you sure you're okay, Dr. London?"

Richard glumly eyed his secretary's sympathetic expression. Why was everyone asking him that today? Had he suddenly started wearing his heart on his sleeve?

Odd that Jessica had accused him of hiding his emotions. No one around here seemed to be having any trouble reading them.

"I'm fine, Marie. But thank you for asking."

Biting her lip, she nodded and started to turn away, after giving him another of those compassionate looks.

"Marie?" he asked suddenly, detaining her.

She turned back. "Yes?"

"Have you ever heard of someone called Nathan Detroit?" he asked, voicing a question that had puzzled him for two weeks.

She looked surprised by the non sequitur, but nodded. "Sure. The character from *Guys and Dolls*, right?"

"*Guys and Dolls*," he murmured. Another theatrical allusion? He was really going to have to start paying more attention to such things. "That's a play?"

"And a movie. It starred Frank Sinatra and Marlon Brando, back when they were young and skinny. It plays often on cable."

From what Richard could remember, Jessica had accused him of being like this Detroit guy. "Was Nathan Detroit a scientist in the story?" he asked, wondering about the connection.

"Oh, heavens, no. He's a professional gambler. One of those who's always setting up an illegal, back-alley game of craps, always one step ahead of the law. It takes place in the thirties, I think."

Perplexed, Richard wondered why Jessica had compared him to such a man. He'd never placed a bet in his life.

Dimly, he remembered another name she'd thrown at him. "And Miss Adeline? Who is that?"

"You must mean Miss Adelaide," Marie corrected him with a smile. "She's Nathan's long-suffering fiancée. She's waited fourteen years for him to set a date, but he keeps putting her off. The thing is, of course, that he doesn't really want to get married. He's just leading her on to keep her around."

Richard winced. "I see."

Obviously well familiar with the plot, Marie continued, "She's a cabaret singer and dancer. Speaks with a broad New Yawk accent. She's watched her youth and dreams fade, and now she suffers from an ever-present psychosomatic cold. She's really a funny character. She even writes long letters to her mother, pretending that she and Nathan *are* married and that they have several children. There's a cute scene where she describes the kids to Nathan and tells him all their names and ages. He's stunned that she's deceived her poor mother that way."

Richard didn't think it sounded so funny. In fact, he thought Miss Adelaide sounded like a rather sad character.

"I just can't go on playing Miss Adelaide to your Nathan Detroit," Jessica had said. Now he understood what she'd meant.

"I see," he said again, slowly.

Marie glanced at her watch. "I'd really better be going. Marv and the kids will be wondering where I am."

"Yes, of course. I'll see you in the morning."

"All right. Good night, Dr. London," she said as she hurried away to join her family for the evening.

Lost in his own thoughts, Richard didn't reply.

Chapter Nine

RICHARD INTENDED to go straight home when he left the hospital, but he found himself driving aimlessly, instead. He didn't want to go to an empty apartment, but there'd been too many surreptitiously inquiring glances in the lab. He'd needed to escape before some other well-intentioned soul invited him to share his troubles.

He didn't deliberately set out for Cedar Ridge, but he suddenly found himself driving down Jessica's street. He slowed in front of her apartment building, gazing wistfully up at her window.

A gleam of light was visible through a crack in the curtains. She was there, so very close to him. All he had to do was stop the car, knock on her door and . . .

What? Beg her to take him back? Promise he would change, when he didn't even know if it was possible? He'd prided himself on never making promises he didn't intend to keep, and he didn't want to start doing so with Jessica. He'd already hurt her. He wouldn't deliberately hurt her again.

He thought he understood her better now. He was embarrassed that it had taken him so long to get it. He should have known this was inevitable, but he'd convinced himself that he'd finally found a woman who would be content with what he had to offer.

It appeared that he'd been wrong.

He'd lost her. And he'd never even seen it coming. If he had, would he have been able to prevent the debacle before they'd both been hurt? Would he have somehow been able to change?

Was it really too late to try now?

Someone honked impatiently, and he realized that he was parked in the middle of the road, lost in his thoughts. Wincing, he pressed the accelerator and moved along.

He might as well go home, he thought, making an abrupt left turn at the next intersection.

He had some grave decisions to make about the rest of his life.

IT WAS FRIDAY AGAIN. A week after Valentine's Day. Two weeks after her birthday. Futilely trying to avoid the unhappy connections, Jessica sat alone in her apartment, working on next week's lessons and nibbling at a dark-chocolate-covered almond from the silver-foil box of candy.

The cut-glass vase still sat on the table beside her, the roses now just sad-looking stalks. They seemed hauntingly metaphoric as their beauty faded, and she hadn't been able to bring herself to throw them away.

She told herself bracingly that she was making headway in getting over Richard. She'd only cried once that day, and she'd only thought of him three or four times every hour.

That was progress—wasn't it?

She jumped when her doorbell chimed unexpectedly. Oh, no, surely it couldn't be Richard. He wouldn't put her through all that again, would he? Maybe it was Denise, instead, here to cheer her up again.

But it wasn't Denise on the other side of her door. It was Richard. His expression was guarded, and he held his right hand behind his back. His hair tumbled over his forehead, looking as though he'd combed his hands through it many times. Something about his expression made him look more vulnerable than she had ever seen him—as though he were painfully aware that she could very easily close the door in his face.

She should, she told herself with a swallowed moan. It would be so much easier on both of them than another painful scene. But something held her back.

Oh, how she hoped there wasn't another fancily wrapped gift in the hand he was hiding from her. What had he brought her this time? Bigger diamonds? More expensive perfume? Keys to a Ferrari?

Hadn't he heard anything she'd told him before?

"Richard," she said with a sigh. "Why are you here?"

He cleared his throat and, with his left hand, tugged at the open collar of his sports shirt, as though it were strangling him. "I—er—I brought you another gift."

She groaned. "No, please. Don't do this to me again. I really can't—"

"No, wait," he said hastily. "Just look at it first, okay? I know it's a week late, but I'd like a second chance at Valentine's Day."

She thought her heart might just break right in two. She could almost feel it ripping inside her chest.

"Richard—"

"Just look at it, Jessica," he urged, bringing his right hand from behind his back. "Please."

It was the "please" that got to her. That and the entreating look in his eyes. He'd never looked at her quite this way before—and she was finding it almost impossible to look away.

She dragged her gaze from his and glanced downward in trepidation at the hand he held out to her. Her breath caught in her throat.

It was a handmade Valentine.

A rather crooked red paper heart had been glued to a white paper-lace doily. Across the front of the heart, in Richard's familiar, precise handwriting, were printed the words, "Please be my valentine. All my love, Richard."

All my love.

Tears filling her eyes, Jessica moved away from the door. "I think you'd better come inside," she said unsteadily.

He didn't give her a chance to change her mind. He closed the door behind him as he entered.

Jessica was still looking down at the valentine in her trembling hands. Her thoughts raced dizzily. Did this mean what she thought it did? Was Richard finally offering the only gift she could accept from him?

She had never realized that hope could be so strong it hurt.

She tried to think of something to say, but nothing came to her. It seemed to be up to Richard to begin.

Slowly, she lifted her gaze to his face.

He looked awkward and uncomfortable, as though he was having to make an effort not to shuffle his feet in embarrassment. "I, er, made it myself," he said.

She nodded.

He cleared his throat again. "I made one very much like it for my mother once. Back when I was a kid."

Hugging the little heart to her chest, Jessica said huskily, "She must have treasured it."

"Well, no," he replied, glancing briefly away. "I—er—found it in the trash the next morning."

Jessica was appalled. "Surely she didn't intend to throw it away. It must have been an accident."

He shook his head. "My mother wasn't one to appreciate sentimental gestures."

Richard had talked very little about his parents, neither of whom were still living. She knew only that he'd been their only child, and that they hadn't been young when he'd been born. Both scientists, he'd told her.

He'd given her no reason to think that his childhood hadn't been a happy one.

"Will you tell me about it?" she asked carefully, sensing how critical this moment was.

He drew a deep breath, his broad chest expanding. He let it out very slowly. "I told you my parents were geniuses. Scientists."

She nodded. "Yes. You said they were both highly respected. Widely renowned."

"Yes. They were two brilliant people with a brighter-than-average child. As soon as I was old enough to sit upright, they began to train me to make the most of my abilities and my advantages as their son. Achievements counted with them, not emotions. Grades were important, but recreation was not. Success was the ultimate goal, happiness was merely an ephemeral concept neither of them really understood."

"They didn't love you?" Jessica whispered, her throat tight.

He shrugged. "In their own way, I suppose. They were certainly pleased with me. As long as I performed to their expectations."

"Oh, Richard." She'd never heard a bleaker assessment of a parent-child relationship.

"My mother," he said, "would have been delighted to receive a state-of-the-art computer for her birthday. It was a practical gift, a functional one. She would have put it to good use."

Jessica shifted guiltily, remembering her own less-than-enthusiastic response to the computer Richard had bought for her.

"As for the diamond necklace—well, she never cared much about fancy baubles, but she would have appreciated the monetary value. Both my parents admired high-quality merchandise and wise investments. The paper heart, the chocolates and perfume, the roses—'' He glanced at the dead stalks in the cut-glass vase. "They wouldn't have mattered to her. Sentiment was a sign of weakness. The opposite of intellect. It wasn't encouraged."

"How very sad," Jessica murmured, thinking of her own happy childhood, her loving, supportive parents. She really should call them soon and thank them for encouraging her to pursue her own dreams, whatever they might be; for loving her for what she was, not for being what they wanted her to be.

"When I met you," Richard continued doggedly, "I knew you were the woman I wanted to marry. We seemed so compatible. I thought you understood me."

"Surely you didn't think I was like your mother!" Jessica said, dismayed by the possibility.

He shrugged sheepishly. "Not exactly, of course. She never would have considered being a first-grade teacher. But you seemed so practical, and so competent and so...well, sensible, that I thought you would be impressed by the same things that had appealed to my family. And that's what I tried to be for you."

Sadly, Jessica shook her head. "All this time, and you didn't even know me."

"I thought I did. Just as I thought I knew myself, and what I wanted from a relationship. During the past two weeks, I've come to realize that I was wrong about us both."

She wasn't quite sure how to take his words. Was he saying that he no longer wanted her as his wife? That he'd been wrong about *that?*

"You accused me of not sharing my feelings with you during the past two years," he said gently. "It seems to me that you were guilty of the same thing."

She looked back down at the valentine, drawing encouragement from the words he'd written on it. "I've already admitted that," she reminded him. "I was taking my cues from you, and I thought we communicated well enough. It took me much too long to realize that I'd been fooling myself—and you."

He seemed satisfied with her admission. He drew another deep breath and straightened his shoulders. "You said you want to know my dreams. My hopes. My fears. How I feel about children."

It didn't surprise her that he'd quoted her so closely. Richard had always displayed a phenomenal memory.

"I've been thinking about the answers I should have given you last week," he continued. "I'm ready to give them to you now, if you're interested."

"I'm interested," she whispered.

"I dream of finding a cure for cancer, a disease that has caused so much suffering—or at least making a significant contribution to a future discovery. I wouldn't mind winning a Nobel Prize," he said. "Not because my parents would have expected it of me, but because it would signify that I'd made a difference.

"I have fears. I'm afraid of failing in my career. Of losing my mental or physical facilities. Of growing old alone."

Jessica started to speak then, but he overrode her. "As for how I feel about children—well, I haven't spent much time with them. Not even when I *was* one. There weren't any other seven-year-olds in the fifth grade. No other sixteen-year-old kids at the college I attended. But I find children fascinating. I'm confident that I could learn to be a good father—if someone would take the time to teach me how."

Her grip tightened spasmodically on the paper valentine. Afraid she would tear it, she deliberately loosened her hold. "That—that wasn't all I asked you."

"No." His gaze softened. "You said you wanted to know how I really feel about you. I'm ready to give you that answer now, too."

She caught her breath, and held it.

Nothing in her life had ever been more important to her than Richard's next words.

Chapter Ten

"I LOVE YOU, JESSICA." Richard's voice rang with a sincerity that brought an enormous lump to her throat. "I've loved you for over two years, I think—ever since I first saw you at that charity thing Dan talked me into attending. I've been grateful to him for doing so ever since, by the way."

Jessica had to grope for something solid to support herself; her knees seemed to have suddenly lost their strength. Her hand closed over the back of a chair, clenched in a white-knuckled grip. "You—" She had to clear her throat. "You never told me before. Never once."

"I know." He somehow looked both grim and sheepish at the same time. "I was a fool. I'd been so well trained to hide my emotions that I was afraid to admit them even to myself. I've always known I wanted you, but I never realized how desperately I needed you until you forced me to open my eyes."

"Oh, Richard—"

"Can you ever forgive me, Jess?" The humility in his expression was new, too. She'd never thought she would see supremely confident Dr. Richard London actually beg for anything. To think that he was will-ing to do so for her made her sway again, her fingers tightened so on the chair that her knuckles ached in protest.

"Why—why were you so reluctant to set a wedding date?" It was the one thing she still couldn't quite understand. "You said you've wanted to marry me from the beginning, but you would never commit to a date."

He shifted his weight, and buried his hands in his pockets. "I think I was afraid," he muttered, the words hardly audible. "Afraid of failure. Deep inside, I've always known that losing you would devastate me. I thought it would be even worse if we'd actually been married first. Maybe—" He shrugged. "Maybe I was also aware that there was something missing in our relationship. And that you wouldn't be willing to accept it forever."

"Richard—are you sure?" It would truly destroy her if he was only trying to meet expectations again, saying the words he thought she wanted to hear. She didn't think she would survive coming this close, only to be left empty-handed and empty-hearted again.

"I'm sure," he answered steadily, his eyes locked with hers. "I'll spend the rest of my life telling you—and showing you. If you'll have me."

"I'll have you," she whispered. "I love you so much it's been killing me to be without you."

She heard his breath catch.

"You love me?"

"I have from the start," she said simply. "I wouldn't have agreed to marry you if I didn't love you.

And that's something *I'm* guilty of not telling you much sooner.''

His lashes closed for a moment in what might have been relief—or a prayer of gratitude. His eyes were unusually bright when he opened them again. She identified the reason with a sense of wonder. Tears? From Richard?

He really did love her, she realized with a soul-deep satisfaction. She would never have to doubt him again. Not after seeing him look at her this way.

''You've given me the most precious gift of all this time,'' she said unsteadily, setting the paper valentine aside with great care. ''You've finally given me your heart.''

''Ah, Jess,'' he said with a tender smile. ''You've had that for a very long time. I simply neglected to tell you before.''

When he held out his arms, she threw herself into them.

To JESSICA'S DELIGHT, they made love right there in the living room. And although it had always been spectacular before, this time was truly ecstatic. This time, Richard couldn't seem to tell her enough how much he wanted her. How much he needed her. How much he loved her.

She knew she would never hear the words enough, no matter how many times he said them. And she would never again hold back her own feelings from him. She loved him, she said feverishly. Now—and forever.

When he'd recovered enough strength, Richard swept Jessica into his arms and carried her into her bedroom, leaving their clothes scattered haphazardly behind them. He'd never left his clothes in a tangle before. Never carried her to bed. Never slept with her in his arms.

Tonight, he did all that and more.

So much more.

EXHAUSTED FROM A NIGHT of demonstrating exactly how they felt about each other, they slept late Saturday morning. Jessica finally had the delightful experience of waking in her lover's arms. Of seeing him tousled and heavy-eyed from sleep, his drowsy smile quickly turning into a gleam of desire.

It was much later when they finally left the bed.

"Marry me soon, Jessica," Richard urged as they shared a slow, delicious shower. "Today. We'll fly to Vegas. Honeymoon in Tahoe."

And then he paused and frowned. "No. Vegas isn't romantic, is it? Where's a romantic place to elope to?"

It meant so much to her that Richard wanted to be married immediately. That he wasn't apprehensive any longer. She found his eagerness so touching that her eyes filled with tears again. They mingled with the shower water already streaming down her face. "Anywhere you take me would be romantic," she said. "But I can't. I have to be at work Monday. And besides, I'd really like to have a real wedding. To have our family and friends with us. You know, white lace and flowers—the works. That is, if it's all right with you."

"Whatever you want is fine with me. Isn't spring break coming up soon?"

She nodded. "Four more weeks. But surely you don't expect me to put all that together in four weeks!"

"You can do it," he said with a smile. "We've been engaged for a year—that's long enough." And then his smile faded. "I don't want to waste any more time, Jessica. I'm no Nathan Detroit, no matter how much I may have resembled him before."

She smiled and looped her arms around his damp, soapy neck. "And I'm no Miss Adelaide," she murmured, planting a wet kiss on his mouth. "I could never be content with waiting that long to be your wife. We'll be married in four weeks, Richard. And it's going to last a lifetime."

"That's a bet even a professional gambler would be willing to make," Richard assured her with a touch of the old arrogance. "I love you, Jessica."

"I love you, too."

She pressed herself full-length against him. His hands came up to haul her even closer. Something told her the water would be cold before they left the shower. But the heat they generated would keep them quite warm.

They were in love. And neither of them was afraid to show it now.

It was the most precious gift Jessica could ever want.

Epilogue

It was Valentine's Day again, and business was brisk at Valentine Delights, especially since the occasion had fallen on a Saturday this year. Hand in hand, Richard and Jessica made their way through the milling customers to the counter, where Papa Valentine, as cheerful as ever, competently handled business while Rudy dashed around town making deliveries.

Papa's face lit up when he saw them. "Dr. and Mrs. London!" he exclaimed. "How nice to see you. It's been a while since you've been in."

"Too long," Jessica agreed. "I'm in dire need of a slice of your Death by Chocolate Torte, Papa."

The older man chuckled. "I'll give you an extra-large slice," he promised. "And a Papaccino to go with it?"

"Decaf," Richard said quickly, wrapping an arm around Jessica's shoulders. "She doesn't need the caffeine."

Papa Valentine lifted a curious eyebrow. "Oh?"

Jessica smiled up at Richard, who was giving her another of those silly grins he'd been prone to for the past few days. Ever since they'd confirmed her hopeful suspicions. "We're having a baby," she announced proudly to their old friend. "We've only known for a week."

Valentine beamed. "What delightful news. I'm very happy for you both."

Richard turned his grin toward the shop owner. "Thanks. We're pretty pleased about it, ourselves."

"That," Valentine said, studying their expressions, "is obvious. What would you like, Dr. London? Your treats are on the house today in honor of this very special occasion."

They made their choices quickly. As he served them, Papa Valentine winked at Richard. "It seems you've finally figured out how to be romantic," he murmured, obviously remembering the conversation they'd had a year earlier.

Richard nodded solemnly. "The secret," he confided, "is to make every day Valentine's Day."

Papa Valentine laughed in delight, and glanced around with pride at his successful business. "That, my friend, is something I learned long ago. I'm glad you finally found out for yourself."

Richard reached for Jessica's hand, holding it gently as he gave her a look that still made her knees go weak, after all this time together. "So am I, Papa," he agreed. "So am I."

Harlequin Romance®

Delightful

Affectionate

Romantic

Emotional

Tender

Original

Daring

Riveting

Enchanting

Adventurous

Moving

Harlequin Romance—the
series that has it all!

HROM-G

HARLEQUIN ⬥ PRESENTS®

HARLEQUIN PRESENTS
men you won't be able to resist falling in love with...

HARLEQUIN PRESENTS
women who have feelings just like your own...

HARLEQUIN PRESENTS
powerful passion in exotic international settings...

HARLEQUIN PRESENTS
intense, dramatic stories that will keep you turning
to the very last page...

HARLEQUIN PRESENTS
The world's bestselling romance series!

Harlequin®
Historical

If you're a serious fan of historical romance,
then you're in luck!

Harlequin Historicals brings you
stories by bestselling authors, rising new stars
and talented first-timers.

Ruth Langan & Theresa Michaels
Mary McBride & Cheryl St.John
Margaret Moore & Merline Lovelace
Julie Tetel & Nina Beaumont
Susan Amarillas & Ana Seymour
Deborah Simmons & Linda Castle
Cassandra Austin & Emily French
Miranda Jarrett & Suzanne Barclay
DeLoras Scott & Laurie Grant...

You'll never run out of favorites.

Harlequin Historicals...they're too good to miss!

THAT'S INTRIGUE—DYNAMIC ROMANCE AT ITS BEST!

Harlequin Intrigue is now bringing you more—more men and mystery, more desire and danger. If you've been looking for thrilling tales of contemporary passion and sensuous love stories with taut, edge-of-the-seat suspense—then you'll *love* Harlequin Intrigue!

Every month, you'll meet four new heroes who are guaranteed to make your spine tingle and your pulse pound. With them you'll enter into the exciting world of Harlequin Intrigue—where your life is on the line and so is your heart!

Harlequin Intrigue—we'll leave you breathless!

INT-GEN

LOOK FOR OUR FOUR FABULOUS MEN!

Each month some of today's bestselling authors bring
four new fabulous men to Harlequin American Romance.
Whether they're rebel ranchers, millionaire power brokers
or sexy single dads, they're all gallant princes—and
they're all ready to sweep you into lighthearted fantasies
and contemporary fairy tales where anything is possible
and where all your dreams come true!

You don't even have to make a wish…Harlequin American
Romance will grant your every desire!

Look for Harlequin American Romance wherever Harlequin
books are sold!

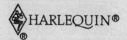

Not The Same Old Story!

HARLEQUIN PRESENTS· Exciting, emotionally intense romance stories that take readers around the world.

Harlequin Romance® Vibrant stories of captivating women and irresistible men experiencing the magic of falling in love!

HARLEQUIN® *Temptation.* Bold and adventurous— Temptation is strong women, bad boys, great sex!

HARLEQUIN SUPERROMANCE® Provocative, passionate, contemporary stories that celebrate life and love.

AMERICAN ROMANCE® Romantic adventure where anything is possible and where dreams come true.

HARLEQUIN® INTRIGUE® Heart-stopping, suspenseful adventures that combine the best of romance and mystery.

LOVE & LAUGHTER™ Entertaining and fun, humorous and romantic—stories that capture the lighter side of love.